# THE MYSTERIOUS ISLAND
## – BEYOND ODIN'S GATE –

### GREIG BECK

SEVERED**PRESS**

# THE MYSTERIOUS ISLAND- BEYOND ODIN'S GATE -

*ISBN: 978-1-922861-40-5*

Expect the unexpected –
where's the fun in that?
Greig Beck

In 1902, famed German archaeologist Robert Koldewey, discovered the fabled Babylonian Gate of Ishtar, that was built around 575 BC. He noted that there were many images of the giant dragon-like creature known as the *sirrush*.

After years of extensive research he decided the images were a portrayal of a real animal because its depiction in Babylonian art was consistent over many centuries while those of all other mythological creatures changed over time, sometimes drastically, but the *sirrush* did not. In addition, the *sirrush* was shown on the Ishtar Gate alongside real animals, the lion, and the aurochs, leading him to speculate it was a creature the Babylonians were well familiar with.

The Babylonian records said the dragon was known to appear, and then vanish for years or decades before reappearing again. But no one knew to where it went, or where it came from.

# PROLOGUE

## 1865 – Lemuria, The Mysterious Island, deep beneath Greenland

Gideon Spilett stood with hands on his hips and looked up into the towering tree. His pants were ragged and tied at the waist with rope, and what was left of his shirt hung in strips from a bony and undernourished frame.

He was the last surviving member of the stolen observation balloon that crashed and trapped him on this mysterious island. After 18 months he knew by now he was no hunter, no fisherman, and no outdoorsman, and mostly he had survived on nuts, mushrooms, berries, and interesting things he found underneath fallen logs. Sometimes he had to close his eyes and hold his breath as he stuffed them in his mouth as a man of his refined sensibilities might end up voiding his stomach and he knew he needed the sustenance more than his manners right now.

Topper, his small and faithful dog, had no such qualms, and as soon as a log was rolled over, the animal darted in and snatched up anything moving. Once they had found a clutch of eggs, each the size of his fist, and though they tasted of fish, Gideon and Top ate well that day.

He nodded. "I think I can do it."

He looked down at Top who stared back unblinking and tilted his head, trying hard to understand his words. The small dog whined.

"I know, it's high. But I need to see if there is anywhere on this island that might lead to a way off. I know you want to get home too."

Topper looked momentarily over his shoulder to the twilight gloom of the overgrown forest, and then back to his tall friend and whined again.

"I'll be quick," Spilett said and turned his face to the upper branches.

The tree he had chosen was at the top of a small slope and seemed to rise above the others. It'd be a good look-out perch, provided he could climb to that height.

Spilett decided on a route and quickly shucked off his rope bag he had over his shoulders but decided to keep his knife as it was the only weapon and tool he had left.

He drew in a deep breath and began to climb.

It was easy work at first and his undernourished body was light, but that also meant it was robbed of muscle so was weak, and he fatigued quickly. He had to pause every so often to catch his breath, and after a dozen minutes he was still only about twenty-five feet up.

He looked down and on seeing him, Topper began to wag his little whip-tail. He yipped, and Spilett quickly commanded him to silence. In this place it didn't pay to advertise where you were.

He climbed on, stopped to rest, and climbed on again. In another thirty minutes he was puffing like a train and his heart was hammering, but he had made it above the canopy line. He edged out to one side and hung there to stare out at the vista – he sighed – it was much bigger than he expected. In the distance there was a mountain reaching up to disappear into the mist line hanging above them.

He stared up at the white ceiling above him; Cyrus had postulated it was a solid roof of ice. It seemed impossible, but in this place the impossible was commonplace. He turned back to the mountain and saw there were mighty trees surrounding it, and he thought there might have been caves on its western slope.

As he watched, something trumpeted, its mournful cry echoing across the landscape, and some of the trees began to shake and bend out of the way as if a creature of colossal size was moving beneath their treetops. He then thought he saw a mountain moving, a huge scaled back perhaps, almost at the tree top level, but thought it must have been his imagination. Nothing living could have been that big, surely.

After another few seconds it sunk down and was gone. Spilett then turned to the east; there was more water, confirming he was on an island. And behind the water, a wall of rock and ice towering into the sky. His spirits sunk; there seemed no way out.

He turned back to the mountain and traced its heights to where it vanished. He thought again of Cyrus' theory of the ice roof; was it solid or could there be a way through it if he ventured inside the mountain; could he then climb via its interior?

He contemplated the journey. He had nothing but time so maybe it was a trip worth undertaking.

He continued to stare but was looking inward as he made plans in his mind, and just then a shadow passed over him and he instinctively ducked. He knew about the giant leathery bat-like creatures and had no desire to tangle with one while perched on a branch.

Spilett moved back to the central trunk and was about to scale down when he paused – there was something carved into the tree – four letters, just four – he traced them with his finger: *N E M O*. Was that a name? he wondered. It didn't sound like an English name, but he bet it was carved by a human hand. He picked at the bark; the carving was dry and healed but not overgrown, meaning it had been carved within the last few years.

Spilett turned slowly, reassessing his surroundings. Someone had stood right here and spent their time doing some whittling.

"Was someone else here? *Is* there?" he asked of himself.

Just then the shadow swooped over him again, and he knew his time was up. He began to scale down, taking as much time on the way as when he climbed up. When he was still fifty feet above the ground, Topper started to bark again.

At first, he thought it was because his small friend had caught sight of him coming back and was getting excited, and probably relieved. But then the barking became manic, and was interspersed with growls, like a tiny machine grinding its gears.

"Top?" Spilett clambered down faster. "Topper?"

There was skittering in the fallen leaves beneath the tree, and he looked down catching sight of the small animal with legs braced, small tail spike-straight in the air.

Topper's teeth were bared, and he shook with either rage or fear at something just at the brush line.

"Top?" Spilett started to come down a little more and stopped to frown. One thing he had found after his time on this miserable place was that some colors in nature didn't exist often. And most creatures opted for camouflage coloring, which was best for hiding or hunting. But every now and then something announced itself with flaring hues – the colors of warning and danger.

As he stared, he saw slowly coming out from under some palm fronds was a blood-red head as large as a shovel. At each side of it was a similar colored pair of enormous and wicked looking pincers that opened and closed.

The thing was segmented, and each segment had a pair of jointed legs. So far, about four feet of it had emerged, but Spilett had no doubt the bulk of it was still to come. And it was coming for a tasty little morsel of dog meat.

"*Back Top, get back,*" Spilett urged, but the small animal stood its ground, trying to block its forward advance.

One thing he had learned about Topper was he believed his job was to keep his human safe, and the brave little fool was prepared to die doing it.

The massive centipede came out some more and its jaws opened and stayed open. It seemed to draw back on itself, but Spilett could tell it wasn't retreating, but instead it was coiling itself ready to lunge forward at his dog. Then, once it had Top impaled on its pincers he would be quickly dragged away. Spilett drew out his blade.

He never thought of himself a brave man. But friends stick together. And Top was the last one he had.

Gideon Spilett, gentleman, newspaperman, lifted the blade and from ten feet up, he dived.

# EPISODE 08

*Don't be afraid to call a dragon a dragon*

# CHAPTER 01

**2002 – Liaoning Province, north-eastern China, border of North Korea**

Lin Bao pulled up in his truck and stepped out. It had been a long and dusty drive, and though as head of the palaeontology division at the Beijing Paleozoological Museum of China he had visited many hard to find and extremely dangerous places around the world, he did not like being so close to the North Korean border.

The NKs were so distrustful of anyone and everyone that they were known for taking pot shots at people who came too close. They were very much of the mindset of *fire first and ask questions later*. Or even, *fire first, and bury the corpses later.*

Bao looked about; the day was hot, and he immediately felt the sun's heat sting the back of his neck. He put on his broad brimmed hat, an Australian Akubra, the best, and one that had been his companion for the last ten years. It was a gift from a fellow archaeologist on a dinosaur dig at Lightning Ridge.

"Ah." He then spotted the dig site and headed over.

Halfway there he was met by Wu Jintao, the dig master, and the person who had personally invited him for the site visit. His cryptic but tantalising references to what he had found had been irresistible. And as he approached, the young man's smile was as wide and bright as sunshine.

Bao waved back. He knew why he was invited as the museum could grant funding to projects they deemed worthy of cultural investment, or if the results ended with significant specimen, then the museum got first rights to it.

"You found us?" Jintao's grin widened and he wiped one dusty hand on his pants and held it out.

Bao shook the young man's hand, feeling the rough callouses. *Good,* he thought. The guy was a working manager and not some university educated guy who did little more than direct traffic.

"Yes, you were easy to find," Bao said. "Just head out of the city and keep going for a thousand miles." He chuckled, but then pointed to the horizon. "Any problems with the neighbours?"

Jintao half turned and grunted. "They're there, and always watching. But they haven't directly interfered with us."

"Good. But be careful; they're unpredictable and trust no one. If they think you're up to no good, they're liable to bomb you," Bao replied. "Now, what have you dragged me all the way up here to see?"

"Something." He turned. "Something amazing."

Jintao guided Bao up the hill and at the top they saw the men and women, dozens of them, working on the hillside like a team of army ants, efficient and tireless, as they excavated, and carried away the tons of rock and soil in baskets.

"A big team," Bao observed.

"It is. And a very good team, but an expensive one." Jintao nodded at them. "And that is why you're here. At the time of our greatest discovery, we are at the limits of our reserves. We need more funding."

"We'll see," Bao replied noncommittedly.

Their first stop was at a large camping style tent, and the hot dry breeze that made the canvas walls flap and tugged at the ropes held in by metal tent-pegs. Jintao used one arm to push back the hanging door flap and held it up for Bao to enter.

Inside there was something on the ground covered in a sheet that was around twelve feet long, and around five wide. And that was all.

Jintao flipped his hat back and the cord held it around his neck. He wiped his brow with a forearm, leaving an orange-brown streak in the perspiration, and walked closer. He crouched on his haunches, fingers meshed, and looked up at Bao.

"You know what the KT layer is, yes?" he asked.

"Of course," Bao replied brusquely. "It is the inch wide layer of clay in the geological strata known as the Cretaceous-Tertiary or KT boundary layer that marks the transition from the era of the dinosaurs, the Cretaceous, to the following post-dinosaur era, the Tertiary."

"Perfect description." Jintao smiled. "It corresponds to one of the greatest mass extinctions in Earth's history when 66-million years ago, a massive asteroid slammed into Earth and wiped out 75% of all living species, including all the dinosaurs. Basically, below the KT layer, we find dinosaur bones. And above it, nothing." He smiled. "Until now."

Jintao's brows came together. "You wanted to know what was so important that I asked you to come out here." He looked up. "Because of this." He flipped the sheet back.

Bao's forehead rumpled as he stared down at the stone and what was embedded inside it.

"Is that…" He squinted, "…is that real?"

"Yes," Jintao replied and placed a hand next to what was inside the stone. He traced it with his fingers. "I believe this thing was around at the time of the dinosaurs, out-competed them, and then outlived them." He nodded. "And maybe even wiped them out."

"I find that an extraordinary assumption," Bao scoffed.

"Maybe," Jintao replied. "But do you know what the largest tooth of a carnivore was?"

Bao replied instantly. "Ah, yes, it was from a megalodon shark, and was around seven and a half inches in length. Found in the desert of Ocucaje, Peru."

"That's correct. But the largest prehistoric land-based meat eater's tooth ever recorded belonged to a T. Rex and was a whopping 12 inches long! Although that measurement includes the tooth's root, so the exposed part of the tooth was 6 inches long."

He held his hands wide over the stone. "But this thing is around 40-inches in length."

"Impossible," Bao whispered and reached out to touch it with his fingertips.

"And yet here it is." Jintao stood slowly, still looking down. "But what creature could it have come from? Nothing like this has ever been recorded in the fossil record."

"A true monster," Bao said softly. "What must it have looked like?"

"A monster, yes, it must have been." Jintao turned to the Museum director. "And that brings me onto the second thing I wanted to show you." He pulled his hat back up onto his head.

"There's something else?" Bao's eyebrow's rose.

"Oh yes. Let's call it, the big picture. Are you up for a short climb?" He smiled enigmatically.

Bao scoffed as he also got to his feet. "Are you kidding? After seeing this I'd walk to the moon. Lead on."

The two men headed for a dusty track beside the dig. And even though the sun beat down mercilessly on the pair, Bao didn't mind at all, as his mind still spun at seeing the unique and bewildering fossil. He couldn't imagine what type of beast it had come from, but its size was so remarkable, it had to have been something breathtaking.

The pair talked as they climbed. "What strata did the fossils come from?" Bao asked.

Jintao grunted. "Most dinosaur fossils come from the shale layers that are dated from the Mesozoic era, between the Triassic and the Cretaceous periods, so roughly between 245 and 65 million years ago. This is from a bed of shale above the KT layer. After the extinction."

"What? Impossible. There were no leviathans on the land at that time. They were all gone." Bao frowned. "Unless it was some undiscovered species from the sea." Bao was intrigued.

"Leviathan? Yes, that is an appropriate reference. And I don't believe this form was aquatic. We're not sure what it is just yet," Jintao replied. "We need to do more excavation. And research."

"And that's where I come in, *hmm*?" Bao half smiled.

Jintao touched his hat and nodded once. "I think this creature had a place of sanctuary. Somewhere it could survive when the asteroid hit. Then it re-emerged."

"Lots of questions," Bao said. "Give me answers."

"And I have some. This way." Jintao smiled and led him on.

The pair of men continued, and it took them another twenty minutes to reach a level path overlooking the dig site. Way down below the workers crowded the huge fossil bed, and Jintao reached into his pocket for a silver whistle which he blew loud and sharp.

The workers stopped, as if expecting the siren call, and all began to move out of the way. Jintao then stepped forward and held out an arm, pointing down at the site. He moved it slowly from one side to the other.

"Behold, the monster."

Bao stepped forward and watched the diggers move aside to reveal the entire excavation site. And the fossil emerging on its surface.

His mouth dropped open and he felt a tingly shock run right through his body from his toes to his scalp, as he stared down at the long dead creature being exposed.

"Oh my great ancestors," Bao breathed.

The fossil was curved in on itself, but emerging from the matrix of the shale bed was a skull, obviously where the tooth had come from. Also, a partial spine curving to a tail that was either still buried or broken off due to geological movement over the millions of years.

But it was the size that took his breath away – the thing was well over 200 feet long, and if the tail was intact, and extended, it would have been even longer.

Jintao put his hands on his hips. "The Argentinosaurus was a member of the titanosaurus family and said to be one of the, if not the, largest known land animals of all time," Jintao said. "It grew to 130 feet and weighed around 100 tons." He nodded slowly. "But this thing would have eaten it for breakfast."

"A new and unknown species." Bao lowered himself to sit on his haunches or he felt he might have fallen over. "And the tusk-like, backward curving teeth tell me this creature was a carnivore."

"Yes, it was." Jintao looked down at hm. "Do we get our funding?"

Bao nodded as if in a trance. "You'll get everything you need." Bao's mind whirled as he couldn't take his eyes from the thing. Mentally, he tried to put meat on its bones, but his mind refused to conjure an image based on any Dinosauria he already knew. It only came up with one image. A fantastical one.

"Can you imagine, what must this thing have been like?" Jintao asked.

"I can, and I'm not afraid to say it out loud: it looks like a dragon," Bao replied.

"A mythical beast, now proved real." Jintao nodded and glanced at his watch. "It's too late to travel back; stay with us for dinner, and we can tell you what we have planned for the removal."

"I'd love to," Bao said softly, barely hearing the young palaeontologist.

*\*\**

The 30-foot long, liquid propellent, ballistic Musudan class missile launched from the outskirts of the North Korean city of Kusong at exactly 8pm in the evening.

Their local spies had informed the Korean military state that excavations for a missile launch base was possibly being constructed on their border. Though China was an arms-length ally, in reality, there were no friends when it came to threats to the hermit kingdom.

Their reconnaissance satellites confirmed two things – one, there was large scale excavation work moving quickly. And two, it gave them a centralized target.

The conventional warhead missile travelled the thousand miles to the site and hit close enough to call it a direct hit. The entire hillside was destroyed, and any structures, equipment, or people there, were vaporised.

The threat had been eliminated, but the North Koreans would stay ever vigilant. As always.

# CHAPTER 02

**Today – Lemuria, somewhere below the ice and snow of Greenland**

Troy and Anne ran for their lives. Troy slashed his knife back and forth to clear a path through the stiff reeds and bullocked through the rest.

They had tried to cross the plain, hoping that the five-foot tall grass-like plants would give them cover. And it did. For a while. But then something found them. And was getting closer by the minute.

"It's coming back," Anne gasped as she stumbled on.

"Gotta go, gotta go," Troy said and reached back to grab her hand and haul her forward.

He could see the tree line coming up, but it never seemed to get any closer as he felt a painful stitch stabbing his side and making his lungs burn like fire.

They had been following an old riverbed but had to skirt around a large theropod hiding in amongst the foliage. So, they took to the plain to avoid predators and sneaking through the long thrush like grasses had seemed a good idea.

But the ground turned muddy and sucked noisily at their boots. And then they found that there were things that hunted in the boggy marsh. And were much bigger and faster than they were.

Troy held onto Anne and pulled her forward. He could hear the creature barrelling through the grasses at a speed that was beyond them.

Anne's background meant she couldn't help identifying it: "*Carnufex carolinensis,*" she gasped. "It means the Carolina butcher."

"That's great, Anne, thanks." Troy kept going but looked across to catch another glimpse of the creature, and felt a further shock jolt his system.

The thing was some sort of alligator that was nearly ten feet long and could run on its long, and incredibly powerful, hind legs. It was only semi aquatic, and its long limbs meant it could leave the water to run down prey.

And right now, a soft human being was just what it had in mind for its next meal.

Troy still had two guns and had been preserving his remaining bullets. He had a feeling he'd be using some of them shortly, and just hoped his aim was good enough to slow down or kill an alligator that was part roadrunner.

Troy's foot finally hit firmer ground and he started up a small incline. The drier ground also meant he could accelerate, but knew that when the creature hit it, it would be able to run them down in another few dozen feet.

The reeds became a little thicker and they were coupled with fern fronds, and the occasional tree now. The cover was welcome.

He let go of Anne's hand and pulled out the gun. In his other hand was his knife which he still swung back and forth like a scythe. The cool mist hung heavily around them, and he just prayed that in his blind rush, he didn't lead them right into anything bigger and badder than what was chasing them.

Anne was falling behind, and he half turned to check on her and saw her flushed face as she crashed along the path he had created. But not more than fifty feet back he saw the reeds being smashed out of the way and glimpsed the long tooth laden head of the predator. Its eyes had been a slitted-green and its mouth hung open in a grin of anticipation at the kill to come.

Troy remembered a schoolyard chant – *beware the smile of a crocodile*. It seemed funny back then.

Troy turned back to the front, knowing he needed some place to defend them, and just then his next step was over nothing. He toppled into emptiness and fell a good twenty feet before striking shallow water. He spluttered and immediately began to get to his feet, just as Anne crashed down on top of him, cushioning her fall, but flattening him back down again.

He pushed her off, blinked away the mud and water, and then held his gun up aimed toward the hole they had fallen in.

Anne rolled over and pulled a knife to hold it up towards the ceiling as well. The pair then waited, lying back, staring upward and barely breathing even though their hearts hammered in their chests.

More seconds passed.

"*Where is it?*" Anne whispered.

"There; 2-o'clock," he replied just as softly.

Just at the edge of the hole in the cave roof was a long, boxy, and very tooth filled head. It peered down and tilted to the left side so one eye could examine the drop. It then pulled back and reappeared a little further along.

"Looking for a way down," Troy said, tracking it with his gun.

"Problem solving," Anne whispered.

After another moment it tried somewhere else. And then it grunted its frustration, pulled back and never returned.

After another moment Troy slowly lowered the gun. "Well, that was intense." He exhaled and suddenly felt how out of breath he was as the adrenaline leaked from his body.

"I think it gave up," he said.

"I know why." Anne pointed. "Look."

He followed where she indicated and saw the bones.

"This is a sinkhole trap. Lots of things have been dropping in here for years, and most creatures dumb or small enough to fall in, were too small to climb out."

"Who are you calling dumb?" Troy turned about and saw that outside the shaft of light they were in, to the west, south, and north, there were walls, but heading east, there was a long cave. And further down more shafts of light.

"Looks like this is or was, an underground water course. Eroded out the soil, and some of it must have caved in." Anne squinted down the cave. "Might be an easier place to climb out further down."

Troy nodded. "Good idea. I don't trust that long legged asshole not to be up there lying in ambush for us." He rubbed his neck, feeling some pain there from the fall. "You okay?"

"Yeah, I'm good." She chuckled. "I had something soft to land on."

"Then just be grateful I fell first, and not me on top of you." Troy reached out a hand. "Let's get moving again." She grabbed it and he hauled her to her feet.

They first climbed over a small line of boulders, and then the pair continued along the sunken riverbed.

Several times, they stopped, and Anne pressed a finger to her lips and the pair eased in behind rocks or into crevices waiting for some predatorial creature to appear, but either it was just echoes, or the animals were more adept at hiding than the humans were at finding them.

Troy just hoped that whatever they were, they were more afraid of them, than he and Anne were of the creatures.

His body was cooling now, but the exertion had raised his temperature and made him perspire. That caused the aromas to lift from him, and though they had been doing it for a while, the coating of a thin layer of dinosaur dung, though repulsive, was the best shield they had to mask themselves from the excellent senses of smell of the huge predators.

However, sight-using carnivores were always an issue, like the running alligator, but at least being downwind didn't automatically ring the dinner bell.

Troy had managed to recover the guns from the bodies of Ord and Lars, and though there were only a few rounds left, it was a comforting feeling to know they had some sort of deterrent if they were cornered by a larger theropod species.

For this expedition, they had set off for one reason – on a previous trek they had crested a hill, coming out from under the canopy of the huge banyan-like tree with branches extending like an umbrella for a hundred feet. Before them was a plain of grasses, with a river cutting through it. But what had caught their attention was the objects on the distant hillside looked like houses, several of them crowded together.

"I knew I saw structures when I was up in that tree," Troy remarked.

"Viking?" Anne asked.

"Maybe," he replied. "They weren't big users of stone, and rather were craftsmen in wood. But then again, someone built Odin's fortress that housed the heart, so maybe it was the same people."

"Speaking of big, why did they make it so oversized?" Anne asked.

Troy shrugged. "Maybe they wanted something big enough to impress a god."

"Impressive and intimidating," Anne replied. She pulled out her flashlight; they both had them but made a pact to not use them at the same time to try and conserve the batteries. And even then, she used it sparingly.

The pair followed the cave for a hundred feet, and though it was a river cave, they could see the water had long dried and they travelled on firm ground.

"I guess this beats navigating monster territory," he remarked.

"Unless we run into something even worse down here," she replied.

"Great pep talk, thank you." Troy grinned.

In another five minutes they had passed under several openings, but none offered an easy means of escape. Continuing, they climbed over an area where the walls had collapsed inwards and saw that the cave then opened enormously. And the ground had been smoothed.

"Was probably quite a large water course that ran to the sea many years ago." She lifted her light beam to the ceiling, that was now a hundred feet overhead. "It's too high; getting impossible."

"We'll give it another ten minutes and then make a call if we need to turn back." Troy pressed on.

"Ten minutes, then another ten, then another." Anne turned. "This was supposed to be a single day's trek, there and back. We don't want to be too far away from the shore when Tygo and your ex-girlfriend returns."

Troy scoffed and turned. "Hey, Elle was not my ex." He put his hands on his hips. "And I put a hole in Tygo's hand. It's only been a few weeks. He won't come back until he is at full power. I know his type; he won't want to be at a disadvantage with a broken paw. He'll give it another few weeks at least before they even set off."

"Makes sense," she agreed. "But someone also has to retrieve Odin's Heart from out of the water."

"Yeah." He sighed. "And I am *not* looking forward to that." He turned and waved her on. "Let's go."

They trekked on and soon were seeing huge hanging fronds of exposed roots from trees overhead, and then came curtains of dried moss or algae proving that once this was a wetter place. Perhaps it had been above ground but the ground had subsided and then somehow been covered over and then burrowed out by the river course over the millennia.

"Hold up," Anne said and crouched beside one of the cave walls and picked up a shard of stone. She used it to work at something in the earth, and soon was able to pull it free. She held it up into her light beam.

"What is it?" Troy asked.

"A piece of jawbone." She scoffed softly. "But look at its size; it's huge."

"Are you sure it's human? Weren't there giant apes once?" Troy asked.

"Yeah, there were. They were called Gigantopithecus, and they grew to nine feet tall." She turned. "But this is not from an ape. It's human."

Troy came closer and she held it out. He took it, and saw it was much bigger than the size of a human jawbone.

He slowly shook his head. "I have no idea." He handed it back. "You're the expert."

She took her pack off, opened the flap and stuck it inside. "This is an important find. I have no idea either. But humans didn't get this big anywhere, any time."

"Yes, they did." He smiled. "In legends."

She smiled back. "I think you mean fairy tales." She shouldered her pack again. "Hope I get to show this to someone."

"You will, don't worry," he said but turned away before she could see the doubt in his eyes.

They headed further down the cave, and it began to broaden and the ceiling got even higher. It was now impossibly out of their reach.

Troy scaled a boulder and at the top saw a light beam spotlighting the cave ahead. He could only stare. At first, he felt like that kid in the museum back in Oslo all those years ago, his imagination now short-circuited by what was embedded in the cave floor before them.

Anne climbed up beside him and was also rooted to the spot. After another moment, she grabbed his arm. "Is that... is that real?" she whispered.

"In this place, it seems anything can be real."

# EPISODE 09

*No secret is safe forever from the march of time*

# CHAPTER 03

**The Kristianstad Basin, north-eastern Skåne, southernmost province of Sweden**

The rain had fallen for weeks. Heavy, unrelenting, and cold. The quarry had needed to be shut down as the ground had become sodden, heavy, and likely to cause dangerous land slips.

Out on the flat grassland areas it was impassable by vehicle and flood warnings were given out. But the area was sparsely populated and had been that way for a thousand years all the way back to the last major villages being Viking settlements.

In the hillside areas, hundreds of tons of water, mud, and rock could give way in seconds, sliding down a slope and destroying property, burying roads, and even diverting rivers. But it could also expose layers below the slip that had not been seen for centuries or millennia. Just like today.

The heavens opened with sheets of rain coming down like the start of a biblical flood. It was a near deafening cascade, but underlying it there was a creaking noise. Those with experience could have guessed what it was – the sound of large tree roots breaking and being torn from the ground.

The area of the Kristianstad Basin hillside shifted an inch, a foot, and then like a giant's rug being dragged out for cleaning, it slid away from where it had sat for over a thousand years.

Down it came, grass, boulders, and tall trees, all sliding the hundreds of feet down to the plain below. The sound was thunderous, birds and ground animals scattered as the soil flowed like molasses, spreading out when it hit the bottom, creating new hills and forested areas.

And then it was over. The rain continued to pummel down, washing the newly exposed hillside clean. And exposing the massive cave that had been bricked in with stones that looked as old as time itself.

***

Anders Ostenson and Freja van der Berg, both researchers working for the Konsthall Museum and also tenured professors for Malmo University, stepped out of the truck, slowly. Both had eyes only for the huge bricked in area revealed a hundred feet up the slope on the ancient hillside.

Freja spoke without turning. "That's got to be 800 years old."

Anders shook his head. "No, older, much older. Those are hand cut stones; more like twelve hundred, or maybe even more. The sedimentary layer was 20 feet thick."

"It has to be Viking," she breathed.

"Yes. But why seal it up?" He turned to her. "Afraid of raiders, maybe?"

"Then, as it's still sealed we can infer that the raiders never found it." She stared dreamily. "But we won't know for sure until we're inside."

Anders let his eyes run over the layered blocks of stone. "We'll need a team."

Freja scoffed. "Phone it in because I'm not leaving this place even for a second. We're here first, and I want to be first inside."

He turned to her, brows up.

"Okay, *one* of the first." She grinned sheepishly.

It took them another six hours to organize some heavier equipment, and trusted students from the university. The team of six selected were a combination of young, physically fit men and women, who could be relied on to keep a secret.

Anders and Freja had made a fire and waved when the two four-wheel-drive vehicles bounced over the rapidly drying mounds of soil.

Anders grunted. "A week ago, and there would be no way we'd have gotten vehicles in here."

Freja stood with hands on hips. "Well, let's hope the rain has stopped for good." She looked up at some of the soil still clinging to the huge hills surrounding them. "Or it'll be us they're digging up in another thousand years."

Anders and Freja called the group in, welcomed them, and gave them each a cup of coffee from an iron kettle they had strung over the fire. They'd brought minimal supplies and hoped to undertake a physical examination of the site over the next few days, and then report in to claim the find. Then they'd tag everything and take it back to Malmo for study.

After rallying the team and allotting tasks, they headed up with picks, crowbars, and shovels.

Anders was first to the wall and used a stiff straw broom to briskly wipe it down, exposing the stones and markings. He finished, dropped the broom, and grinned broadly.

"Runes, *runes*!" he spun to Freja who joined him. "As we hoped."

"Viking," she breathed.

On the wall and carved into each and every stone was a runic prayer, and Anders traced it with his fingers.

"It's old lettering, um, *Här sover drekka*." He moved to the next. "*Här sover drekka*." Then the next, and the next. "*Här sover drekka* – they're all the same."

"Here the dragon sleeps," Freja translated. "In here? Is that what it's telling us?" She faced him. "Behind this wall?"

"Must be allegorical, surely." Anders stood back, looking up at the wall of stones for a moment before clicking his fingers. "A dragon boat. That's what it must mean."

Freja pressed her hands together as if in prayer and grinned. "Please let it be a tomb with an intact longboat. Please let it be true."

"They never sealed them in like this. In fact, they never sealed anything in like this; this is rare." Anders placed a hand against one of the stones. He took out a knife he had on his belt and turned it around and used the hilt to bang on the rock. The sound was deep and heavy, and the vibration caused some clods of earth to rain down on them.

"Thick stone," he said and looked up. "We can't use heavy equipment. I think the slip has finished, but I don't want any further soggy soil to come down on our heads."

"Then we have to do it carefully, by hand," Freja said.

Anders nodded but couldn't help feeling troubled. The small prayer-like script was carved in every stone as if it was some sort of religious invocation. Or a warning.

But curiosity burned at him as well, and between he and Freja they organised the team and decided to work on a single stone to begin with – they'd remove that as a test piece and then peek inside before doing anything on a larger scale.

The group set about chiselling around one of the waist-height stones. As they went, they couldn't help damaging the stone, but as the wall over the cave opening was 10 feet high and 6 wide, Anders estimated that there must have been over a hundred of the 2-foot by 1-foot solid granite blocks.

It took an hour to loosen the simple mortar around the stone, and instead of trying to pull it out, they instead used a rubber mallet and then a boot to kick it inwards.

It fell inside with an echoing thump and the group stood around the open hole looking at each other. Anders handed Freja a flashlight. "The honour is yours, my lady."

Freja leant forward quickly to kiss his cheek, took the light and held it in both hands, beaming back at Anders for a moment before getting down on her knees. She switched the flashlight on and shone it into the hole.

Anders got down on his belly behind her. There was nothing but blackness. Freja crawled forward and put her face right up into the dark void and shone the light slowly from one side to the other.

The area inside was a large room, but sparse, and though there might have been something interesting on the rough-hewn walls, there seemed little else.

"What can you see?" Anders got beside her.

"No longship..." she said, her voice dripping with disappointment. And then: "wait, I think there's a burial plinth, and a body. It's a crypt." She moved her head from side to side, still peering in. "There are other things in there, but it mostly looks empty."

"Could it be something other than Viking? They don't usually have crypts like this?" Anders frowned. "But seems so much older."

She half turned. "Looks like a cave rather than a room, but I can't see the end of it from here." She drew back a little and turned to him. "Well, there's no other option; we need to get inside and have a look."

"We should report it to the museum first." Anders knew that all Viking artefacts needed to be reported to the authorities under the heritage act. If not, they could be shut down, fined, or even imprisoned if they tried to keep any.

"Yeah, but I suggest we get inside and see what it is we need to report first," Freja replied.

"Makes sense to me." Anders stood, and then looked over the stones. He pointed. "We remove these stones here and create an opening. Be gentle, people, and be mindful of any soil and rock slippage. We don't want any broken skulls."

The group set to their task and after another few hours of painstakingly slow stone removal, there was finally an opening wide enough for a person to slip through. Freja first, and then one after the other the team entered.

Anders went in last and breathed shallowly as he swung his light around. "Been sealed for a long time. The air's thick, and not very healthy."

Freja went straight for the body, but the rest of the group moved to each area of the cave that was only around 50 feet square. There was weaponry, beer urns, and something that might have once been furniture but was now just a pile of mouldering sticks.

"Murals," Anders said as he approached one of the walls. He quickly saw the runic writing talking of the battles, gods, and Ragnarök, which was common in Viking murals. And there were also references to something like Odin's secret place.

He then went to join Freja at the body. It rested on a platform that had partially collapsed and the skeleton lay amid a pile of decaying rubble. The man was probably huge when he had been alive, well over six feet.

Anders and Freja crouched. She pointed to the skull. "He was still young; had all his teeth. And look here, this guy certainly saw some action."

The bones had many places of healed breaks and fractures. "Here's something." She picked up a piece of wood that had runic writing carved into it.

"Here lies Halfdan the *DrekkaWathe*." She looked up and grinned. "The dragon hunter." She read more. "He passed through something called Odin's Gate."

Anders looked down the body and saw the item in the skeleton's hands. He teased it free from the curled bones. It was cloth wrapped around more cloth, the last one tied. And inside that there was a parchment.

He carefully unrolled it. "Wow, I think this is important."

Anders knew that very ancient Vikings did not have lengthy written histories or committed much at all to print. So, when something was recovered, it was usually of great significance.

"It's a map," he observed.

The starting place was the representation of a Viking holding his hand out and something small and round on his palm. "It's a *Drekkafinneri*," he read. "A dragon finder?"

"What?" Freja stood and came to look over his shoulder.

The next images showed a crude map of what had to be Greenland, and a picture of a Viking ship sailing towards somewhere just above the island's mid-point on its east coast. There was a shaded area that might have been cloud or a fog bank that half obscured a massive wall of rock or ice. At its center there was a tall ice crevasse and further in there was a dark cave.

There were just a few words written underneath and Freja spoke them almost reverently. "Lumeria – *drekka heimr*." She looked up at him and grinned. "Lemuria, home of the dragon."

"It was just a myth," he said. "But this map implies it is a real place and that something was there that was so important. And this Viking, Halfdan, needed to visit there before he could cross to Valhalla."

"We need to spend some time with that to study it," Freja said.

Anders nodded and finally carefully rerolled the hide and then held it out to one of their assistants. "Tag this as a priority artefact. It could be of monumental importance."

One of the university students brought in a larger lamp which he placed in the center of the room and turned up to maximum. It chased away many of the shadows and illuminated the far wall.

Freja crossed to it. "What are these?" she asked. "Are they some sort of shields?"

Mounted along the wall were three objects, each around five feet in length, a triangular shield shape, and were not quite flat.

Freja approached one and lay her bare hand on its surface. The object wasn't smooth but raised and its edges were fraying or splitting like an unkept fingernail. She leaned forward and narrowed her eyes as she examined it. "It looks like it's made of some sort of resin, or hard wood."

Anders pulled it away from the wall a little so he could see behind it. The object wasn't that heavy, and on its back it was smoother, but covered in some sort of mesh like dried and stringy gristle. "*Hmm*, I've seen something like this before."

As he looked at its rear, Freja had her light pointed at its front. "What?"

"Hey, keep your light there." He leaned in even closer behind the shield object. "Yeah, like I thought, there are things running through it that look like roots. Or veins." He looked up. "Like it was grown, rather than made."

"Are you telling me it's biological?" She grinned. "From what?"

"I'm not sure… yet. Or even if it's plant or animal." Anders let the shield drop back against the wall. "We'll let the science department take a look and they can let us know what it came from."

Freja turned away and headed towards the only other thing in the room. There was a staff in the center of the cave, and at its top it finished in a carved bulb that might have been painted red at some time. She moved her flashlight beam over it.

"Hello." She reached up and placed her fingers on the top. And twisted. The top half lifted away revealing inside it was a small cup that held an orb. "It looks like an eye. An eye made of jade."

"That's beautiful." He looked from the front to the rear. "It's sort of looking…" he lifted his head over the small green orb to where its pupil was facing – toward a wall of the cave that had an alcove still in darkness, "…there."

Anders lifted his lantern and walked toward it. He brought his light closer. "It's looking here, at this." He turned, smiling broadly as Freja joined him.

"Wow," Freja whispered.

"Odin's Gate," he whispered. "Like on the map."

The rear wall had a huge painting covering it from floor to ceiling. It was like on the map but in much more detail. It had been easy to miss as it was mostly dark colors, but toward its center there was a mighty wall of ice, that was split open. Just visible inside was a darker hole with the name below it; Odin's Gate. The final detail was a tiny Viking ship heading inside the pitch-dark hole.

"That's where they went," Freja said.

Anders looked back at the green eye. "That's what it's looking at." He walked back to it, and then squinted at the pupil. He picked it up and then quickly rummaged in his pocket for a small magnifying glass. He held it over the pupil and read the ancient runes on the front. "*I see the heart.*" He grinned and looked back at Freja. "Any ideas?"

"No idea." She shook her head. "We'll get it all checked out back at home base." She turned away. "Okay, people, I want everything photographed, tagged, and packed like it was your newborn baby brother. I want it all back at the museum by this evening."

Anders replaced the green eye on its cup-pedestal and walked away. No one noticed that it slowly moved to correct its position to look back at the drawing on the alcove wall.

He chuckled as he watched Freja; she was like a miniature bulldozer when she wanted something and getting this find catalogued and home was her priority right now. They'd come back and perform some excavations later to see if there was anything buried, but for now, removing, preserving, protecting, and analysing the artefacts was the main objective.

It was thankful that there were few objects to pack, but by mid-afternoon they had everything in the Land Rovers. They set off for the long drive back home, and though everyone was exhausted after a long day, no one would have begrudged a second of the time spent. It was rare to come across a find as exciting as this, and they looked forward to doing more research to understand exactly what they had.

Anders typed the finds into his university catalogue and included photographs. The records would be kept in the non-public folder, meaning when they had something to display to the public, they could do it, when they knew more about what they had.

\*\*\*

In just two weeks, they had some preliminary research results, and information back from experts across the country. Their original information received from the archaeologists, and then biologists was deemed too fanciful, so was then sent on to external specialists.

The results came back the same. The material the *shields* was made from was keratin – the same substance found in hair, fingernails, and scales. In effect, they *were* giant scales and believed to be reptilian as there were no embedded marine elements that suggested an aquatic lifeform.

The other anomaly was that the substance was not fossilized, and instead was carbon dated at just 10,000 years old. At that period in Earth's history modern humans walked the planet and there were definitely no saurian species, especially of that size.

Not a single scientist was able to identify what it came from, and most simply suggested it was a clever fake. Although none could venture how it was possibly constructed.

The next item was the small jade eye, which was an interesting but unremarkable artefact, and the Malmo Museum had agreed to take it. Freja had requested another few weeks to study the item as she was determined to at least find some provenance of the thing so they could supply the history along with the artefact. That way it assured that their names were associated with the find.

But one thing Anders suspected – the eye was the same as the thing the figure was holding on the map. There was something up there in the frozen north, he was sure of it.

Anders had logged all the information into the internal cataloguing site, along with the images, and where they had found the items. A dig was now ongoing back at the cave, but as yet there were no significant new discoveries.

He sighed and shut the system down, and then let his eyes slide to one of the huge scales. A fake, they had said. He tried to imagine what it could come from but his mind kept coming back to the final words in the inscription in the tomb – the *drekka Heimr* – the home of the dragon.

*Dragon scales*, his mind whispered.

"Impossible," he said softly in the darkness. But deep inside himself he didn't think they were fake at all.

# CHAPTER 04

### City of Aarhus, eastern shore of Kattegat Sea, Denmark

Vissen Tygo sat in a huge leather armchair, fingers steepled, and simply stared at the almost complete urn that was spot lit on the plinth. The missing piece still mocked him, but that wasn't the reason for his dark mood.

There was supposed to be something else sitting there, something so valuable that gods and kings had coveted it. He muttered curses into his thick beard as his tormented mind worked; he'd had it. In his hand. Odin's Heart. And he had lost it.

He held up his hand and looked at the scar where the bullet had taken a piece out of the side of the palm. His hand would forever ache as there was nerve damage. But it would heal and be strong as ever.

He made a fist with it, feeling the shooting pain, and cursed himself again for not ignoring the agony when the bullet struck and made him drop the magnificent ruby.

They had spent several days out on the Arctic Princess trying to plan a return, but in the end gave up, as Troyson Strom with a weapon, and him with a damaged shooting hand, meant the risk of total failure, and death, were too high. In the end they returned to port like a pair of beaten dogs.

And that's where it got worse. Tygo turned to Elle who frowned down at a computer screen. The woman had promised, and offered, so much, and then in the end he ended up with nothing. And worse, as he found out she had dropped the *drekkafineri*, thrown away the all-seeing eye, so now they had no way to navigate their way back through the mist.

His eyes shifted to her again, and for a few moments he watched the tall Nordic-looking woman with the patch over one eye. "We had it," he said darkly.

"And you dropped it." Elle didn't look up from the computer screen.

His jaws worked. "As you did with the all seeing eye."

She looked up at him briefly, her single green eye glinting for a moment before she went back to working at her screen.

He laughed softly. "And as we sit here, our time runs out. Soon the cold season will be upon them, and the seaways will once again be locked down. The ice rift may close and take with it Odin's Gate."

He knew the two fools trapped on Lemuria had probably already become food for the great beasts inside. But that was little comfort as he would be forever haunted by never finding the entrance again. His fist clenched again; he had been there, seen it, and knew it was all real. He would never rest until he set foot back on that mysterious island, Lemuria, and recover the All Father's beating heart.

Elle began to laugh, and he turned to face her. "What?" he demanded. "Do you mock our predicament?"

"No." She pushed the computer back on the desk. "I've been searching the Internet, overtly and covertly, and using intrusion software to investigate anything interesting." She turned to him. "And I finally found something. Something very interesting."

He stared at her with a flat gaze.

She folded her arms, her own gaze half lidded. "And I think I just found us a new compass." She reached forward to turn the computer around so the screen faced him. "The Malmo Museum's Natural History Department has located several artefacts, some large objects like shields, that are made of keratin." She raised her eyebrows. "They're the scales of the drekka, but they don't know it."

Tygo got to his feet. "And the other thing?"

She smiled sweetly. "A decorative, green jade eye. That seems to point north, but not true north."

Tygo's mouth curved into a smile.

*\*\**

Anders was working from his home office on the outskirts of the city, and Freja was in at the Museum studying some of the artefacts they had pulled from the Viking tomb.

They had both felt energised and electrified by the discoveries. It was the most unique and wonderful thing they had ever found. Or anyone had found for many decades. He had never seen Freja so animated. Her eyes blazed with excitement when she talked of the artefacts, and he loved seeing her like this.

Even after her initial investigations, Freya was sure now that there was a place, a hidden land, that might be the basis of the Lemuria myth, and there must be an artefact there, an idol, geological formation, or something of great value, that all the Vikings went and paid deference to. She was adamant that if there was anything of such cultural significance, then it should be in a museum. *Their* museum.

He had smiled, assuring her that no matter what, they would find it and bring it back. After all, he would do anything for her.

He sighed and brought himself back to his own tasks. He looked down on the draftsman's platform; before him was the map they had discovered. As he thought, it had been crafted on vellum, a parchment made from calfskin, and had been dated to around 200 BCT – and possibly one of the oldest Viking forms of writing ever discovered.

He smiled, still hardly believing he was the one to discover it. After years of only ever turning up tiny bits of bronze, jade, and broken pottery, he had finally found something of great importance that was going to add to their knowledge of Viking history. As his mother always said; *nice things happen to nice people.* Eventually.

He adjusted the magnifying goggles he wore and looked down at the precious map. Soon the dragon document, as he was referring to it, would be stored flat, pressed into a special folder, and then stored in a box or drawer in a climate-controlled area. But until then, it was all his.

Beside him was his computer open at a map of Greenland and he used it to compare to the map's diagram. The first thing he noted was how accurate the map was – the Vikings had obviously circumnavigated the landmass and had used surprisingly sophisticated measurements to create the map.

He photographed the ancient drawing, uploaded it, and lay it over the online map. He then hit some keys and latitude and longitude lines appeared. Anders leaned forward, noting where an area continually covered in fog that was known locally as *the dragon's breath* was situated.

There was writing on the map – Odin's Gate – Lemuria.

He rubbed his chin. The area around there was isolated, distant, and uninhabited. "It's possible," he muttered.

If there was really something hidden up there, then it had to be somewhere as remote and inhospitable as this, and that meant it could still be there.

There was only one thing left to do. "We need to have a look." He pushed himself back from the desk, got to his feet and went to the phone to call Freja.

***

It was midnight, and Freja was finishing some work on another dig site that was opening the next week. They had supplies to obtain, a team to build, and funding to apply for.

They'd done it before and parcelled out the tasks between themselves. She looked up at the picture of the blond-haired man she worked with and smiled – they were a pretty good team and had on occasion after too many drinks celebrating or commiserating a project, fallen into bed with each other. Anders had been her best friend, and part time lover for years. They had fun together, and she always felt better when she was with him.

She picked up the picture. Did she love him? A little. Did he love her? She thought, yes. They had a lot in common and she guessed she could grow to love him even more over time.

Maybe he'd ask her to marry him – she laughed softly – maybe she'd ask him to marry her. After all, she was a very modern woman.

She finished her funding request documentation, attached it to an email and sat back, watching the message shoot from her outbox. She waited a few moments for the automatic receipt to come back from the administration department.

As she did, she glanced across at the jade eye sitting on her desk. They had deciphered the old runic writing. It hadn't been easy as some of the symbols were new to her, or rather old, *very old*, but eventually the translation succumbed to them.

*I see Odin's Heart*, it had read.

The interesting thing was, the writing was contained in a small circle in the center of the eye, making it the pupil. Anders had postulated that it might have come from the dragon head of a long boat.

There was an example of this in the Oslo Viking Ship Museum, but unfortunately just on a year ago it burned down taking all the artefacts with it. All they had was some black and white pictures from old brochures.

And now it was lost forever. *We were so close and never even knew*, she thought.

She placed the eye in her drawer, and then a small sound from outside her office caused her to frown and half turn to listen. There was silence again, but Freja's neck prickled, and she felt uneasy. She turned slowly to the door just as the phone rang, making her jump in her seat.

***

Tygo moved through the museum like a wraith. For someone 6 feet 5 inches tall and weighing around 250 pounds, he was silent and light on his feet.

In the dark building, he had made his way to where he knew the orb was being kept for research. The pair of scientists had not yet given it over to the museum storage vaults, so they hadn't placed it anywhere overly secure. That was their first mistake.

Their second mistake was being amateurs and not recognizing the object for what it truly was.

Tygo got to the door and paused to lean his ear up close to it and listen. There was a phone ringing, and then the soft squeak of a chair, and then to his surprise, the door handle turned, and it was pulled inwards.

It was the woman, and he bet he was a lot less surprised by the encounter than she was – her eyes went wide and were dark pools of fear as she stared up at the mountain of a man filling the doorway.

She was frozen solid with fear, and he grabbed her by the throat and squeezed, cutting off her voice and breath. He then pushed her into the room, and still holding her with one hand, slammed her back into a chair. He pointed his gun into her face.

"Where is the eye?" he growled.

The woman couldn't speak.

Tygo used his free hand to slap her across the face so hard he saw her eyes roll back in her head momentarily as she nearly blacked out.

She blinked watering eyes and held her face as he leaned closer.

"Where. Is. The eye?" he repeated.

She wouldn't look at him as she said in a small voice: "Do you mean the orb?"

"Ye-*sss*." Tygo never blinked.

With a shaking hand she opened her desk drawer and pulled out a small tray. She then took out the orb that was nestled in a box, swaddled in cotton wool.

Tygo holstered his gun and carefully picked it out. He then held it up to the light, seeing the flecks of something inside, like the one they had formerly possessed.

He grunted his pleasure as he read the tiny inscription on the pupil – *I see Odin's heart* – it was as he hoped – perfect, and undamaged. He slid it into his pocket.

"Is that all?" the woman said nervously.

"No," Tygo replied.

"What else do you want?" she asked meekly.

"Your silence." Tygo shot her in the temple, and her body crumpled.

He then arranged the woman's body in the chair and slumped her forward onto her desk. He wiped the gun down, placed her hand on it, and lifted it, her finger on the trigger.

The last thing he did was use a bottle of whisky he brought with him to douse her, her furniture, and then start a fire. He watched it catch, and then satisfied, he headed out the door, fast.

Though he didn't expect his suicide ruse to fool a competent investigator, the authorities rarely sent their best and brightest first. And all he needed was to buy enough time to be well away from the city and country.

As he left the building, Tygo turned to see the boiling glow of fire spreading in the upper floors of the museum. He reached down to feel the all seeing eye in his pocket and smiled as he jumped into the car. Elle was waiting with the engine running and she held out her hand.

The big man placed the orb in her palm. "The luck of the Valkyries is with us," he said.

Elle held the orb up on her flat hand, and it gradually shifted in her palm to face slightly northward.

She nodded. "The warm season is coming to an end but the gate is still open." She smiled. "And this time, we'll be ready."

"Almost ready." His brows lifted. "I need a new team."

As Elle pulled out into the dark street and sped away, Tygo lifted his phone and dialled a number. It was answered almost immediately, and he stared straight ahead. "Send them out."

*** 

Hilda Bergensen opened her door to the courier and was handed a large envelope with a package inside it. It was small but had some weight and before the guy could answer any of her questions he was away.

She glanced up and down the street. Ever since she was released from jail, she distrusted strangers. She also distrusted the government, ex-friends, and family, and everyone else in-between.

She shut the door and took the package inside, opening it as she went. There was a small cloth bag, and a note. She opened the bag and tipped the two 20-Kroner gold coins into her palm.

Her eyes went wide; they were real, and each worth about €650 apiece. She then opened the accompanying note – intrigued – she wondered who the hell sends you a gift of over a thousand euros?

She read: *These coins are to get your attention. There is a job, for one week. Your skills are needed.*

She had been a marine biologist in her former life before being convicted of serious fraud. Now she was unemployable in her profession and worked in a bar. A fall from grace her now dead father reminded her of too many times to count.

There was more to the note: *On successful completion of job there will be a payment of one million euros. Your discretion is mandatory.*

Hilda's mouth dropped open and she quickly read the rest, but barely registered it as her head spun: *The job is not illegal but must not be discussed. The job is urgent and may be dangerous. Your marine biology experience, and diving skills are of value to us. There will be a team of seven. You will be one of them.*

The final conditions were that she must be prepared to travel this very evening. There was a location she had to be at midnight. If she wasn't there at that time, she could keep the coins and someone else would fill her spot. There was also a contact name: Tygo.

Hilda held up the two coins. "Dear Tygo, damn right I'll be there."

\*\*\*

Anders had cried himself out. A week had gone by and he was still coming to terms with the loss of his beloved Freja.

He would never see her face again. Never hear her laugh. Never see her eyes light up with excitement on an archaeological dig. And he would never hold her again. He missed her so much it physically hurt his chest and made him feel sick.

The depression remained, but only now was he able to function again. But that just showed him clearly how he had not only lost her, but lost her data, her advice, and all her work.

He hadn't known what to do next, until the police invited him in with some new information. The fire authorities had at first suggested that the fire started in her office, and was probably due to an electrical fault. Until the coroner had examined the body and found the bullet wound in her temple. That triggered a fire investigation, and then the accelerant was found.

He was asked: *Would she have committed suicide?*

*Never, ever,* he had replied. And especially not now after they had found something of monumental importance. She was more excited and alive than she had been in years, he had told them.

The fire hadn't burned down the museum but had totally gutted their offices, so Anders was able to recover little. Even the jade eye was gone. Though jade can resist high temperatures, sometimes with sustained, higher heats, splintering can occur, so not even a shard of the orb was found.

He was about to give up on it, when the detectives had shown him the security camera footage of the huge man making his way into the offices, and then leaving. And as the man was leaving the fire had commenced. Naturally, he was a chief suspect.

"Do you recognise him?" he was asked.

Anders shook his head as he lifted his gaze to the two detectives. "So, not suicide then?" His jaws clenched as his teeth ground in his cheeks.

"We're following all leads," the detective had replied professionally. "And this is a person of interest, and the accomplice who drove him away. At this stage the investigation is ongoing."

They'd left with promises to keep him informed. But his gut told him, they'd never find out who or why Freja was killed. What was the motive? She wouldn't hurt a fly. And in turn, she had been shot in the head and then burned.

He guessed sometimes bad things happened to good people, twisting his mother's old saying.

Hours later Anders was still sitting in the darkness turning things over in his mind. There was only one thing of value Freja had – the green jade eye. And he knew in his soul that the giant had come in, killed Freja, and taken it.

But how did the man know about it? And what value did they put on it?

His sorrow gave way to a furious anger. And not just his own; Freja's younger brother, Oder, had been incandescent when told of the police investigation and its findings.

Oder was an engineer by trade, but was a big, fit man, with a cyclonic temper. The young man wanted revenge and wanted to extract it himself. So did Anders, and he had told him to be ready, as they would have their satisfaction.

His eyes went to the map spread on the tabletop – he hadn't uploaded that to the museum's catalogue – like he did with the eye. Was that how they found out about it? If he had uploaded it, then maybe he might have perished in a fire as well.

Anders crossed to the ancient parchment and looked down at the figure holding the eye up, and at the destination. After a moment, his resolve was set.

He looked again at the police images he had frozen on his screen of the giant exiting the building. His back teeth clenched that hard his face ached.

He straightened. "I will find you."

# CHAPTER 05

**Lemuria, somewhere below the ice and snow of Greenland**

Troy and Anne stood dumbfounded as they stared at the object embedded in the floor of the underground basin.

"How?" Anne said.

It was a Viking ship, no sail, but almost perfectly intact even though the years had covered much of it in mosses and strange, twisted growths.

"A thousand years ago this must have been a river cave," Troy said. "I bet they rowed up, it shallowed out, and they got beached."

"No, no, I'm thinking much older." Anne stepped forward. "This is one of the oldest Viking ship designs – see, no sail – like from the famous petroglyphs on a coastal wall just outside Frederiksted, in south-eastern Norway that depict Viking-like long ships, but without sails. And they've been dated as being well over *5,000* years old." She turned to him. "We're not exactly sure how old the Viking culture extends back, but its cultural roots might stretch all the way back to the Mesolithic age."

"The cool air down here has kept it intact." Troy quickly shone his light about but saw no danger. "Let's check it out."

"You bet," Anne replied.

They headed down, and on the way she grabbed his arm. "I know this is probably a dumb question, but if we somehow got it to the water, could we…?"

He chuckled and reached out to grab her arm and felt her muscle. "How's your rowing arms?"

She tugged her arm away. "Okay, okay, it was just a thought. Or maybe a hope."

They closed in on the boat and Troy paused to look up at the roof that was a good 120 feet above them now with only a few small holes and cracks in the rock ceiling that let in shafts of brilliant, white light.

As they got closer, they saw the remnants of the broken oars lying around it and the dragon head prow still intact, but this one with just carved wooden eyes.

"It's a warship," Troy remarked. "Built for speed and attack. Would have been just eight rowers, four a side. But they would be the strongest of them."

The boat was sunken into the earth and tilted toward them, so up close Troy could see over the gunwale. There were no skeletons above deck, but there was a shield and axe with forged iron head and stout wooden handle. He reached in to grab and lift it, but the handle fell apart like it was made of dust.

"Rotted. Of course." He let the flakes drop.

Below him, Anne was digging into the rotted side of the boat, the planks shredding like tissue paper.

Troy stood back to watch her and folded his arms. "Still think we could row her home?"

"Hardy-har-har, and no, of course not." She went back to widening the hole she was making. "Just having a look inside to see if there's anything we can use."

"I'm hoping for a couple of AR-15s, and a box of ammo. Also, a satellite phone." He crouched beside her, reached in and pulled more of the rotted wood out.

In minutes more there was a good-sized hole and he shone his rapidly yellowing flashlight inside.

He slowly shook his head. "Guess now we know what caused them to run aground."

Inside the hull was treasure, piles of it in mounds surrounded by rotted wood that might have been boxes or baskets. Anne reached in and grabbed something. She leaned back and opened her hand. It was a green emerald, smooth and the size of a sparrow's egg; it hung on a silver chain.

"This also tells me they were arriving and probably had all this to pay tribute to Odin in his fortress." She put the chain over her head.

"Nice," he said. "You're really going to turn heads back home wearing that baby."

"I only plan on turning one head." She smiled and held his gaze for a moment before she blushed and turned way. "Whatever," she said softly.

She rested on her haunches for a moment. "Well, one thing this tells me, is they obviously never came back for it all."

"They stayed. Whether they liked it or not." He wiped the wooden

35

fragments on his pants leg. "Maybe those structures I saw in the highlands…"

"If that's what they were," she interjected.

He nodded. "Maybe that's what happened to them. The Vikings had both male and female warriors on their voyages, so who knows."

She snorted softly. "This is no place to raise a family." She looked back inside the hull of the ship.

Anne spotted something else. "Hey, this is…"

From behind them off in the darkness, there came a soft scratching noise. Both spun to it, with Troy holding the flashlight in one hand and gun in the other. Anne froze with her arm still buried in the boat, listening.

After a moment, Troy relaxed. "Maybe just water dripping, or something knocked into the cave from above."

He glanced up at the tiny rips in the ceiling letting the misty light in. Anne grunted and turned back to the dark hole, just as a massive insectoid head appeared.

She screamed and fell back. The creature emerged to follow her. Troy spun and fired, hitting the foot wide head right between the plate-sized compound eyes, and leaving a finger-sized hole.

The creature continued to emerge but looked like it was short circuiting. Anne scrabbled backwards. The massive insect then dropped half out of the hole in the boat.

"*Jesus!*" she gasped.

"What the hell is that thing?" Troy grimaced.

"If I had to guess, I'd say it's some sort of prehistoric horntail wood-wasp." Anne stood on jittery legs. "*Ypresiosirex orthosemos*; meat eater, and guess what? They prefer to live in hollows in trees, logs, and posts, so a nice empty wooden boat would be perfect."

The wasp jiggled. And Troy spun back, gun up.

"We should get out of here," she hissed.

"Muscle spasms. I'm pretty sure it's dead. We're okay now." Troy lowered his gun.

"No, we're not. Wasps aren't solitary, they're hive insects," she said.

"Oh, shit." Troy looked back at the thing as it came fully out of the hole. But it dropped to the ground making a hard noise like plastic striking a hard surface.

Then they saw that it hadn't emerged, instead had been pushed out. Another head appeared, and this time they heard the hum of activity from behind it.

"Here comes the rest of the gang." Troy backed up. He knew that one creature he could deal with. But a swarm? He'd run out of bullets in the first few seconds. *"Run."*

The pair sprinted away, and Troy glanced back over his shoulder, to see huge bug after bug emerging from the hole. To him, they looked more like ants, but the powerful wood-cutting mandibles and barb sticking from the abdomen was the only clue to their real lineage.

"No wings. So flightless," he shouted.

"But they're ruthless hunters of meat. And that's us." Anne leapt over a pile of tumbled rocks.

Troy followed, but his boot came down on a fist-sized stone that skidded out from under his foot, and he went down hard, hitting his head. His gun and light skittered away, and everything went black for a second or two.

He began to come to, with Anne pummelling him, and slapping his face. "Wake up, Troy, wake up…please…" She tugged at him.

"I'm. I'm okay," he said, but his legs wouldn't work, and everything swam before his eyes. "Damn." He felt the trickle of something warm run down his temple. "I just need…" And then he heard Anne whimper in fear.

She used all her strength to drag him back, then towards the cave wall, and there she wrapped her arms around him to protect him.

Troy blinked and saw the wasps moving in that quick, jerky movement, like robots. Each was the size of a large dog, but if they were like normal insects, they probably had the strength of elephants, and would easily carry them back to the hive to be dismembered and eaten. While they were still alive.

He looked to his gun and saw it, and the still lit flashlight, now too far away to be of use.

"Gotta get the gun," he said.

She held on tighter. "You'll never make it."

"We're as good as dead here," he replied, but guessed they were as good as dead either way, but at least he'd die trying to do something.

Troy lifted a rock and tossed it hard at the closest bug. He struck its middle section, the thorax, he remembered it was called. The fist-sized stone bounced away as if it was a grain of sand.

No choice. He sucked in a breath, trying to map a way around the bugs. From the wall above and behind them, they heard that scratching sound again.

Before they could even turn, something dropped down and landed on one of the wasps. The new arrival was as big as a buffalo but angular, with sharp corners. It had long legs with gripping claws, and whip-like antenna. But the killing mechanism was a long sharp probiscis like a spear.

The huge creature pinned the wasp down, and the probiscis punctured the abdomen with a loud crack. Ignoring the other wasps, and the humans, the creature began to drink the internal fluids, sucking them straight up and out of the body.

"*Reduviidae*," Anne gasped. "Assassin bug, giant size." She pulled Troy backwards.

More of the huge bugs dropped down amongst the wasps, and each one picked a target and as soon as the wasps were grabbed, they were as good as dead.

Seeming to recognise the threat, the wasps gave up their pursuit of Troy and Anne and began to retreat. But more of the huge assassins dropped down looking for a meal. And Troy knew that soon all that would be left to eat was the two soft-bodied humans.

"We need to go." Troy grabbed Anne.

He plotted his course. "Count of 3, 2... *go*."

He ran, wobbling as he went, but Anne took off in another direction. "*Hey!*" he yelled as he watched her sprint out, scoop up his gun and flashlight, and then put her head down to accelerate back to him.

She held them up, grinning.

"You fool," he seethed but was thankful she did.

The pair ran as the sound of more bugs landing behind them receded. Glancing over his shoulder, he saw the assassins, like six-legged tanks, making their way to the wasps' home. It seemed the Viking ship was about to be boarded.

*Good*, he thought. *Kill them all.*

After running for another five minutes they came to a bend in the cave, and Troy looked back before rounding it – there was no pursuit, so he slowed to a walk, sucking in deep breaths.

Anne held a hand up and stopped to put her hands on her knees. "I feel like I'm going to be sick."

He came closer and put a hand on her back and rubbed it. "You know something? You're even madder than I am."

"If that's a compliment, I'll take it." She looked up red faced and grinned. She then handed him his gun and kept the light. "Thought we might need these."

"You bet we do." He took the gun and tucked it into his belt. "Thank you." He turned about. "I think we need to find our way out of here. I've decided it's not that safe down here, after all." He chuckled.

She nodded, straightened, and dragged in one last long breath through her nose and let it out with a whoosh. "I should have known if this island had been here long enough then there'd be mega insects. It makes sense that they'd be in sheltered areas and not compete with the saurians above. This place is perfect for them."

"That big?" Troy scoffed. "They were never that big, were they?"

"Yes and no." Anne, now holding the flashlight, waved it back and forth, and then upwards. "Insects first appeared about 400 million years ago during the lower Devonian period. They got supercharged in the Carboniferous and Permium era around 320 to 250 million years ago. Many grew wings and took to the air. But they grew huge because they had an oxygen rich atmosphere that allowed primitive lungs to work just fine. Plus there were no predators."

Anne looked back over her shoulder. "Nothing like those guys is in the fossil record, but insects don't fossilize very well, and who knows what changes have occurred on this island over the millions of years."

"What about the creatures up above?" Troy asked.

"What do you mean?" She turned.

"I mean, could they have undergone changes as well?" He waited.

"Sure they could. But insects can adapt and change super quickly due to short life spans and hundreds of offspring. The animals above certainly can change but it would be slower." She shared a crooked smile with him. "You do remember the dragon, don't you?"

He nodded. "Yeah, I do." He looked up. "Still up there somewhere."

Anne shut her eyes for a moment, tilted her head back, and exhaled. "I just want to be home and leave all this madness behind."

Troy put his arm around her shoulders. "Soon. Soon."

# CHAPTER 06

## Birch Point Beach, State Park, Maine, USA

The north-easterly wind was up and whipping the sand along the shoreline. It wasn't a day for swimming or surfing, and even though the Atlantic's waters were unusually warm this time of year, even the sailboarders who would normally brave the waters in full steamer wetsuits were taking the day off.

It was the beginning of autumn, and a beach was a beach, so people were still drawn to the sand and water. After all, there was always something interesting to see. Like today.

The group gathered with the hoods of their jackets held down over one side of the faces to shield their cheeks from the flying sand and shell grit.

"Shark's head," Chris Ansted remarked and scratched at a silver beard. "Great white, I think."

"What could do that?" a woman asked. "It's a giant."

The group stared at the massive lump of meat at the tide line.

"Yep, probably a twenty-footer. Or was," Ansted snorted. "Tried to take on an even bigger great white, I guess."

Charles Whalen took off his shoes, rolled up his pants and then walked into the water. He went around the back of the head to inspect the ragged edges. He squinted in at the massive wound. "Hey." He reached into the neck meat and jiggled at something stuck in the exposed spinal column.

"What've you got?" Ansted asked.

"Hang on, it's stuck." Whalen gripped the object with two hands and tugged harder. He strained until eventually the thing came loose, causing him to nearly fall back in the water. He held it up. The thing was the size and shape of a small banana, but ivory white.

Ansted's jaw dropped. "Damn, is that a tooth?"

"Yeah, and you're right about something bigger taking this guy on." Whalen held up the eight-inch tusk-like thing. "But it wasn't no shark."

# CHAPTER 07

Troy and Anne continued down the broad cave for another ten minutes until they found the first skeleton, or rather bits of it.

"Viking?" Anne asked.

Troy crouched. "Looks the right age."

He held out a hand, thought about it, and then grabbed the skull and lifted it. It was without a jaw and was age-browned with some lichen growing on it. There was a circular hole in the cranium, the size of a silver dollar.

"That'd give you a headache." He turned to her. "Our assassin bugs?"

"Possibly," she said. "They might have been pursued all this way." She pointed. "There's more."

Scattered about there were the remnants of weapons, and bones, lots of bones – a moss coated ribcage, a femur, and two more broken skulls.

"I'm not liking this." Troy stood.

The pair turned about slowly, listening. But there was no tell-tale scrape or skittering of hard shelled, pointed legs in the darkness. Troy felt the hair on his neck prickle, and suddenly hated being in the darkness anymore.

"We need out. Down here is not good for our health." He turned and waved Anne on, and the pair headed further down the cave. Finally, the ceiling began to drop and the cave narrowed, and more shafts of light began to appear.

"Look." Anne pointed at the largest light beam.

At the roof was another hole around ten feet wide with water dripping down. But beneath it there was a huge cave-in making a landslide of tumbled boulders. The most encouraging aspect was that it looked climbable.

"Looks like this is where we get off this crazy ride," Troy said.

The rocks were slick from the years of dripping water and proved difficult to climb. Both slipped and slid back off one or another of the boulders and when they got to about 30 feet in the air, it became dangerous. And then they reached the top, and the last 10 feet had no more rock ladder.

"We're damn short," Anne said.

There were long grasses tipping into the hole, but Troy doubted they'd be strong enough to hold them. Plus, the stones they climbed were too big to move and many welded together from perhaps centuries of resting in the same place and constant water dripping to glue them together.

Troy got to the uppermost rock and found himself about 6 feet too low. He looked from the hole back down at Anne who perched on the next, green-slicked boulder below him, and judged her weight and height.

"You ever seen those guys on television make a human pyramid?" he smiled down at her.

"Yes, I have." She raised her eyebrows. "But don't remember seeing any of them attempt it on a prehistoric island, while underground, at the top of a pile of slippery rocks. And held up by a guy who was knocked out a little while ago."

He chuckled and held out a hand to her. "Always a first time."

Anne carefully scaled up to stand precariously beside him and he held her as he looked back up. "You'll need to climb up on top of me. Then reach up to that low lip of stone."

"I'll do my best." Anne felt around her back for her pack. "I've still got my rope. So I'll tie it off to whatever I can."

"We can do this," he said.

She took a few deep breaths and grabbed his shoulder. She paused to look him in the eye. "You better catch me if I fall."

"How could I not? I've grown quite attached to you." He grinned, but he saw her blush even through her mud-streaked cheeks.

"Yeah right." She looked up again. "Hands."

Troy made a stirrup with his meshed fingers, and she stepped into it and bounced for a moment.

"*Allyoop,*" she said and he hoisted her up about 4 feet. She stretched to reach up but was still too low.

"Another 2 or 3 feet," she groaned.

"Step up on my shoulder," he said.

He held both her hands, and she wobblingly rose higher.

"Reach up." He set his jaw as he tried to keep himself, and her, still.

"I'm not quite..." She cursed, "... give me, just, a little bit, more."

She gradually let go of one of his hands and reached up toward the lip of stone. Her fingertips brushed it, and she stretched an inch more, and then she was able to rest her fingers against the stone ledge – not high enough yet to grip it – but it gave her something to lean on.

Much to Troy's discomfort, she used the stone lip for balance and stepped her other boot up onto the top of his head. He tried to brace his neck, but the hard sole of her boot on his head freaking hurt.

"Near-*rrrly* there." Anne strained, her fingertips reaching for the lip above them.

Troy held her ankles and tried to lift on his toes to give her an extra inch or two. He looked up, his eyes as slits to ward off the grit raining down on him.

Just as her fingers came close to a handhold above the lip of stone, a huge hand reached down to grab her wrist. A *very* huge hand.

Anne squeaked as she was lifted up and away as if she weighed nothing.

"Hey?" He stared upward. "*Hey!*" he yelled. But she was gone.

\*\*\*

"*Hey!*" Troy yelled again and tried to replay what he had just seen and was sure the hand and forearm was huge, in fact, enormously bigger than a human hand.

"Oh god, no," he thought, hoping it hadn't been some sort of animal that had been poised above them, waiting for them to make an appearance.

Troy looked about, trying to work out how he could drag and stack rocks to try and climb out now he was by himself, and just as he was near panicking, a rope came down.

He grabbed it and looked up. "*Anne!*" he called, but there was no response and no one up there peering back. He tugged on it. It was solidly attached to something.

He sucked in a deep breath. "Here goes," he whispered. And began to climb.

When his head and shoulders got to the rim he was roughly grabbed by the neck and hauled up and out.

Troy struggled with the tight grip at his throat but was let go and he stumbled forward. Anne was standing there, her hands bound and eyes wide.

Troy only glanced at her, as his eyes went to who had pulled him out, and also who stood on either side of her.

He guessed they would have been called a hunting party as there were four men and two women. All were dressed in ancient Viking garb but instead of furs the clothing they wore was made from some sort of leather and a down-like covering was draped over their broad shoulders

– dinosaur feathers? he wondered.

Each held a spear that was around 12 feet long, tipped with iron, and was as thick as his wrist. It would have been a formidable weapon even against medium-sized dinosaurs.

Vikings, *real* Vikings, he thought. But that wasn't the astounding thing; each individual was around 8 feet tall, and not the gangly or awkward giantism found back home where the extremely tall usually suffered from acromegalia and had oversized features, hands, and feet, and ended with arthritic limbs by the time they were forty. But this group was long and clean of limb, powerfully built, with not unattractive features.

Troy was pushed in the back and he stumbled toward Anne.

"Are you okay?" he asked.

She nodded and lifted her hands, showing him they were both tied at the wrist. "They haven't hurt me, but the big woman did this. I can't understand them." She looked up, her eyes round. "They're giants."

Perhaps, the frost giants of legend, he wondered. One of the tallest with a huge scar running down the side of his face and his neck attesting to some fierce battle he had obviously won or escaped from, stepped forward and pulled Troy's pack from his shoulders.

Around his waist there was a belt hanging with reptilian skulls, and bones, and also a single human skull without the jawbone; trophies, he guessed. The skull didn't look that old, as it was still white, but he thought it was no more than a few hundred years – maybe one of the last members of the fateful balloon crew that crashed on the island back in the 1800s.

Troy didn't fight the pack removal as he had no doubt the guy could have torn him in half with little trouble. He still had his gun but knew that even their skulls would be monumentally thick, and he had only had four bullets left, so not enough to take them all down before he and Anne were crushed like bugs.

The huge warrior upended the bag and let the contents fall to the ground – the night goggles, the rope, and then other items Troy had gathered. There was obviously little that interested the giant, so he dropped the bag on top of the small pile.

Troy bent to scoop everything back in and was surprised they let him. When he finished, another of the towering men grabbed him and Troy jerked away from him.

"Be still," the giant growled.

Troy recognised the words; it was the most ancient of Viking languages and though he had trained himself to be proficient in the ancient runes, he guessed it'd take him a while to adapt to hear the words actually spoken.

He tried to articulate some of them. "We are friends," he said.

The giant stopped and stared, and that effect told him his words were understood.

Troy tapped his chest with a fist. "My name is Troyson, from the family Strom."

The giant turned to the scarred one wearing the belt of skulls. This one stared, his pale eyes never blinking. Troy felt he was being examined at a detail that was like an X-ray looking right down to his bones.

"How did they get here?" Anne asked softly. "How did they survive?"

"I don't know," Troy said out of the side of his mouth. "But look at the size of them; they'd need to be this big to compete and survive."

Troy looked at each of the hunting party in turn; all looked back with stony expressions as if they were examining a new form of animal they had just caught, and it started talking. Which is exactly what happened.

Troy's gaze rested on the closest giant woman who had been staring at him. She was nearly as tall as the men, and probably just under 8 feet tall. She had blond hair in braids, a grimy face with the upper part painted black like a mask over her eyes and nose. Her features would have been called more striking than pretty.

She also had some jade, bits of cloth, and small bones tied into her twin braids as adornment, and there was something like a silver medallion around her neck. Troy smiled at her.

She continued to stare, but he noticed that the vertical frown line between her eyes became a little deeper and he didn't know if she was surprised by this action or disgusted by it.

Troy turned back to their leader again and repeated himself. This time he thumped his chest with a fist and raised his voice. "I am Troyson Strom."

The giant's lip curled into a sneer and at last he spoke. "No, you are fœða." He motioned with his hand to the one who tied Anne, and he was pushed toward her. He and Anne were then dragged along behind the group.

"What did they say?" Anne asked.

Troy walked in deep thought for a few moments, and now had an idea how the skull was appropriated around his belt.

He shrugged. "I'm not really sure."

He didn't meet her eyes, because he knew exactly what the huge man had said they were: fœða, which was the ancient word for food.

The hunting party made their way back through the forest, the giants leading Anne and Troy behind them like children.

# EPISODE 10

*At the heart of every legend is a seed of truth*

# CHAPTER 08

## 5000BC – the mountain – Greenland's surface

Harald, the group's leader, stopped and the line of men behind him did the same. He tugged the fur-lined hood down lower on his face. He already had another cloth over his nose and mouth as the stinging wind carried sleet that stung the flesh, and its dryness would have turned the flesh to flakes in minutes if it could get to any bare skin.

It was a time of peace in their lands and had been for many years, and the ice sheets had grown so broad there was no chance to sail to the hidden island of Lemuria. But it was said there was one other way, a secret way. However, it was also the most testing way.

Harald looked up at the mountain peak, and at its top was *Himmelens Mor* – the Mother of the sky, and up high in the clouds it was sheer fingers of rock thrusting upwards. Up there, somewhere, was an entrance, and he was following a story laid down by the clan elders as no one living had travelled this path for many generations.

He and his group hoped to find the entrance, scale down to Lemuria, and leave their tributes – he didn't bring much, just some captured gold and jade, and a handful of eye teeth pulled from the heads of dead enemies. It would be given as tribute and proof of their worthiness to be granted admission to the great hall of Odin on their deaths.

He turned, and Birger nodded to him. He looked down the line of his twenty strong clan group, all now walking in his footsteps of the knee deep snow – he could make out Birger, Srgne, Sune, and a few of the strongest women, Inga, Tora, and the beautiful Sif, and all the rest, with hoods pulled down.

They were already tired, but their arduous journey would only get harder from here. He turned to point up at the peak.

"Above even where the eagles fly." He turned back. "And now, we climb to find a way in."

A few nodded but none responded as it was a waste of energy and breath, and the words were usually snatched away by the bitter, howling wind. Harald put his head down and trudged onward.

The climb took longer than expected, and it was another half day before they stood at the base of the sheer shaft of stone rising to the clouds. They had ropes, axes, and some spare unfinished knife blades and a hammer to pound them in to use as footholds. That was all.

Harald knew some would die on the climb. Maybe all of them. But they had judged it a worthy price to pay. He looked up, trying to plan a path – he saw there was a crack, that began as a hairline split, and opened to a half body crevice in a hundred strides – that would be his way.

He stepped forward and drew forth one of the unfinished knife blades which was more a flattened spike, and his hammer. He pounded the iron blade into the rock at about shoulder height. He placed a hand on it and tugged – it was firm.

He then called to Sune, the wiry one, to lead them up, and the man grabbed the spike, hoisted himself up and stood balancing on the iron. He then reached into his pack for another spike and began to pound that in.

In another hour, Sune was a hundred feet up and had reached the crack. Behind him, balancing on each spike was Harald and the other warriors. It was a brutal climb, and they only lost one of their group, Tiam the ox, whose massive weight was against him. The blade had shifted under his foot, tipping him backwards before he could get a grip on the crevice of stone.

He tumbled 500 feet to the ground and would be dead or dying down there. And if he lived, then maybe they would see him on their return. But Harald doubted it.

They climbed the entire day, slowly. The gloves they wore were thin enough to allow them to grip with fingers that were freezing to numbness. And any cuts were bloodless as the blood had drawn to their bellies.

Harald knew they needed to find the cave soon and start a fire to warm their extremities, or their fingers would blacken and become useless – he had seen it before.

The leader chanced a look back down, and saw his group strung out in a long line. The ones at the very rear were lost in the mist and snow falling around them. He hoped he lost no more of them.

Up ahead of him, Sune yelled – he had found the opening, and Harald smiled and rested his head against the rock face for a moment to give his thanks. He then turned to yell the good news down to his team and ensure their spirits would be buoyed in knowing their climb was nearly over.

In another hour, they had found and entered the opening in the rock face. It was only shoulder width, but inside it opened out, and even without a fire it was warmed from not being in the chill of the moving air, but also from some sort of heat from within.

Sune was already stacking debris and tinder he had found into a pile and chipped at the fire stones to start a flame. It caught quickly, and the warmth and light spread. Harald looked around.

There were bones, people slumped against the walls, their desiccated skin tight across their faces, making their mouths drop open in perpetual screams. But there were other things. He dragged a flaming stick from the fire and headed in deeper. There was something that looked like a giant bat with a long beak that had half finger length teeth in its beak.

He grabbed it up and took it back to the fire where he tore up its dried, leathery body and tossed it on the flames where it burned magnificently.

With the added flame came extra light. All his group had their gloves off and hands thrust forward. Others chewed on dried beef. He would let them rest, sleep if they could. But not for long. There wasn't enough fuel to burn to stay long, and they must press on.

"Srgne, Inga," he called.

The pair stood, waiting.

"Find us this pathway to Lemuria," he said.

The pair pulled a bone each from the fire, that had dried skin burning, creating a torch, and headed to the dark rear of the cave.

Harald already knew they would find it, as there was warm air coming from deep in the darkness like the breath of a giant beast.

He took out a lump of dried meat and tore a good strip off with his teeth and chewed. The climb had been hard. But he knew what was coming would be far harder.

# CHAPTER 09

## The Met Office UK's national weather service – Operations Centre, Exeter, Devon

"Hey Bill, check this out." Rae Klemetski pushed her chair back.

Bill O'Reilly, her supervisor, came and looked over her shoulder at the screens that showed the weather patterns for the northern seas and the swirling colors of the sea currents.

"Lot of movement," O'Reilly remarked.

"Yeah, that's what got my attention. But now look at this." Klemetski switched to thermal, and they saw the ocean temperatures overlaid on the currents. "This time of year, should be near freezing up there."

O'Reilly whistled. "Looks like we got some hot water highways."

There were streaks of warm water running through the Atlantic, all the way down along Scotland and then onto the east coast of America.

Rae Klemetski then changed the screen. "That's not all, look at the atmospheric readings."

"*Hmm*, warm thermals moving southward as well." After another moment, Bill O'Reilly shrugged. "We'll keep an eye on it, and just mark it up as another of those climate change anomalies. Keep me informed."

# CHAPTER 10

## Attlee Park, Beddington, Northern England

Raqual Humphries opened the door of her Jaguar beside the park and let Fru Fru, her medium-sized labradoodle, out. The overexcited dog exploded from the car, sprinting out across the emerald-green grass, air barking as he accelerated.

Raqual smiled. After a night and morning in the apartment, he was probably busting for a poo and wee, but had to first stretch his legs, and check if any of his doggy buddies were there.

She shut the door and sipped at the coffee she bought from her local café and served by Eduardo, her favourite barista of all time, who she was sure had an eye for her.

She walked slowly out onto the park following Fru Fru. The sun was up, but it was still cold, and they had it to themselves. She turned her collar up and sighed; the grass had a coating of dew that she knew would dampen her boots and wished she had worn her rubber wellingtons.

Under her arm she had a ball tosser with a tennis ball in the end and after Fru dropped his poop bundle, for someone else to clean up of course, she called his name and he turned in an arc to head back to her, mouth open in that huge doggy grin of his, tongue lolling, and eyes alive with excitement.

She held up the stick, and the dog already knew the game and began to turn. Raqual drew her arm right back and flung it forward. The ball shot out, travelling at a rapid velocity into the air, heading out towards open space. Fru Fru had already turned to chase after it.

She sipped her coffee, her mind going to today's duties, planning some articles for the magazine, and organizing for photographs to be done to accompany them.

As her mind wandered, a shadow passed over her. She thought

nothing of it as her eyes were unfocussed and her mind looking inwards.

It was Fru Fru's scream that brought her head up, and she looked out to where she expected the dog to be. But there was nothing there but a bouncing ball that quickly rolled to a stop in the wet grass.

She lifted her head. Something that she thought looked like a small airplane was just vanishing over the treetops at the edge of the park. But then its broad, membranous wings flapped, and she was sure there was something that was the same brandy coloring of her dog's fur held tightly beneath it.

"Fru?" She dropped her coffee.

# CHAPTER 11

"Why haven't they tied you as well?" Anne held her bound hands up.

"You're obviously the greatest threat." Troy half smiled.

"Oh yeah, comedy, that's what we need now." She shook her head.

Troy turned to look at the huge 8 foot tall beings around them. He doubted they saw either of them as threats.

"Maybe they think you're my mate and guess that you being bound means I won't leave you behind." He shrugged. "It's all I can think of."

"We do make a fetching couple. Always thought so." Anne's smile, and bravado, was brief. "I guess we're about to find out what those structures you spotted were. Might be their homes."

"They're the right size," Troy replied. "Unfortunately, we can't stay. We've got a giant ruby to retrieve."

Anne turned to watch them for a while. She turned back. "Do you know who the tallest people in the world are?" She turned to him.

He shook his head. "Nope."

"The Dutch. Average man is six feet one inch. Average woman is five-eight." She nodded. "Same stock as the Norse."

"Could they be the remnants of a lost group that came here several thousand years ago, and stayed?" Troy asked.

"Surviving in a place like this would be extremely difficult and favor the more robust. But do I think human beings could evolve to grow two feet in a few thousand years? No." She faced him. "It takes hundreds of thousands of years for significant evolutionary effects to become apparent." She nodded. "Unless…"

"Unless?" he asked.

"We don't know what radiation that ruby was giving off. Or other buried fragments from the potential asteroid crater. Radiation can last for many millions of years. I still think that massive dragon beast was a mutated aberration."

He nodded. "Everything is bigger here. Even people."

Behind them the huge woman gave Anne a shove in the back, and she stumbled forward.

"*Hey*." Anne spun. "Piss off."

The giantess raised a fist that was nearly the size of Anne's head. Given the woman's broad shoulders, Troy had no doubt it would have broken Anne's neck if the blow landed.

"No, no," Troy stepped between them, fully expecting the blow to land on him. But the giantess stayed her hand, lowered it, and then snorted her disdain and turned away.

Another of the giants who had been leading Anne tugged on her lead and pulled her back to her feet as the small procession marched on.

On their trek, several of the warriors peeled off for a while and returned carrying the remains of something that looked like a kangaroo with black fur or plumage, and a brilliant red throat.

"Dinner?" Anne suggested.

"Yeah, I certainly hope so," Troy replied.

They continued for another hour and Troy felt confident that because he still had his guns and knife, he could break them both away. But that needed to be before they made it back to the village and somehow constrained them. If they took a rest break, he would seize his chance.

Often, he had caught the tall woman looking at him. He stared back, and smiled again, and once winked. She snorted in either disgust or scorn. But then she looked back.

Though she was nearly two feet taller than he, he thought it was more than just his ego telling him that she was intrigued by him. Vikings sometimes had wedding rings of bronze or copper and she had neither. But other times Viking men and women just entered into a form of contract between families.

However, if she was interested, any way he could use that, he would.

Over the course of the trip he had found out that her name was Yrsa. He knew that meant female bear, and given her size it was apt.

The men's names were Skarde, who was the oldest with a streak of grey at his temples and seemed to be their leader. Also, there was Odger, Gorm, Birger, and the particularly bad tempered and battle-scarred mountain of a creature called Birwulf.

As the woman approached him, Troy nodded to her. "You look like a powerful warrior, Yrsa." He smiled again.

She nodded. "I am." And she held his eyes, not turning away with derision or contempt this time. "I'm a huntress." She nodded to Anne. "Is that your woman?"

"She is not my wife, she is my friend," he replied.

Yrsa grunted and turned away, satisfied perhaps with that answer, or maybe losing interest. But after another moment, she turned back. "Where did you come from?"

"Across the frozen sea," he replied. "But we lost our boat. So we are stuck here."

She snorted. "Not good for you."

Troy was thumped in the back by a blow that knocked the wind out of him. It was Birwulf, and his words to Yrsa were harsh. Suddenly, he realised that just because she wasn't married, didn't mean there might not be interested mates.

But in the next instant, Birwulf's venom was not directed at Troy but at the huge woman. He struck her with the back of his hand, and she stumbled backwards.

But she didn't go down and instead braced her stance and came back at him. Yrsa was big, muscular, her teeth were bared, and her eyes flashed with fury behind her face paint. But she was still no match for one of the men who had half a head on her, a barrel chest, and arms like tree trunks.

The other men just stood back with smiles as if this was a common occurrence and none gave a hand and they even seemed to encourage it. The only one whose expression remained neutral was their leader, Skarde.

Birwulf's closed fist smashed into the side of her head, and this time Yrsa went down onto all fours. As she shook her head to clear it, Birwulf took a step and began to drag his leg forward – Troy saw exactly what he was going to do – kick the young woman in the face.

He'd had that done to him once on a mission, and all he remembered was waking up afterwards with two loose back teeth.

Yrsa asked for no quarter, and just held a hand up to try and ward off the blow. As Birwulf started the swing, Troy ran. The huge warrior probably weighed close to 500 pounds and more than double that of Troy. But mass and velocity were wonderful things when applied just right – Troy ran, dived, and at the last moment rolled himself into a ball that struck the back of Birwulf's knees like a cannon ball.

The big man grunted and was knocked down and to the side. Troy felt the pain of the impact but rolled and began to get to his feet. He remembered hearing Anne call his name and seeing the shock on Birwulf's face, and the look of confusion on Yrsa's.

Then something hit the back of his head and neck and the lights went out.

***

Troy opened his eyes. Or rather one eye as the other was gummed closed. His world turned to pain as his face, neck and entire upper body screamed its agony.

He groaned, and Anne came closer. He saw her face was ripped with concern. Also, that she had a black eye and a blood crusted nose.

He realised she was walking beside him and that he was being dragged, his arms up over his head and bound together, his boots leaving twin drag marks in the dirt.

"How do you feel?" she asked

His other eye finally broke the blood stickiness and popped open. He was at least happy to see it still worked.

"Like I just fell out of an airplane." He coughed and he tasted blood. "How do I look?"

Anne grimaced. "Like you fell out of an airplane and then when you hit the ground were run over by an eighteen-wheeler."

He laughed, but then winced. "Ouch." He sucked in a breath. "What happened? How long was I out?"

"You've ben unconscious for around two hours. After you hit the big guy, one of the others knocked you down. Then the big bruiser came and beat the sticks out of you. I tried to stop them." She pointed at her face. "It didn't help. It was the woman who stopped them from killing you. Also their older leader. I think he was impressed that you attacked and knocked down one of his best warriors."

"Anything broken?" He looked up at her.

"I had a quick look. Not that I could see or feel. But they wouldn't exactly give me time to fully examine you. Can you stand?" she asked.

"I'll try." He pulled on his arms and then spun and sat up, so he was being dragged on his ass for a second or two. He then jerked himself upright. He hopped for a while as one of his thighs screamed from a large cork, and his shoulders were agony, more so from being dragged with them above his head for several hours.

He nodded. "Not too bad, everything works. I'll live."

Troy noticed that all the hunting party had turned to look at him. Some with interest or admiration. Birwulf, his attacker, also looked at him. But his lethal stare promised more violence and Troy knew that given the chance the guy would finish what he had started.

Yrsa was the only one who kept her eyes on him. A small smile lifted her lips, and she gave him an almost imperceptible nod. Maybe a thank you for intervening, he wondered.

Troy looked down and saw that his blade was still in the sheath on his belt, but he couldn't feel the gun at his back. And just as bad, there was no feeling of weight on his shoulders. "Oh shit, my backpack."

"Gone," she said. "They ripped it from you but I couldn't grab it before we were pulled on our way."

He groaned. "The guns."

She nodded. "Gone."

Troy looked down and saw the bulge of the jade eye in his pocket and exhaled with relief. At least that was something. He also knew that they had left some meagre supplies, equipment, and the goggles back close to the beach at their base camp for when they attempted to retrieve the heart. They just needed to get there; harder now, he had less weapons.

"Maybe we can get the guns on our way back," Anne said with raised eyebrows.

"Yeah, that's the plan," he replied, but knew that first they needed to escape, then find their way back, and survive while doing it.

Troy glanced at his captors and knew that sprinting away was out – the top speed for a human being was around 23 miles per hour. And by the look of the long and strong legs of the hunters, he bet they could get to 40, easy. He'd hate it to come down to a running race.

As they trekked, the group only had to pause and go to ground once when a large therapod carnivore eased through the forest. They watched it move and Troy and Anne marvelled at the size and stealth of the great creature as it stalked.

Their group was downwind of it, so their scent never carried, but the way it moved, all ten tons of it, was sure footed, placing each monstrous clawed foot carefully and softly before it, pausing to listen, and then taking another step. It too was hunting.

He saw that Anne was open mouthed and wide eyed in awe as she stared at the beast. The thing was covered in a banded green and brown texture over its body that could have been fur or pressed down feathers.

The group stayed down for five full minutes after it left. Troy was wondering what they were waiting for, and he turned to Yrsa, who put a finger to her lips and then nodded back at the forest – then he saw – a group of smaller meat eaters, around four of them and each around six feet tall followed the great beast.

They were probably fleet of foot, and only weighed in at about 300 pounds each, but he bet they hoped to take advantage of any scraps left behind by the alpha predator's kill.

After another few minutes, Skarde sent out two scouts, who quickly checked the forest and returned to announce the way forward was clear. And then they crept forward and away.

It was just on another hour that they approached a wall of rock, around 50 feet high and near sheer. They followed it for a while until they came to an arch of natural stone, entered, and then exited to an open space that had another wall, this one of giant sharpened stakes surrounding it.

"I'm guessing to keep out unwanted visitors. Big visitors," Anne said.

"What about dragons?" Troy asked. "This would be kindling to that behemoth."

"Hope we get a chance to ask them. And learn more about them." Anne looked about as they came out of the spear barrier and headed towards the village made of a mix of wood and stone blocks.

"Seems we might have just found the people that made Odin's fortress," Troy said.

As they approached, yet another gate was opened; this one looked like it was fortified by extraordinarily thick cross beams. They entered, and they saw men, women, and children come out to stare. Some grinned, some waved, and some looked at them with disinterest, and Troy noticed that many of the older children were taller and more robust than he and Anne were.

"Look," Anne whispered.

He turned to where she motioned. There was a wall that was decorated with trophies, mainly carnivore skulls of varying sizes but in amongst them there was several human skulls, *normal*-sized human skulls.

"More of the balloon crew, or maybe some of Ulf Skarsgard's kin?" Troy asked.

"Let's hope our skulls don't join them," she replied in a small voice.

He heard the tremor in her words and turned to her. "Don't worry, I will never let that happen."

The pair were led to one of the buildings and a door drawn back. Inside there was nothing, no furniture, windows, or even a bucket for waste.

The door was pushed closed, and Troy immediately pulled out his blade to cut Anne's ties. She quickly moved to the door and put an eye to the crack while Troy paced the interior, looking for any place they could squeeze out, but there was not even a sliver of light showing.

It was a very effective jail, so he went and stood with Anne to first check the door – solid – and then glance out through cracks in the wood beside her.

"Can you see anything I can't?" he asked.

"Just men, women, children. Some animals that look like some form of synapsid..." She turned to him, "...weird creatures that shouldn't be here – they're transitional creatures – not quite dinosaurs and not mammals either. Very ancient."

Troy pressed his eye to the crack and saw what she was referring to –

there was something that looked like a flat faced cow, but with two upward curving tusks at each side of its face. It had a rope around its neck and was being led away by one of the older men.

He changed his angle and saw some children playing, another group making or repairing weapons, two men cutting up some meat, and just beyond them a wall of stout poles, and something happening just on the other side of it.

"We need to learn more about them," Anne asked. "This is astounding."

"No, we need to get the hell away." Troy turned to her. "Otherwise we might end up in their cooking pot."

"What?" She frowned.

"I didn't want to tell you this…" He sighed, "…but I think they might be cannibals."

"Wait, *what*? Why would they be? With all the game available." She shook her head. "No Viking clans, ever, were cannibals."

"No Viking clan grew to eight feet tall either. Or lived on a lost island below a ceiling of solid ice." He leaned back against the door. "And I'm not sure they see us as real people. So all bets are off."

"Oh boy," she scoffed softly. "Yeah. Okay, I suddenly agree immediate escape is the best option."

The door rattled, and Troy leapt away from it. "Get behind me."

The door opened and Yrsa entered the room with some bread and what looked like dried meat.

"The condemned last meal?" Anne asked.

Yrsa put the food on the ground. "Eat." She stood with her body blocking the doorway.

"Why?" Troy asked. "You're going to kill us anyway."

"No, not you," she said but didn't look at Anne. She briefly glanced over her shoulder as if to check if anyone was listening, and then lowered her voice. "Why did you act as my shield?"

Troy snorted softly. "It's what a real warrior does. Where I come from, true warriors do not attack the weak."

Her brows came together. "I am not weak."

"Of course not. I meant less strong than Birwulf," he replied.

She mulled this over. "My father is Skarde, the chieftain. Birwulf wants to be my mate, and then lead the clan. He is ambitious."

Troy nodded. "I know men and women like him. He cannot be trusted and would not be a good leader."

"I have no choice," Yrsa said. "My father grows old and knows he cannot lead us for much longer. Birwulf is strong. If he challenged my father, and they fought, then Birwulf would win. Then all will be his,

60

including me."

"Winner takes all?" Troy asked.

"Not if I marry him, then the succession will be without blood." She half smiled.

"But you don't want to marry him?" Troy pressed.

She shrugged. "It is our way. If I marry him, then there will be peace in the clan."

"You deserve better," Troy replied.

Her mouth turned down in a regretful smile. "Perhaps. But no others will fight for me."

Troy guessed this clan was as close to real Viking culture as ever existed. He knew that many held to a tradition of *Ta gjennom krigen* – it meant *take through war*. If Troy could somehow defeat Birwulf, then all his possessions and status could become his.

"Yrsa," he said, and she looked to him. "If someone did fight for you and win, then they would inherit, *ah*, own all Birwulf's property?" he asked.

"Property?" She frowned.

He tried again. "His goods, his weapons, house, everything he owns."

"Yes. But no one would dare challenge Birwulf." She shrugged massive shoulders. "So what will be, will be."

Troy stared back at the huge woman with the painted face, twin blond braids hung with small skulls and feathers, and saw the look in her ice-blue eyes.

"I have a question," he said. "Seeing you are the daughter of the chieftain, would you lead the clan… if Birwulf didn't exist?"

"Yes." She straightened. "But he exists." She turned to leave.

Troy saw perhaps an opening for escape. Right now, they were probably marked for death. Or at least Anne was, and he might end up a slave. He knew he'd rather die fighting than let anything happen to Anne.

"Wait," he said.

Yrsa turned.

Troy folded his arms. "Then I would challenge him."

Yrsa smiled, showing strong white teeth and reached out a hand to touch his face and stroke it. "Such a big heart in a small body." She lowered her hand. "But I have no desire to see you killed." She then pointed at the food. "Eat." She withdrew from the room, locking the door.

Anne had her hands on her hips. "You two seem to be getting on like a house on fire. What did you talk about?"

He snorted softly. "Clan politics. And our future."

"And?" Anne asked, breaking off some bread and handing it to him.

"And, our time is running short." He paced back to the door to look out. "But there might a way." He turned. "All I need do is challenge an eight foot tall Viking in a fight to the death."

# CHAPTER 12

Tygo and Elle landed at the Port of Reykjavík and went immediately to the port master to rent a boat – they didn't need a crew, as they already brought a full crew with them. What they really required was something of size with a strong hull, could take plenty of spare fuel, and had a couple of large life rafts.

Tygo let Elle take the meeting and negotiation as she was the pleasant face of their team. He turned to look at the group of men and women he had assembled – Hilda Bergensen, chosen for her diving skills and her knowledge of marine and other biology. It would be up to her to locate and retrieve the heart of Odin from the bottom of the island's lagoon.

Tygo grinned; he had told her it might be dangerous. But he didn't tell her just *how* dangerous it might be.

Diving with her would be Joren Karlsen, ex Korps Commandotroepen, the special forces unit of the Royal Netherlands Army. His eyes were pale and unblinking, and he had not laughed or even smiled since he had joined them. His expertise was as a sniper, but his special forces training meant he was also skilled in diving.

Aksel Gundersen was a hunter and tracker, and was now flat broke. His business had been destroyed ever since pictures of him with one of his customers appeared in the press with a dead rhino – he had been fired, erased, and now couldn't get a job selling pencils from a tin cup.

Then came the two brothers: Borg and Gunner Hagen – both former rugby players who did debt recovery work for one of the criminal gangs. They were his muscle – not very bright, but strong as oxen, violent, and compliant. They'd come in handy if Mr. Troyson Strom happened to survive and was stupidly lying in wait for them.

Elle rented them a 52 foot 1940's motor yacht with lifeboats and pivot crane. It was high cost given they had little choice and even less time, but Tygo had no doubt that by their return any expenses they incurred would seem a worthwhile investment many million times over.

Elle was in the wheelhouse and Tygo went to cast off. He unlooped the ropes and threw them onto the deck and then flexed his large hand. The star-shaped scar of the bullet wound entering in the meat between his thumb and forefinger had healed, but there was some nerve damage. But that didn't mean it didn't hurt; it always hurt, night and day.

He made a fist and let the pain come – he cursed the man who did it and was only mollified by the thought that Troyson Strom had probably long been torn to shreds by one of the gargantuan denizens of Lemuria. He smiled, feeling better already.

But if by some miraculous means he managed to survive, then that might please him even more. He turned away from the gunmetal grey, freezing water to enter the wheelhouse with Elle.

While his team were below deck drinking coffee, smoking, and generally distrusting each other, he had Elle ease the boat out through the harbor. She turned to face him, her single eye almost luminous in the cabin.

Tygo took the wheel with one hand and in the other he held up the all-seeing-eye. It swivelled to face a direction north, but not quite true north.

"And so we begin." He pushed the throttle forward.

\*\*\*

Two hundred and twelve miles to the north, Anders Ostenson and Oder van der Berg, Freja's little brother, had sailed from the port of Ísafjörður, a town in the Westfjords region of Northwest Iceland. It had dramatic glacial landscapes with rugged rock covered in a coating of green and gauged deep by ancient titanic ice flows.

Anders and Freja had undertaken some Viking digs in the past around the town, and many of the locals still remembered him.

He'd rented a fishing boat, the Sjøspray, complete with the single-man crew, owner, and captain of Olaf Linberg, in his 60s. He was delighted to offer his services as the fishing was getting to be difficult as his fingers were bent with arthritis and his back ached when pulling in nets. A large commission where he needed to do little but motor sail for a week, and sip the local strong brewed tea, was too good to pass up.

Anders and Oder sat in the small mess room below deck, and both worked on their own tasks. Anders used his computer to plot where he thought they needed to go – already, the software he had created had used satellite images, and measured them against the map he had found and given him an approximate destination – he thought its accuracy was only a few miles in or out, so if his luck held, he could find whatever it was the map said was there.

He sat back and folded his arms. The glow from his computer illuminated the desk he worked at and the scraps of ancient map, and old tomes open at marked pages, all created a mosaic coloring in the lines of a larger legend.

"*Lemuria,*" he whispered.

Oder looked up. "What have you found?" he asked.

"A pattern," Anders replied. "And perhaps one that has been going on since before time began." He waved him over. "Look here."

Oder joined him around the long bolted down table and Anders opened his collected list of strange sightings and ran through the list.

"There is a reason these people stole that artefact from Freja." He nodded slowly. "It was because it pointed the way to somewhere that has been lost for a thousand years."

"Where is this place? What is it?" Oder asked.

"Lemuria," Anders replied, keeping his eyes on the screen.

"The lost continent?" Oder scoffed. "But it's just an old myth."

He smiled at his brother-in-law. "Not to these people. And perhaps not at all." He looked back to his screen. "I think that once every warming period that some sort of doorway opens, and access can be obtained. And I think other legends prove this." He tilted his head. "Are you familiar with the Loch Ness Monster?" he asked.

"Of course. In Scotland." Oder's brows came together. "What does that have to do with anything?"

"Because if people can get into this hidden world, then it stands to reason, that things that live there, can get out."

"Oka-*aay.*" Oder sounded sceptical.

Anders turned his screen to the side so they could both see. "Look here, another one; the Mokèlé-mbèmbé, a supposed large, water-dwelling creature which lives in the Congo River Basin. There have many sightings over the centuries and many expeditions have searched for it – all of which being unsuccessful. Many people believe that Mokèlé-mbèmbé, or a group of them, are sauropods, that simply arrived one day and never left. Ancient rock paintings indicate it has been there for at least a millennium. Maybe longer."

He went on. "Then there were too many to count on the north American coastline: A large, aquatic creature apparently living in Lake Champlain, a lake in North America. It was suggested as being a remnant plesiosaur, or even a Tanystropheus. Then came the Cadborosaurus, living off the Pacific Coast of North America. Its name is derived from Cadboro Bay in Greater Victoria, British Columbia, and the Greek root word "saurus" meaning lizard or reptile. These creatures were seen in coastal waters or appeared in lakes and lagoons after one year's heavy flooding or prior to silting which marooned them.

"The list goes on with sightings dating all the way back to the time of the Babylonians, Vikings, and ancient aboriginal tribes of northern Australia, all depicted in their cave art. And importantly, the timings of every one of them were clumped in generational warm periods."

Oder sat back. "But I don't..."

"Wait." Anders held up a finger, and then quickly brought up another report he had compiled. "And now, just in the last few months. There was a strange unidentified creature attack in eastern Australia. Then, a dog taken by a large, winged creature in the United Kingdom, and this..."

Anders pressed a key, and the film of a fishing boat landing some sort of giant sea reptile was displayed in all its blood-filled glory.

Oder watched it with half lidded eyes, and then lifted them to Anders. "So, it's happening again?"

"Yes, it is. And I think these bastards that killed Freja planned to go there and the artefact somehow showed them *how* to get there." Anders folded his arms.

The fire burned again in Oder's eyes. "Where is it? You must know as we are on our way to somewhere. And I doubt you hope to run across them in the entire northern sea."

Anders nodded and hit a few more keys on his computer. He then entered their locations into his chart, and then overlaid it with a sea-current diagram.

"I think all the creatures might have been swept there or borne along by a warm sea current that originated in the northern hemisphere. You see, the beasts were transported to their new locations on a highway. A warm current from..." He pointed.

"So, Greenland," Oder confirmed.

"I believe so," Anders said softly. "Lemuria is somewhere on, near, or maybe under, Greenland."

"Big place." Oder raised his eyebrows.

"The warm water corridor leads all the way from the north-eastern coast of Greenland. That's where we're heading now." Anders smiled. "And then it's up to you and your technology."

Oder looked across at the large case stacked against the wall and nodded. "If there's something there, then we can find it. And them." His expression hardened. "For Freja."

"For Freja," Anders agreed.

His eyes watered at the thought. Freja would have given anything to be with him. In fact, she *had* given everything, and someone had taken that everything from her.

"We'll make them pay," Oder said.

Anders nodded and put his hand in his pocket and felt the hard steel of the pistol there. He took it out and held it in his hand. It was still warm from being close to his body and he stared down at the dark black-blue steel. He hoped to find this hidden and mysterious island. But he also hoped to find the person responsible for her death.

"I hope we don't need them," Anders said softly.

Oder's eyes were half lidded. "Just remember, they did this. They killed Freja. They deserve everything that's coming to them." He patted his own pocket and glanced again at the large case he had brought. "We'll be ready, and we are not defenceless women like Freja."

There was a knock on his cabin door, and Anders quickly tucked the gun back in his pocket.

"Come." He sat back.

Captain Olaf stuck his bushy eyed head around the door and grinned. He then held out two steaming mugs of sweet tea.

Anders took them and handed one to Oder. His brother-in-law nodded.

"Extra strong, thank you, I need it." He nodded at Anders. "He snores, with his mouth open wide enough to catch flies."

"I've never heard myself snore." Anders chuckled, and then raised his mug in a toast. "You spoil us, Captain Olaf," Anders said.

The old man shrugged. "Your money will help my family. And it is easy going."

"No icebergs this time of year?" Anders asked.

Olaf shook his head, his mouth turned down. "There should be, but the water is very warm." His brows rose. "Unusually warm water surge I think is running in the current."

Oder grunted softly. "No bergs is good news."

"The warm water will show us the way." Anders sipped again, his vision turned inwards.

# CHAPTER 13

**Forty feet down – Blackmar's reef, St. Augustine, Jacksonville**

The warm water corridor from the far northern seas branched out like a lot of tentacles all around the globe.

In some areas it dissipated and left any passengers stranded in freezing water where they quickly succumbed. But in others, the warm flows stretched all the way to meet with other welcoming warm water currents. And from there, a new life awaited.

\*\*\*

Brady Allen and Tris Tolhurst drifted lower and hung mid water about 40 feet down. Visibility was good, and they knew the wreck they wanted to visit was just another few dozen feet to their east.

Though the waters were warm and teemed with numerous fish and tasty crustacean species, today they came with just a camera and a sense of adventure. They'd never dived Blackmars before; it was a magnificent diving zone that offered a natural reef ledge system and had five wrecked-ships, two planes, and plentiful marine life making it an enthusiast's paradise.

It was attractive to divers like Brady and Tris, because Blackmars was one of the reefs located along the edge of the continental shelf, an underwater landmass that resulted in moderately shallow water, spanning more than 40 miles wide off the northeast coast of Florida.

Brady had the camera, and so far had taken a few shots of Tris on the descent. He'd take more when they were on the wreck or if anything else took his interest.

The pair had been engaged for six months and dated for years before that. They were brought together over a love of diving. In fact, when it came to birthdays, Christmas, and anniversaries, the gifts were always dive knives, new flippers, dive masks, or even airline tickets to some pristine water bay somewhere on Earth. Brady had even proposed to Tris underwater and had floated in front of her and opened the small box revealing the diamond ring.

Both judged themselves competent divers, and they knew the risks, planned for them, or compensated for them when something unexpected occurred. Today was just a fun dive not far from the shoreline, and more a start to the season to blow out the cobwebs and test the equipment that had been in storage for a while.

It was Brady who felt the change first; maybe it was a diver's intuition, or that all the fish species suddenly disappeared like a magician's trick. But the next thing, he had the skin crawling sensation on the back of his neck that told him they weren't alone.

Then he saw it; looming out of the azure water from the great beyond, was a 16 foot great white. It first glided past them like an open mouthed torpedo, and one of its soulless black eyes swivelled to take the pair in.

*Keep going, keep going*, Brady prayed.

But it didn't; with a tiny flick of its tail it began to circle them.

Tris glided back towards him, her face turned to the shark. She knew the drill; no sudden movements to attract or excite the predator. She seemed serene, but Brady could see that her shoulders were hiked, and knew she was as nervous as he was.

Brady watched the shark, now just faintly visible out at the limits of his vision. The thing about great whites was their unpredictability. Most times they came in to see if you were some sort of long seal, and then after giving you the once over, simply went on their way. Other times they might even give you a little bump.

But then there were the times when they just decided that *what the hell*, I'm going to eat that thing anyway.

He felt a shiver as he had a bad feeling in the pit of his gut, that this was going to be one of those times. The big shark circled some more, each time coming closer and that big ole black eye was watching them the entire time.

The circles got smaller, and it began to speed up. Brady knew what it was doing – deciding which one of them it would take.

He glanced up at the surface – the sunshine so warm, inviting, and safe. Their boat was about forty feet up and a hundred feet from where they were – not that far – but heading up meant they'd be vulnerable, and great whites loved to strike from below.

Brady eased his hand down to the diving knife on his calf. It was more to bolster his courage as he knew the six inch blade was near worthless against the huge predator and he doubted he'd even be able to penetrate its hide.

He motioned to Tris – *down* – she nodded, also knowing it was better to wait it out on the bottom.

As they glided lower, the huge shark veered away, fast. James felt his heart rate kick up as he knew what that meant – it was going to turn somewhere out in the dark blue water and then accelerate to take a run at them. It would come at them like a freight train, huge mouth gaping wide and teeth like serrated knives extending forward, ready to grab with the bite force of around 4,000 pounds per square inch. Then it would clamp those big bad-ass jaws down and shake its head from side to side to saw through muscle and bone, shredding everything.

Brady felt a wave of nausea run through him and he tasted bile. He glanced up at the surface again; he suddenly wanted to be back on deck sitting in the sunshine with Tris more than anything else in his life. He reached out to pull Tris behind him and readied himself.

Brady shivered, suddenly cold, but shook it away; sometimes you just gotta man-up, his father used to say whenever adversity struck.

He felt an elbow into his side and saw Tris float from behind him, her own knife gripped tightly in her hand. He tried to smile at her, but his mouth wouldn't work, and he turned back in time to see the large, dark shape come out of the blue gloom toward them.

Its jaws were wide, showing all the teeth, so many teeth – Brady screamed into his mouthpiece and went to slash forward with the dive knife, just as the shockwave from the impact threw him and Tris backwards in the water.

But it wasn't the shark colliding with him, but something even bigger than the great white colliding with it. And it wasn't just bigger, but *enormously* bigger.

Brady's eyes bulged and he barely felt Tris' hands dig into his arm as he saw the gigantic creature swim away with the shark hanging from each side of its mouth.

At first, he thought it was also a shark, as it had a shark's tail. But before it vanished into the dark water, he saw it had four large flippers, and a long, tapered head that was mostly finger-length conical teeth.

It kept going, not even paying them the slightest notice. It went. It went, and then it was gone.

Tris grabbed his arm and together they rocketed to the surface, sped to the boat, and he pushed her up and in. And on his turn, he knew he had never gone over the side of his boat so quickly in his life.

He lay on the deck in full wetsuit and pulled the mask off his face to feel the warmth of the sun. After a moment he grabbed Tris' hand, squeezed it as he pressed it to his lips. And then burst into tears.

# CHAPTER 14

Troy put an eye to the crack in the door and watched as several men led a 6-to-7 foot tall, biped dinosaur with its mouth bound in through a doorway opening through the tall wooden wall. He saw now that the structure was circular, and he had the feeling it was some sort of open arena, and he guessed by the way other villagers were streaming in through other entrances the show was about to start. And his gut told him he and Anne might be featured.

"That was a raptor, a, *ah*, medium-sized therapod." She pulled her face back from the door crack. "What's happening in there?" she asked.

"I think the evening's entertainment is about to kick off," he replied and stood back a step. "Tell me, those therapods, what are their weaknesses?" he asked.

"Compared to each other, or to us?" She faced him.

"To us. Just in case we had to fight one." He half smiled.

"*Pfft,*" she scoffed. "Well, my first bit of advice is, *don't* fight one." Then she must have seen the look on his face and her eyes went wide. "Oh god no." She suddenly seemed to understand what was going on and pressed her eye back to the door again. "That's like their version of a colosseum, isn't it?"

"That's what I'm thinking." He sighed. "So, what have you got?"

She frowned as she thought for a moment. "*Um,* well, that raptor was only about 250 to 270 pounds, and six and a half feet tall. But it will be able to move fast on its powerful hind legs. Each big toe will have an extended talon, like a long knife." She paced away. "Plus, it has backward curving teeth, all close together, and strong jaws, meaning significant bite and cutting force."

He laughed softly. "Let me know when we get to the weaknesses part."

"I'm trying." She scratched her head. "We now believe they were pack animals, so it will be vulnerable by itself." She spun and held up a finger. "Got it, one thing, and it's an old dino-joke – raptors would be bad at football because they can't sidestep."

He raised his eyebrows. "Is that true?"

She slowly hiked her shoulders. "Maybe. We think they can't easily change direction because of the bio-mechanical structure of their hip girdle. But how could we ever prove it?"

He nodded. "If it's all we got, then I'll take it."

Troy paced away and put his hand on his knife blade. His pack had been taken from him and probably lost. He had no doubt the giant Vikings had no idea what a gun was, so left everything in the pack. If he had a chance, he could retrieve everything. But that didn't help him now.

All he had was his knife, leather belt, and the gloves Anne had made him carry after the tree climb. He half smiled; he had one more thing – a wicked sidestep from college football.

Troy turned to her. He just hoped that he was sent in first, or at least they went in together. Even though he thought his chances of prevailing were less than even, he bet they'd be considerably better than Anne's if she was thrown in solo.

He turned to her. "We need a plan."

"Let me guess, it's high risk?" She lifted her chin, waiting.

"High risk, high return." He smiled.

She shrugged. "Then you know me; I'm all in."

***

That evening, fires were lit behind the wooden barricade walls, and more people were entering – men, women, and even older children.

"A real family affair." He laughed darkly. "Nothing like a little bloodshed for the kiddies before bedtime."

"Here they come," Anne said and stepped back.

The huge door opened, and the huge form of Birwulf and another warrior stood there. He glanced at each of them and then motioned for Anne to come forward.

"Are you afraid I will kill your pet too quickly?" Troy said in the ancient language.

Birwulf's huge bushy brows meshed and he turned slowly. He began to grin. "I will enjoy watching you be torn to pieces. And then I will eat your meat." He turned to Anne again and held out a log-like arm "Don't make me hurt you. Come."

Troy stepped forward. "In my culture, men fight men. We don't need to hurt women. That is for weaklings."

Birwulf swung an arm backwards and connected with Troy's head.

72

The blow knocked him down and his head felt like he was swimming under deep water. But he got straight back to his feet.

"Coward," Troy snorted with disdain. "This is a weak blow, from a weak warrior. I only wish it was you I was facing."

The warrior behind Birwulf made a noise in his throat, and Birwulf lunged forward and grabbed Troy by the neck. He lifted and shook him and looked about to strike him with a huge fist which would have broken Troy's neck.

But a soft word from the warrior behind reminded Birwulf he would rob the clan of their night's entertainment. Birwulf let his fist hang in the air for another moment as his lips pressed flat with rage.

He threw Troy to the ground and roared. A crafty look then stole over his face and he turned to Troy. "Then you will get your wish. The *dýr* waits for you. And it is hungry." He reached down to grab Troy's ankle and dragged him to the door.

Troy glanced at Anne and nodded. But she seemed frozen in shock. He knew the meaning of the word *dýr* – it roughly translated to *beast*. And sometimes, *monster*.

As he was dragged out, the other warrior reached down to pull Troy's knife from his scabbard.

Birwulf nodded and grinned. "No teeth for the little man."

***

Troy was dragged toward another smaller door in the barricade and pushed inside. The door was locked, and he saw it was a cell, and there was a similar door on the opposite side but this one with ribs of wood and a small, barred window. He walked toward it and peered through – as he suspected, inside there was a spiked wooden wall around a dirt arena.

He crossed back to the door he had entered through; this one also had a small window and he looked out at the crowd heading towards another gate – the viewing stands, he bet. He looked at their faces and saw the smiles, the laughter. Obviously, the games or executions held here were a big favorite of the villagers.

After a moment, his sixth sense told him someone was out there, just out of sight and close to the wall.

He took a chance. "Yrsa?"

The huge figure came a little closer and he saw her arm, recognising the swirling green clan tattoos. She continued to face away, perhaps lest she be caught talking to him.

"I am here," she said.

Then she quickly ducked down to look in at him. Her hand came in palm up. He wasn't exactly sure what she wanted, but he reached out to take her hand. It was bigger than his, and the palm rough; it was a fighting warrior's hand.

"You said…" she began, "…that you would fight for me."

He squeezed her hand. "I did."

She ducked down to look him in the eyes. "Did you mean it?"

He stared back. "You know I did."

After a moment, she nodded. Her hand squeezed harder. "No one has said that to me before."

"Perhaps no one has needed to," he replied.

There was silence for a moment more, and then she sighed. "I wish I was from your world."

She let his hand go and pulled her arm out. But it came straight back, and this time it held his knife. She handed it to him.

"Today, Troyson Strom, you must fight for yourself." She looked around and then brought her face closer to the window. "There will be no mercy asked or given. You must be ferocious and fearless."

He nodded. "I will."

"I will ask Odin that he gives you the speed and strength of Tyr." She reached in again, this time her finger and thumb holding something small. He took it and saw it was a small carved jade heart.

He smiled at the affectionate gesture from the giant warrior woman. "Thank you."

"Swallow it," she said.

"What?" He looked up, not sure he had heard her right.

"It is our custom. Swallow it, and it means you will carry my heart inside you into battle." Her face was deadly serious. "Then I will be fighting with you."

*Oh boy,* he thought and looked at the quarter-sized stone. At least it was smooth, he thought.

Troy popped it in his mouth, worked it around to draw up some spit, and then swallowed. Luckily it went down. He couldn't imagine what sort of insult it might be if he gagged it back up in front of her.

"Thank you," he said, but when he looked up, he saw she was already gone.

Troy stuck the blade in the empty scabbard on his belt and sighed. *The strength of Tyr,* she had said. That was good, he guessed, as he was the powerful Viking god of war. The only downside was that god had only one arm as he lost the other one while trying to fight a giant wolf named Fenrir. He hoped he had better luck.

The door behind him opened and he turned expecting it to be Yrsa again, but this time it was another warrior who entered. This one had a shortened spear that came to his shoulder, and above Troy's head. The huge man glared at him and then thumped the butt of the spear on the ground. "Prepare yourself."

Troy knew what the guy's job was – when the door was opened, he was the one to *encourage* Troy to leave.

Troy stood at the door and glanced out through the bars – there were stands where people stood and some sat, and lit torches illuminated the stands. There were also lit torches placed all around the edge of the arena. He guessed they were there to light up the killing field and probably also to stop whatever beast they had inside from leaping over the fence. To make doubly sure of that, there were sharpened wooden spikes all pointing inwards.

From across the arena and behind an opposite door, there was a hissing roar, and from time to time a shadow passed by the bars. It would be his adversary, and his hand automatically went to feel his knife for reassurance. He also reached into his pocket to draw out the length of rope – only about ten feet of soft cord, but it was strong, and he rolled it around and up his forearm. It would serve as his shield and also, he hoped, his weapon.

From above his head there was a sliding noise and then he saw the barred door over his cell begin to be pulled upwards.

From behind, the warrior grabbed his arm. Troy turned, expecting to get some sort of insult or shove. But instead, the big man patted his shoulder.

"Yrsa has friends," he said and from under his tunic produced a long claw like weapon with a handle at one end.

He held it out and Troy took it. He nodded, and then held it up. "For Odin."

The warrior smiled. "May his strong arm be with you on this day. And if not, may your courage carry you to the Great Hall."

"Good enough." Troy turned back and sucked in a deep breath all the way to the bottom of his lungs.

He hung the claw weapon on his belt just as the door was pulled all the way up. Surprisingly, he didn't feel nervous at all, and he didn't need to be pushed, but instead stepped boldly out.

The air was warmer against his skin than he expected, probably due to all the lit torches hanging over him. The crowd of now more than fifty cheered when he arrived and he looked up, only just making out a few of the Vikings he recognised from the hunting party – there was Skarde, sitting on a throne that was the skull of some mighty beast with the snout rising behind him and the teeth all forming a crown over his head.

Next to him was Yrsa sitting on the edge of her chair and staring down with apprehension with one of her hands curled into a fist at her throat. Seated beside her was the scowling Birwulf, his mouth twisted into a cruel sneer – he was obviously hoping for a brutal and bloody death for Troy. Troy laughed back in his face, trying to look more confident than he really was.

There were a few others of the party who captured them, and he walked slowly around the arena. Beneath his feet was hard packed clay that was stained in large areas with blood, some fresh and red, and some an ancient brown. The arena had been used often and for many years.

Troy walked closer to the chieftain's seated area and felt the older man's eyes on him. Yrsa sat even further forward.

Troy knew the spectacle was everything in these events, so he held his arms wide and raised his voice. "I am Troyson of family Strom. I gladly submit to your challenge." He began to turn slowly taking in the entire crowd, his arms still wide. "I will win this day." He stopped and pinned Birwulf with his gaze. "Because I am a man of honour and bravery." His mouth curved at the corners as he knew exactly what he was going to ignite. "Unlike some whose stink of cowardice even reaches me here."

Birwulf's eyes physically bulged as the crowd turned to look at him. Everyone knew who Troy was referring to, and he was making it personal.

Birwulf screamed a command to someone out of sight and immediately at the opposite end of the arena, the door began to slide up. His adversary was about to make an appearance.

Troy waited. There was nothing but darkness behind the door, and he backed up a little. He pulled out the knife and balanced on the balls of his feet.

Still nothing happened, and he felt like he was in a vacuum as all external sights, sounds, and smells vanished around him and he could only focus on that dark mouth of a doorway.

And then it came, fast, exploding out of the darkness.

The creature was probably a little taller than Troy, but its forward jutting head sat on a powerful neck of muscle, and it was now down and pointed forward. Its tail was rod straight out behind it, used for balance as a pair of powerful legs propelled it forward as it gathered speed.

Just as Anne had predicted, on each big toe was a dark, curved talon which he knew could have disembowelled him at a stroke. A theropod raptor, Anne had called it.

From the crowd there were a few laughs, some *oohs* and *aahs*, and a few rousing cheers. And as the creature came, its body dappled in the fire-light, it hissed like a train jamming on its brakes.

It crossed the distance between the doorway and Troy in only a few seconds, and Troy jinked to the right, and then immediately hard stepped the other way.

As he hoped, the theropod went in the opposite direction. From what Anne had told him, it had the binocular vision of a hunter, and its skull size meant it was probably at least as smart as a dog, so he didn't know how long he had before the thing would adapt to his strategy.

It skidded to a stop and came back. Troy could only think that it had been starved as it seemed furious in its desire to get at him, and given the upper and lower rows of razor-sharp teeth and powerful jaws, he couldn't afford to let it get a single bite out of him.

It accelerated again, and this time as well as the blade clamped in his right fist, he drew out the single long claw on the handle the Viking had given him and he opened his arms like a matador as it bore down on him.

Once again, he feinted left, and stepped hard to the right, but it had adapted already, and it didn't swerve this time. He threw himself aside, as it sailed past, this time its jaws snapping so close he smelled the stink of its carnivore breath and saw into the red furious eye as it went overhead. But Troy didn't waste his chance and as it passed over him he slashed upward with the long dark talon weapon, jamming it into the thing's throat and leaving it there.

It coughed and shook its head, and then staggered. Blood spurted as it used one leg to lift it like a dog and try and use its claws to dig out the thing sticking in its throat. Troy didn't wait to see if it could and sprinted at the therapod.

It heard him and began to turn. But he was on it before it finished its spin, and he jammed the knife blade into the eye socket where it sunk in a good six inches.

The theropod staggered away and Troy thought for a moment that maybe he hadn't sunk the blade in deep enough and perhaps missed the brain. But the creature ran straight into the wall, and then turned. It walked back slowly towards him, the talon weapon hooked deep in its neck and the blade protruding from one eye. And then it collapsed, shuddered, and lay still.

Troy crossed to it and put a foot on top of it and yanked his blade out. He wiped it on the creature's downy feathers and then looked up at Skarde. "Where I come from, the people are brave." He yelled his words and turned slowly. "The clan here are brave. All except for one."

He sucked in a breath. *Here goes nothing*, he thought, and pointed his knife at Birwulf. "And that one is Birwulf. Birwulf, the coward."

The crowd audibly gasped. Skarde sat forward, his eyes wide, and Yrsa's eyes blazed but sat straight with a smile lifting her lips.

Birwulf was on his feet, his face blood red and visibly shaking with rage at the insult from the small person, and one he was more used to killing and eating than being offended by.

Troy sheathed his blade and reached down to rip the talon weapon out. He tucked it into his belt again. He stood with hands on hips.

"I challenge Birwulf, the coward." He began to walk around the arena. "If he wins, you may feast on my bones." He stopped in front of Skarde and Yrsa. "But if I win, I demand safe passage."

Skarde smiled and sat back. The crowd silenced and the chieftain lifted his voice. "What say you, Birwulf? Will you accept this challenge? Or the insult?"

Birwulf's face was rage red, and he roared. "I accept." He pointed and was handed a battle axe that probably weighed as much as Troy did.

He hefted it and glared down at Troy. "But we will not be able to feast on your bones, little man. For there will not be enough meat left on you to feed to a *skrnlnk*."

Troy had no idea what a *skrnlnk* was but assumed it was some sort of small animal.

The huge man didn't need to find his way to any stairs but instead leapt out over the spikes and lit torches to land in the arena. Troy felt the thump as he hit the ground.

He stood to his full height, and Troy gulped. The man was not only a physical mountain, but hugely muscled. He must have weighed 500 pounds, easy. And he wasn't a lumbering oaf, but fast and agile.

Troy did his best to hide his trepidation and smiled. All he had was his blade and talon weapon against the huge axe, but watching the big man swing it, the thing looked heavy, even for Birwulf, and would not be easy to adjust its angle mid-flight.

Troy had no doubt that even a glancing blow from that massive weapon would be his end. And then when down, Birwulf would chop him to pieces. As Yrsa had told him: expect no mercy. Did she know it would come to this? Or she just hoped it would?

Troy went into a crouch and began to circle the big man. One of the things that his agency training had taught him was where the vulnerable places were on a human body – the eye sockets, the temples, the nape of the neck, up into the armpit, the diaphragm, and of course, the groin – a good deep strike into any one of those areas would debilitate the giant.

The thing was, with the short blade, he had needed to get in close to deliver the killing blow. And that was going to be the challenge.

Birwulf lifted the axe, one hand on the handle end and the other hand just behind the huge iron double bladed head. His eyes were on Troy and his mouth twisted into a confident smile.

Troy could tell the giant wanted his blood more than anything else, and he decided to stoke his anger even more because a furious anger made for bad decision making.

"I can smell your fear," Troy laughed into the giant's face. "It stinks, like all cowards stink."

Birwulf roared and charged. As he came, he drew the axe to one side and swung it in a horizontal sweep. If Troy was Birwulf's size, the attempted blow would have forced him to leap back or try and counter it. But for someone Troy's size, a measly six feet two inches, he was able to duck under the blow, and slash out with his knife, catching the giant Viking across the thigh.

He opened a three-inch wound, painful for sure, but it was far from enough to slow him down. And Birwulf refused to acknowledge or even look down at the wound as it streamed blood down over his knee.

He grinned. "You will need a thousand pinpricks to bring me down." He readied his axe again. "I will need only one."

Troy knew he was right. He could not let the giant land a single blow.

Birwulf charged again and feinted to the right. Troy dodged left, but Birwulf was much quicker and smarter than the raptor and jabbed back with the hilt of his axe to catch Troy in his mid-section and sent him rolling across the hard packed dirt.

*Bastard*, Troy thought. He'd used the same strategy against Troy that he used against the dinosaur.

Birwulf pressed his advantage while Troy was on the ground and swung the axe in an arc to bring it down onto where Troy lay.

Troy rolled as the massive axe thumped down and buried itself a foot into the dirt. He felt the impact right through his body and was up and sprinting away to the cheers of the crowd.

Birwulf grunted as he drew the axe out and chased him.

Troy headed for the wall of the arena, and the Viking followed fast, gaining on him. The huge man probably thought he was going to corner Troy, and he spread his arms wide, hoping to either hook him with the axe head, or grab him with his plate-sized other hand.

Troy glanced up and saw Yrsa with eyes wide, and he accelerated at the barrier, leapt up on it, and then used it to spring back – directly at Birwulf. He moved far too quickly for the big man to act and as he flew past, he slashed out with the blade, catching him this time in the side of the neck.

Troy landed and spun. He saw that this time the wound was deep, but not a kill stroke. However, it bled heavily, and that meant that now the longer the fight went on, the more of Birwulf's energy would drain away like his blood poured from his body.

Troy knew there was another way to bring the fight to an end as he knew that if he goaded Birwulf into more high energy activity while he bled out, his heart would struggle to find oxygenated blood – so that's what he did.

"If you submit, I'll let you live," Troy said.

Birwulf's eye burned, but he breathed heavily, and he seemed to find the axe heavy now. Troy glanced up and saw the crowd had begun to jeer, not at him, but Birwulf.

The thing about bullies, Troy had found out over the years, was that while they were strong, the crowd went along with them. But once they began to lose power, the crowd quickly regained its voice and hungered for them to lose. All those he had bullied in the past, now wanted him to fall.

Birwulf sucked in a few deep breaths, filling his chest, and then he roared his frustration and anger. Troy bet that in the past his battles would have been a toe-to-toe slash and bash fest with mighty blows rained down upon shields and opposing massive weapons. And not against a foe that simply avoided being hit.

Birwulf sucked in and blew out breaths like a bull about to charge. His eyes were red rimmed with fury and then with an almighty shout, he came at Troy again. But this time the movement of the axe was sluggish in his hands.

Troy didn't wait but sprinted to meet him. They closed the space between each other fast, and Birwulf managed to swing the huge axe forward.

But Troy wasn't where the axe cut the air, and the rotation of the heavy weapon pulled the big man off balance. As he staggered, Troy slashed downward at the back of his heel, cutting through the achilles tendon.

Birwulf was hobbled, and the arena was now turning red with his blood. He went down on one knee and Troy ran at him and lowered his shoulder to collide with the center of his back. Even though Troy bounced off, jarring his own bones, the big man was thrown forward, and his axe flung from his hand.

Troy walked to the axe and dragged it back to the man. He looked up into the stands. Skarde returned a flat gaze, but Yrsa's eyes shone with excitement, awe, and something else, was it adoration?

Around the small stadium a chant began to rise: *Strom, Strom, Strom.*

After anther moment, Skarde gave him an almost imperceptible nod. Troy looked down at Birwulf. He knew the man would never be on his side, and if he allowed him to live, then sooner or later the giant would take the opportunity to crush his skull. Even now, the big man stared up at him with a hatred that bordered on psychotic.

He knew Birwulf would never let the insult of the defeat go unchallenged. And Troy couldn't live with that threat hanging over he and Anne's heads while they remained stuck on the island.

Birwulf's face was drained of color as his lifeblood ebbed away. His eyes slid away from Troy and looked up toward the heavens. "Valhalla," he whispered.

"You fought well," Troy said softly. "And you will be welcomed by the Valkyries."

Troy sucked in a breath, drawing all the strength he had left, and raised the huge axe over his head and brought it down on the man's neck. The strike was good, and the axe stuck in the dirt. Birwulf's head was cleanly severed and bounced away across the arena leaving a trail of dark blood.

The crowd cheered and Troy let go of the axe handle and then turned to hold his arms wide. "I am Troyson Strom. I come in peace to your lands. All I ask is safe passage."

Skarde, still expressionless, nodded again. He turned to whisper something to Yrsa, and then left his seat. Troy breathed heavily and felt all jittery. As the adrenaline left his system his body began to crash from all the traumas. He was covered in bruises, cuts, and abrasions, and he suddenly felt like he wanted to throw up. But he would never do it in front of this crowd.

The barred door from his waiting room slid upward, and the Viking who had given him the talon weapon smiled and waved him in. Troy went to the door, and the man slapped him on the shoulder, nearly knocking him over.

"You are a great warrior." He leaned closer. "But I wagered you would be killed quickly, so I lost my bet."

Troy grinned. "Thanks. But I for one, am glad you lost."

\*\*\*

The outer door was opened, and Troy saw an old Viking woman was waiting for him. He saw that her long silver hair was woven through with bones, feathers, and little bags probably of mystic herbs. He knew enough about the culture to tell she was the clan's healer, and he must have garnered enough respect to have her tend to him.

He would have preferred Anne to treat his wounds, but right now, he didn't want to upset anyone with a cultural insult. He just hoped he did enough to get his pack and weapons returned to him.

The night was rapidly cooling, and he shivered, perhaps feeling the cold more as his energy levels lagged. She led him to a wooden dwelling and inside it was dry and warm as there was the embers of a fire still glowing in a fire pit.

There was a large platform, probably a bed, covered in the softest hides and feathers. The healer gave him a warm drink that he thought was some sort of fermented beer but had a meaty flavor that burned the back of his throat as it went down.

She then motioned for him to lay flat, and she began to remove his torn and bloody clothing. *What the hell?* he thought, and then he let her. He lay naked and shut his eyes and let her wash and bathe his wounds. Her hands were rough, but he could tell she did her best to be gentle and he ignored their abrasiveness.

After a while the hands left him, and he heard the healer moving around the room. Troy kept his eyes closed and drifted, feeling relaxed and comfortable.

He thought about Anne and wondered if she even knew he had survived. He bet that if she thought he was dead she'd be terrified right now, and he needed to get back to her. He also wondered about Tygo and where and what that asshole was up to. And the island, getting home, and the drekka. He must remember to ask the Vikings about the dragon. So many things on his mind. He sighed. For now, he'd just let it all go.

And then the hands were back on his body, rubbing a smooth scented oil over him. This time the hands felt less rough, less weathered. They rubbed his chest and stomach, softly now, almost caressing.

And when they slid even lower, perhaps it was the scent of whatever was rubbed on him, the warmth, or the sensation of it all, he couldn't help himself become aroused.

He was too embarrassed to open his eyes so decided to just pretend he was asleep. And then the hand gripped his hardness.

His eyes flicked open.

It was Yrsa, and he tried to sit up, but she pushed him back down with one hand while the other still held him in her warm, oiled grip.

He continued to watch her as her pale blue eyes never left his. She smiled almost dreamily at him as she leaned closer to whisper her words.

"No one has ever fought for me, Troyson Strom."

She released him and began to unpick her clothing – a strip of armored leather from her chest, gauntlets, a small cloak, the dress-like tunic, and she let them all fall to the floor.

Yrsa stood before him, and he couldn't take his eyes away. He knew from home sports that there was a Polish female basketballer that was seven feet two inches tall. But Yrsa would have been another half-head taller and had a strong athletic figure.

Her muscular frame was covered in green tattoos of runes, sworls, and depictions of shields, swords, and axes, and he could smell more of the scented oils as her body glistened so she must have anointed herself as well.

She wasn't bashful at all, and she held her arms wide for him to admire her. The whole scene was just, impossibly, erotic.

She came forward and leaned to press her mouth over his. It had been ages since he had made love to anyone and when she began to climb onto the bed, he couldn't help his hands reaching for her

*Forgive me, Anne*, he thought.

# CHAPTER 15

Troy woke the next morning still in the healing hut. He sat up and threw his legs over the side. He stretched his muscles and groaned from the aches and pains that plagued his body and wasn't sure if they were from the battle with the theropod and then Birwulf, or from the torrid lovemaking with the giant Viking woman.

He laughed softly. He had never felt so overpowered in his life. After their third time, he had felt so drained that he fell asleep cradled in her arms right after. And looking about the room, he saw his clothing had been cleaned and there was rough stitching holding the tears together. Plus, his missing pack was in the corner.

"Yes." He quickly crossed to it and ripped it open. The guns, night vision goggles, and the last of their supplies were still there.

The door pushed inward, and Yrsa returned with a bowl of fruit, and one of dried meat. Plus a jug of water, he hoped, because he didn't feel like a heady beer first thing in the morning.

She put the plate down, crossed to him, and he stood. She grabbed his face and bent to kiss him again.

"Because of you, I am now free." She straightened. "And unless there is a challenge, I will be the clan chieftain one day." Yrsa continued to stare. "Birwulf was a mighty warrior and had high clan status. That is now yours, as are all his possessions and claims that were taken in fair battle."

Troy nodded; it was as he hoped.

She tilted her head, her eyes warm. "I think I would be a good ruler. But a better one with a strong husband beside me. And now I can choose my husband."

She reached out to rub her hand up his side and looked him up and down, and he realised he was still naked. He eased back a step and took

84

her hand in his.

"I'm glad. We should all be free." He pulled on a sad expression. "But I must return home soon." He pointed to a chair. "But stay while I eat and dress and talk to me. Tell me about your clan."

Yrsa's cheeks reddened a little at the rebuff, and she took her hand back. But after a moment she sighed and nodded. Troy pulled on his trousers and then popped a large, succulent looking berry into his mouth. It was so sour it nearly made his eye twitch.

"My people have been here for... a long time. This is a magical place, the home of Odin and the frost giants." She held up a hand. "And it has been good to us. It made us grow strong and tall."

"So you were normal, *ah*, I mean our size, when you first came?" he asked.

She nodded. "I have seen some of the most ancient burial places broken open, and the bodies were smaller. This island has many ferocious beasts and the extra strength Odin gifted to our tribe was a good thing."

"I'll bet." He looked up at her. "I have a question. You are some of the best boatbuilders in the world. Why didn't you leave? Try and return home?"

"Some did." She shrugged. "But the rest felt that this is now home. There is nowhere else we want to be. Things stay the same here. Though our lives can be hard, it is these brutal challenges that will allow us to earn the right to cross the rainbow bridge to Valhalla."

"Of course they will." Troy, now full dressed, perched on the edge of the bed and began to consume the breakfast in earnest. He realised he was starving, and the salted and dried meat was an odd flavor but delicious.

"What is your world like, Troyson of the house of Strom?" She lifted her chin, her eyes glowing. "Are you a chieftain or a great warrior?"

"No, I am a normal man. Better than some, not better than others." He smiled. "And my world is fast, and crowded. Many people live in large cities, like towns, with more people than you can count." His mouth turned down. "But there are still wars, and we have damaged some of our land and water. Made it dirty."

She stuck her tongue out. "I would not like that. And I think you would not either. You should stay here." Her voice grew soft. "With me." She looked away as her cheeks flushed crimson.

The silence hung in the air between them for a few moments until Troy sat forward and took her hand.

"I need to get home, Yrsa. If I can." He leaned closer, still holding her hand. "Do you remember how you got here? Your clan."

She bobbed her head. "There is a story about how our clan came to be here. They say we descended from the *Himmelens mor*."

Troy translated it as being something called the 'Mother of the sky'. "What is that?" he asked.

She shook her head. "I do not know, Troyson Strom. Not even the elders remember anymore. It is said the story of our clan's birth is hidden in the caves of the drekka."

"The caves of the dragon." He thought he knew where that might be. "I think I've seen where the drekka lives."

She quickly rounded on him. "Never enter that place. The drekka guards it day and night and any who enter leave their scent behind, and it will follow and find you." She got to her feet, her eyes wide. "Promise me, Troyson."

He smiled. "I've seen the drekka. It is a monster. Does it bother you here?" he asked.

She shook her head and sat again. "It does not come here to the highlands. That is why we are here," she said.

"Where did it come from?" he asked.

"It has always been here." Her brows came together a little as if his question was a silly one. "Some legends say it fell from the sky as an egg. And hatched."

"The meteor crater," he whispered.

"Meteor?" she asked.

"Doesn't matter." He looked up. "Is there only one?"

"Only one drekka?" She shrugged. "I do not know. To the drekka we are all food. Even the other mighty beasts. We stay out of its lands, and it stays out of ours."

He nodded. "Good advice."

After a moment, she looked up. "Troyson, will you stay?"

After a moment he shook his head. "No, I can't. I need to let Anne know I'm alive. She will be worried."

"I knew it. She is your mate." She snorted. "I could kill her. Then you would also be free."

"No, she's not my mate. But she is my good friend. And besides, if you hurt her I would not be free, but instead be bound by my hatred. For you." He stared hard at her.

Yrsa held his gaze for a moment before dropping her eyes and making a guttural sound in her throat. "I would not want that." She stood.

He sighed and nodded. "If, when, I leave, will I have safe passage?" he asked.

She sighed and finally turned back. "Yes." She smiled. "You did my father, Skarde, a great favor by defeating Birwulf. The clan would not be better with him as leader."

"Thank you." he said.

"Where is your camp… on the island?" she asked.

"Near the coast. Past the fortress that holds the heart of Odin," he replied. "Another place protected by the drekka."

"It draws the clans like a precious bloom draws the bees." She laughed softly. "I would not enter there if I was you."

*Too late*, he thought.

"Skarde will ensure you have safe passage, and I will obtain a map for you," she announced.

She reached out a hand and Troy took it. "Thank you," he said.

"But promise me this, Troyson Strom. There are worse things than the drekka that live in these lands. Always be on your guard."

"I will." He smiled.

The huge woman leaned forward and grabbed his face in both her hands and pulled him closer. She then kissed him hard and pulled back a little but still held his face a moment more, looking deep into his eyes. She then stood and took the medallion from around her neck and hung it over his head.

He lifted it in both hands and read: It was an image of a tall warrior with a long beard holding a spear and shield. It was like one of the earliest depictions of Odin that existed and was found on a cave wall on the island of Gotlan from around the 13th century.

She grabbed both his hands, still holding the medallion in one of hers and she closed her eyes. "May his gaze be upon you, and you forever have his luck." She bowed her head just a little and then turned to the door. She paused there to look back at him for a moment, her ice blue eyes on his and the gaze penetrating deeply. Then she turned and was gone.

"Thank you," he whispered as the door closed.

***

Later that morning Troy was let back into the small hut like dwelling where Anne was waiting.

"Troy!" On seeing him she rushed to him, grabbed him in an embrace, and then held him back to look him over. "Oh my god, you're a mess."

"You should see the other guy," he chuckled.

She leaned forward to sniff him. "But you smell fine. Did they wash you?"

"Yeah, I got a bit bloody and dirty. But the good news is I won, and they're going to let us go." He held up his pack. "And gave me back our gun, and supplies." He handed her the smaller pack.

She grabbed it, checking inside and then brought out the remaining iodine and bandages. "Do I need to check you for wounds?" She took hold of his arm.

"I'm okay," he replied.

"What happened?" She held onto him.

"Not much. I just had to fight a dinosaur, and then one of their warriors." He raised his eyebrows. "Considering what we've already been though it was a walk in the park."

She scoffed.

He wasn't sure she believed him, but he had been lucky. He had won their freedom. Because if he had of been killed, the pain was over for him. But Anne might have ended up on the menu. He had to remember that about Yrsa; these people were cannibals.

She squinted at his shirt, and then pants, and walked slowly around him checking all the stitching holding his ripped clothes together. "Who's your tailer?" She grinned and then stopped in front of him and lifted the medallion that was hanging around his neck. "What's this?"

"Oh that… One of the warriors gave it to me. I guess it's like a medal of freedom," he lied.

"I like it." She nodded and let it drop against his chest. "I've seen that image before somewhere."

"It's a very old depiction of Odin." He pressed against the door and found it still locked from the outside. "We should get ready to leave as soon as we can."

"Okay." She scoffed softly. "As a scientist I'd love to learn more about this clan of people. Plus, I'd like to get a DNA sample to find out how they grew this big."

He smiled. "Skarde told me we are permitted to leave. But I doubt that would extend to taking blood from his people."

Troy put the pack over his shoulders and tucked the gun in the back of his belt. "Ready?"

Anne nodded slowly, and then exhaled. "Okay, I'm good." She nodded to his chest. "Let's hope that medal of freedom is good for two."

"If you must stay behind, at least you might end up taller. You always wanted that, right?" He chuckled and turned back to the door and banged on it.

The bolt was pulled back and the warrior outside nodded deeply to Troy. "Strom."

It was about mid-morning now and the misty sky was throwing down a diffused white light. It was cool but not cold. Many of the clan had come out to see them, whispering and watching as the pair of small humans passed by with the warrior escort.

"Which way?" Anne asked.

"I guess we head back the way we came," Troy said.

"Troyson."

Troy turned to see Yrsa coming toward him. She was an awesome sight with hair braids twined with all her hunting decorations. Her tunic was sleeveless and allowed her strong tattooed arms to be displayed. He noticed she had reapplied the streak of dark color across her face that made her eyes shine like lights.

She smiled and held out a roll of softened animal skin. "For you."

"The map." He took it and opened it.

Yrsa pointed. "We are here."

There was a tiny image of a village, and the rest was mountains, plains, rivers, with designated areas that had small pictures of different animals, obviously for hunting, or some large two-legged variety to avoid.

There was even an area he knew well, named *drekka lund*, the dragon's land, and Odin's fortress. It was a valuable map as the detail gave him a good idea of where he was and where he needed to get to.

He nodded as he looked at it briefly. There were areas of the mountains and coast he needed to study further, but for now, he had what he needed to get going. He rolled it back up and looked up at the tall, striking Viking woman.

"Thank you, Yrsa. Thank you for everything."

She reached out a hand and lay it on his shoulder near his neck. Two of the fingers gently caressed his skin. "No, thank you, Troyson Strom." She shared a broken smile with him, and her eyes glistened a little. "May we meet again, in this world, or in Odin's great hall."

She seemed to remember herself and drew her hand back and straightened. She nodded again, and then turned on her heel.

"I can't understand what she said..." Anne's brows came together, "...but, looks like you certainly made a friend there."

"I set her free." He turned to her. "The asshole I had to fight wanted to take over the clan, force her into a marriage union. She didn't want that."

"Where is he now, this giant Viking you beat?" Anne asked.

"On his way to Valhalla, I assume." He smiled.

"You killed him?" She blew air between puffed cheeks. "Holy shit."

He exhaled and nodded. "Yeah, it was him or me."

He unfurled the map again and holding it up on one hand traced a path with his finger. "We start back the way we came but let's avoid the grasslands with those damn long legged alligators." He traced another trail that led back to the coast. "This way."

"Works for me." She hefted her pack.

"Let's get going. We don't want to miss Tygo, and I still need to work up the courage to go diving in a prehistoric sea for the heart of Odin." He started off.

Anne stayed at his shoulder as the giants watched them pass by, commenting and nodding as they went.

As Troy spoke to a few of the massive Vikings he recognized, he saw the admiration in their eyes, possibly reassessing him now after his win against Birwulf. He looked up towards one of the largest dwellings on a slope and saw Yrsa standing out front.

He lifted the medallion she had given him and kissed it. The Viking woman put a hand against her chest, then curled her hand as if she was grabbing something before she then motioned throwing it to him – her heart – he pretended to catch it and put it to his mouth. He was keeping her heart within in.

Yrsa then raised her hand and continued to watch him go.

He and Anne passed without incident from the village and then headed down the trail. He let the medallion drop. He just hoped the talisman gave him Odin's luck as it was supposed to, as this place had a million ways to kill them in the blink of an eye.

# EPISODE 11

*Fear has many eyes, and can see you everywhere*

# CHAPTER 16

**Ain Diab Beach, Casablanca, Morocco**

Like specks of dust the larvae of a myriad of tiny animals poured from the warm waters behind Odin's Gate. They drifted in the temperate currents, aimless, and in their billions.

Many that fell outside of the warm water corridor immediately died, shocked by the significant change in temperature. Others were scooped up by the large oceanic plankton eaters. And just some, like the larvae of *Pennichnus formosae*, the extinct giant sandworm, found their way to warm, clear shallows, where they immediately settled to the bottom to burrow into the sand to begin their new life.

The *Pennichnus* was closely related to the modern-day Bobbit worm, which was also large and predatory, and sometimes referred to as the 'sand striker,' because as it sensed vibrations with its antennae, it then launched itself from its sunken burrow to grab its prey with powerful jaws, and then drag it into its sand burrow to be dined on at its leisure.

The ancient *Pennichnus* was like the Bobbit worm, except it was three times the size, and was an aggressive hunter of the shallows. With a fist-sized head, viciously spiked jaws, and a muscular body that extended up to twenty feet below the sand, it could, and did, take on prey much bigger than it was.

\*\*\*

Sam Ibn Abadi dropped anchor in the shallows and stood on deck, bare chested, in a pair of swim shorts. He raised his binoculars and slowly looked along the beach front. He was on an extended holiday from the company and planned on doing nothing but swim, snorkel, sunbake, and eat extremely well.

It was mid-morning and still quiet with a few joggers, some

sunbakers toward the middle of the long beach, and further down, a dog chasing a ball at the more popular southern end.

Ain Diab Beach was about two miles long and lay between the two rocky peaks of the Corniche and the Sidi Abderrahman marabout, and Sam turned back to the northern end where the reefs were submerged below the water. He was planning a morning of snorkelling and if he could spear a fish or two, then his lunch was set. And he had his camera ready to send the pictures back to the office.

He went below deck, grabbed up his hand spear, face mask and flippers, and threw a towel over his shoulder. He then eased himself over the side where the water was chest deep and he made his way to the shore while he held the towel and his gear over his head.

He grinned; he had it to himself and the water was bath warm and crystal clear. He wondered why he never did this sooner – this was living, real living, and not the loud and bustling, and manically fast life of a modern office and city.

Sam came up on the beach and walked the extra few hundred yards to the cove-like northern end. He dropped his towel on the dry sand, placed the dive mask and snorkel on his forehead, and lifted his flippers and spear and walked down toward the water.

It was high tide, and he guessed at low tide this area was a huge sand flat. But with plenty of extra tide water it would allow the bigger fish to come in closer – *Perfect*, he thought.

He looked down at the water and frowned – there was a bunch of grey, white, and black feathers and a single webbed foot. From the coloring he guessed it was the large, black-backed gull that had met its demise.

Too shallow for sharks, he thought, and looked about; maybe a dog got hold of it. He turned back to the mess; if it was, it must have been hungry as it left nothing but feathers.

Sam looked back down towards the southern end and wished more people would be responsible dog owners and keep them under control. Sam shook his head, sighed, and continued into the water, determined not to let it annoy him.

When he was just ankle deep, he dropped the flippers and slid his feet into them. Then he turned to walk backwards out to the deeper water.

And then his left foot became stuck on something, nearly tugging his flipper off.

Sam looked down into the clear water that was by now just under a foot deep. It looked like a dog's paw had grabbed onto his flipper.

*What's that?* he wondered and tugged on it. But the thing had come up out of the sand and fixed tight to the rubber fin top and wasn't going to let go. As he watched, the sand parted on the other side and another one came to the surface and this time latched onto the rubber heel.

Sam used the butt of his spear to jab at one of them, but it was like a bristled pipe of solid muscle that resisted being dissuaded. Whatever the things were they were alive and had decided to try and make a meal of his flipper.

Then to his alarm, more began to rise, and one grabbed his other flipper, now pinning both his feet. While he was distracted another had surfaced and latched onto his heel, this time above the rubber and getting onto the skin. The pain was immediate and excruciating, as whatever mouthpiece the thing had in its head it seemed to be full of needles and began to quickly bore into his flesh.

Sam swore loud enough to scare some gulls on the beach and dragged his feet out of his flippers, and stepped back as he prepared to sprint to the shore. But the worm was still clinging to the rear of his ankle, and in the seconds it took to reach down to try and dislodge it, another surfaced to grab the top of his other foot.

Once again, the pain was white-hot and worse than anything he had ever experienced in his life. This time Sam screamed, yelled, and tried to get someone's attention, but his choice of an isolated swimming area was working against him as the nearest person was around 200 yards down the beach.

He waved his arms, and then tried to use the sharp end of his spear to stab the worms. He was successful as the sharp tip pierced their rubbery flesh, but in those lost seconds he spent stabbing, all around his feet and ankles became crowded with more worm heads and he became locked in place.

The water around him began to flush pink, and with tears streaming down his cheeks, Sam tried to step away but couldn't and just fell backwards. The blood in the water, and his vibrations, by now had attracted dozens more worms and they were already just below the sand waiting for him.

They latched onto his thighs, the small of his back, and one of his hands. Slowly but surely, he was being pulled flat in the water and towards the sand bed.

It was just deep enough to cover him, and he screamed as he was dragged down by the bristling pipes with their round lamprey-like teeth that sawed and burrowed into his skin and muscle with a furious energy.

Sam's face went below the water, and he held his breath, but only for a few seconds, as he couldn't help the scream blasting from his lungs, and once that was gone, then in came the salty, warm water.

In another hour, what was once Sam, was some shredded lumps of flesh and bones that were gradually separated and dragged into separate worm burrows.

Eventually, all that remained of the man was a broken dive mask, a pair of ragged flippers, and a small sailboat anchored a few dozen feet from shore that no one would ever come to claim.

# CHAPTER 17

Troy waved Anne down and together they crouched on a rise that was a slope, leading down to the coastal waters.

"There." He pointed to the tops of the massive forest-like rib bones rising on the shoreline. "We're nearly home," he said.

"*Home*?" Anne scoffed.

"Well, home base," Troy corrected.

"Better." Anne pulled out her binoculars, the last pair they had, and scanned the water line. "No sign of anyone. But they may have beached their boats already."

"Maybe, but I doubt it," he replied. "I think they'd be anchored offshore and diving for the ruby as soon as they got here. I doubt they'd want to hang around."

"They might if they just wanted the ruby. But the big guy you shot may also want to settle the score. With you." She raised her eyebrows.

"Good point." He looked back at the water. "We need to get back down there, find where I left my dive mask and then get old Odin's Heart before they do."

"Then what?" she asked.

"Um." Troy scratched his chin. He hadn't really thought that bit through to its conclusion. They needed to get home, so needed a boat. He doubted Tygo or Elle would trade a ruby for their boat. Unless…

"Let's hope they bring two boats. They can have the ruby if they leave one for us."

"Don't worry, I've got your back. And something else." She held up one of her small fists. "See this?"

He nodded, grinning. "Yes, very impressive… and scary as well."

"Damn right; it's for that bitch, Elle." She punched it into the palm of her other hand.

"Ooh." Troy pursed his lips and sucked in air. "She's as good as dead." He laughed softly and placed a hand on Anne's shoulder to squeeze it.

Anne quickly put a hand over his. "Thank you."

He turned back. "For what?"

She shrugged. "Well, I'm pretty sure I'd be dead by now if it wasn't for you."

"And I'd be dead if it wasn't for you. But thank me when we get home." He smiled. "And I'm pretty sure if we never met, you wouldn't even be here."

He went to pull away, but she held onto his hand. "Troy…?"

He turned back. "Yeah?"

She stared back into his eyes for a moment, and then snorted softly and shook her head. "Nothing." She let his hand go.

*Strange girl*, he thought. He turned back to the slope, and then reached out to take her binoculars. He scanned the forest and after a moment of not seeing anything on the ground or trees, he handed it back to her.

"Let's go. Nice and quiet. We don't want to alert any predators, dino or human." He headed down the slope with Anne right behind him.

# CHAPTER 18

Tygo held the small jade eye in the palm of one hand, and the other rested on the ship's wheel. He had no lookouts for bergs because even though the freezing mist was like a London fog, the warm water meant they had all melted.

Elle stood beside him with her arms folded, her single green eye staring straight ahead with its usual hawk-like intensity.

She spoke without turning. "We're close now. I can feel it."

The wheelhouse door opened, and Hilda Bergensen entered. The marine biologist shook her head. "Unbelievable; the water's 72 degrees, almost tropical. We brought cold temperature wetsuits. We'll overheat if it's like this."

Elle half turned. She was a full head taller and looked down on the woman. "Wear them, don't wear them, we don't care." She fully turned to face the fit young woman and smiled at her with zero warmth. "But I'd take my speargun if I was you."

Tygo laughed darkly.

"What does that mean?" Hilda frowned. "Exactly what might we run into down there?"

Elle turned away. "We'll put you right over the artefact position. You drop down into water that will probably be under 50 feet, grab it up, and return to the surface. Joren will dive with you and have your back."

"Why am I not liking this vagueness? You're not paying me enough to commit suicide." Hilda stepped closer. "So I'll ask again…"

Elle spun to her and grabbed the front of her thick coat, pulled her close for a few seconds to glare into her face, and then pushed her back a couple of steps. "If need be, Joren can take over your job. Then you are not needed. So look around you."

Hilda bared her teeth and grabbed Elle's hand. But she briefly glanced out the windows at their bleak, mist-filled surroundings. She then turned back to Elle.

Elle craned forward until she was about three inches from the woman's nose. "This is not a good place to be pissing off the management. Is it?"

Hilda stared back, but then must have realized where she was and what she was pushing her way into.

She shrugged. "Hey, no problem. Just like to have as much information as possible before I dive."

"Of course," Tygo said over his shoulder. "We are not far away now, and I suggest you prepare your gear. We'll be taking to the boat soon."

Hilda saluted. "On it." She backed out of the cabin.

"Insect," Elle said as she took her place next to Tygo.

He chuckled. "But a needed insect. Be nice to her." He turned. "Until she surfaces with our prize."

Elle grunted. "As far as I am concerned, as soon as we have Odin's Heart and are back on board, then we don't need any of them anymore."

Tygo's smile lifted his beard. "They are just tools. And once we have finished with them, then it would be better for our security, and finances, if they all stayed behind.

"*Ahh*, I feel it." He held up the eye again. "It grows warm in my hand. It sees the heart." He cut the engines and let the boat glide. "Time to go to work."

# CHAPTER 19

Six hours later Olaf slowed his fishing boat. "The fog is too thick; I can't see anything, and the compass and sonar are both going mad." He turned to Anders and sniffed twice. "I can smell land, but I don't know if it is a hundred feet or a mile from us." The old man grimaced. "Sorry, son, but I don't think I can risk going in any further."

Anders nodded. "I expected this." He exhaled through his nose. "I feel we are close." He turned to his brother-in-law. "I think it is time."

Oder went below deck and reappeared seconds later with his large case. He took it out onto the foredeck and opened it. He fiddled with a control box, raising small antenna, and then almost as if by magic, a drone lifted from the case and straight up into the air.

The drone was a SkyQuad X, and the small black drone was fitted with inbuilt gyro and gravity sensors to allow it to navigate complex trajectories and stay out of trouble. It was fast, had an extremely long range, and was strong enough to be fitted with different accessories.

Olaf's mouth dropped open as he watched it hover above his foredeck. The drone was three feet long and two and a half wide, with a propeller at the end of each arm spoke. Its noise was little more than a gentle whine, and at its center there was a camera lens.

Oder came back into the wheelhouse with the now empty huge case, and the controller in the other hand. "And we're away." He stowed the case and leaned back against a bench and piloted the drone higher into the air.

On the small screen Anders could just make out their ship through the mist. But on another panel, there was a red blip and a segmented map – a position plotter.

"I've just loaded it with the tracking pellet and the camera for now. When we need something else fitted, I'll recall it and resend," he said

Anders knew what he meant by 'something else fitted' and looked across to the case that was still open – he saw the other attachments slotted in their foam cradles. And one of them was a 9mm handgun shining darkly. He smiled; like him, Oder had come ready for business.

"You're right," Oder said, looking at the screen. "Radar says we *are* close. Just under half a kilometer. I'll take it in, lead us, and then all we need to do is follow the drone on the tracker."

Olaf shook his head, and Anders put a hand on his shoulder. "Don't worry, we'll take to the rowboat. Just wait for us for two days, as we agreed."

The old man looked relieved. "I've plenty of tea, rum, and tobacco." He smiled. "I'll be here."

The old captain turned back to the front window which showed nothing but a billowing fog. He shook his head. "I'm not sure what you'll find out there." He turned. "But be safe."

# CHAPTER 20

### 5000BC – The Mountain – Greenland interior

Harald stood at the edge of the pit in the cave floor. He got down on his belly and held his burning torch lower and saw there were handholds chipped into the rock face.

He opened his hand and let the torch fall. As it dropped, he watched closely as the flame illumined the long pipe of stone. He saw that the handholds kept going ever lower. They weren't large, but they would do.

This was it; this was where they needed to go. He got to his feet.

"Brothers and sisters, this is our path." The small clan group had drawn down their masks of cloth as inside it was warmer, much warmer, and the breath of heat rose from the pit to warm their bones and unstiffen their fingers.

*Good*, he thought. Because they would need nimble fingers and stout muscles for the climb. He looked along their faces; their cheeks and noses flared red as the blood returned to them. In their eyes he saw fatigue, but they were all eager and none would complain. But he still needed them to steel their hearts.

Harald straightened to his full height. "We will climb down, and it will be long. And I cannot tell you how long." He slowly smiled. "But when we reach the bottom, we will find ourselves in Lemuria, Odin's home. And there we will prove ourselves worthy to the All Father, and we will receive the promise of a place in Valhalla for us and our kin."

The group hooted and raised arms. Many drew weapons and brandished them. Harald was proud of them, and their courage. And he hoped all would make the return journey with him.

But Harald knew the rest of the legend. And he knew that only those strong enough, brave enough, and cunning enough would survive the journey. Where they were going was the home of Odin's beating heart. And there were many foul beasts protecting it. None more so than the fearsome drekka.

Sune once again requested to climb first. The long and wiry man was an adept climber and had no fear of heights.

Harald would go second, and then the warriors would come down. There would be no ropes and Harald had ordered that they leave two body lengths between each person. If one were to slip, there was less chance of knocking the climber below off their handholds.

He looked again at the small, chipped ledges in the stone – they were little more than a half finger-length gouge in the rock. It was good that their fingers had thawed out, and that the rock was dry. He just hoped there was no moisture below.

When he had thrown the torch down it had fallen and fallen until the dot of light vanished completely. It would be a long climb, and he knew an even more arduous one on the way back.

Sune had started, and Harald adjusted his woven bag and then tied it closely to his body. Everyone had done the same as there had to be no swinging objects to unbalance them.

The last thing they all did was take out a small ember pot that had a length of thin rope tied to it. They packed it with dry wood, and then flicked some lit embers into its top. The glow from the ember would stay alight for many hours. It was only miniscule illumination, but in total darkness, even a speck of light was like sunshine.

Like the others, Harald hung his around his neck and then edged over the rim of the almighty pit, found a toe hold, and lowered himself down. Another toe hold, a finger hold, and then he began in earnest, working methodically, foot, hand, foot, hand, minute after minute, hour after hour.

His team above and Sune below continued down. He heard the groans from above and he tried to push thoughts from his head of wishing for a ledge, or anything he could stop on for just a few minutes to flex his hand and rest his aching shoulders. But there was nothing, and he knew their survival would come down to something beyond body strength, but the toughness of their minds.

Harald began to softly sing; it was an old song about battle, and victory, and Odin's great kingdom to come. Many of the warriors joined in, and the sound echoed in the pipe of rock they scaled down within.

Then they lost one.

Harald felt the body pass rather than heard it as it silently hurtled on its way to the dark depths. He turned to watch it and in its tiny pool of light he saw it bounce against the wall once on its way down to oblivion.

"Who was it?" he called.

From above he got his response.

"It was Tora," Inga replied. "She knew she was tiring too much. She didn't want to hold us up or ask for help. She let go."

Harald rested his head against the cold stone for a moment. Of course she let go. It was the Viking way. In times of battle or duress, you never ask for help. When the war was done, only then can you expect aid.

"Farewell, brave warrior." Harald said it softly but in the silence they all heard him. "We will see you in the great hall soon."

He then looked upwards, but there was nothing except the pinpricks of light from the ember pots above him that made his clan's faces glow a hellish red. "Steel your hearts, your flesh, your bones, *and*, your minds," he said. "We are nearly at our goal."

He said the encouraging words, but he knew he had no idea how much further they needed to climb down.

He faced downward. "Sune."

The man grunted and began his climb again.

*** 

Harald had felt the air warming for a while now. Through Odin's mercy on their way down, they had found a small perch of rock, they had taken turns resting on it. Just enough time to sip water, flex fingers, and then they continued.

After a time, Harald inhaled, drawing in the scents of damp soil, plants, and fresh water. Then the most encouraging words he had heard for years.

"I see light," Sune shouted up at him.

The group redoubled their efforts but knew to cling harder to the rock and not make a mistake in the final moments of their task.

Sune jumped down to a cave floor, and soon all the warriors had joined him. Many collapsed to lay flat, others rolled shoulders, or just bent over, hands on knees.

Harald saw there was a long slit in the stone, and watery, white light seeped in. He crossed to it, and carefully peered out. His face broke into a broad grin.

"This is Odin's land," he whispered.

The first thing he noticed was that they were up high and looked down on towering trees of a thick forest below them. They were on, or rather still in, a mountain. The rocky edifice rose above the forest, and in all directions, there was green, with a mist filled light filtering down. In the distance he could make out the sparkle of water, but he couldn't tell yet if this was ocean, lake, or river.

Harald gripped the edge of the crack and leaned out to look down. It was steep, and in some places treacherous, but after what they had just been through, the climb down was going to be the easy part.

He let his eyes roam over the forest; it was far bigger than he imagined. And now here, they had nothing but ancient legends to chart their path. He lifted his gaze and watched as a flock of giant bird-like creatures glided over the treetops. Given the distance it was hard to judge their size, but they looked bigger than an eagle, and perhaps even bigger than a man. His mouth watered at the thought of a giant chicken roasting on a fire.

Harald could hear down in the forest that all manner of creatures hooted, cawed, hissed, and roared, many with throats sounding of massive proportions, and not one of them he recognized.

He knew he needed a direction and the elders had told him that he had to follow the drekka's breath, and then enter its lair. In the distance and just over a hill, he saw steam rising and a soft red glow – if anything looked to be the breath of a dragon then that was it.

The danger didn't matter anymore. The group needed to hunt and feed as strength was going to be needed for the arduous tasks to come. And they could only do that in the forest.

He turned. "Let us find this dragon's lair, and pray it allows us safe passage through its lands. And if not..." He smiled, "... then one day they will sing of us as our names become legends."

The group raised hands and banged their chests. All looked weary, but their eyes still shone brightly.

"We head into the forest. Srgne and Birger will hunt down some game, and we will make camp and rest." He turned back to peer out at the forest and spoke without turning. "All need to be on guard, as this place will challenge us like no other."

This time he led them. "Follow." He stepped out.

# CHAPTER 21

Troy sat with Anne under a clump of trees with branches that hung around them like willowy curtains to give them shelter. He held his dive mask in his hands and stared out over the water – it was dark, and the silvery light filtering down only penetrated down a few feet and from then on, the shadows ruled.

"I can do this," he said more to himself than Anne.

"I don't like it," Anne whispered and then looked up. "Want me to come with you?"

He turned to smile at her. He nodded to his gun in her hands. "Thanks, but I need you here. If anything comes at me on the surface, I want you to take a shot at it. I'll deal with anything below."

"With just a knife?" She looked away.

He shrugged. "It's all I got. But believe me, I don't intend to be in there any longer than I have to." He held up the green orb that pointed straight out at the dark water. "I'm hoping this will point outwards, and when I'm over the top of the heart, then point down. So I swim down, grab it, and then head back to the shore like my pants are on fire." He grinned.

Anne looked from the orb to the water. "At least it tells us it's still out there, so Tygo hasn't arrived yet."

"Good," Troy replied.

Anne's expression remained unmoved. "I still don't like it."

Troy sighed and looked back at the water. "You said that. And I don't like it either."

"Um…" She got to her feet.

"Yeah?" he asked.

"What happens if you don't come back?" She shared a fragile smile.

He chuckled. "Then it would be safe to say that my day turned out a lot worse than yours."

Troy looked up and down the beach. There was nothing on the shoreline, or at the tree line he could see. But that didn't mean there wasn't some sort of ambush predator watching with hooded eyes, waiting for some soft prey animal to make an appearance.

He also couldn't see anything in the water, which was glass smooth and with a few vapour ghosts lifting from its surface, at least that was something he thought; not having to worry about the cold as it would probably be warmer beneath the water than out if it.

He checked the small green eye one last time and it swivelled a little, pointing to the water as always. He marked its position. "Okay, here goes."

Troy reached down to check his knife was still in its scabbard and then stepped out, pausing to look up and down the sand again. He hyperventilated, more to suck in courage than air, and then quickly headed to the water.

"Good luck," he heard Anne whisper as he waded in. As he went in deeper, he tried to make as few ripples as possible. He knew that many of the creatures were just as attracted by sound and vibrations as they were by sight and movement. In seconds he was up to his waist and pulled the mask down over his eyes and sunk down.

Once under the water, he saw that even though it was gloomy and shadow filled, it was at least crystal clear. He opened his palm and saw the green eye still pointing outwards so began to slowly one-arm stroke out into deeper water.

The bottom was covered in seagrasses and some of the sandy areas were lined with sea snail tracks and in only a few strokes the sandy seafloor quickly fell away.

He continued stroking outwards and came to the surface to take a quick breath and turned back to the shoreline. He could see Anne and was surprised how far out he had come already. She waved, and he gave her a thumbs up, before turning again.

He ducked back down and saw a school of silver fish darting about, and his near empty stomach told him that any one of them would have made a good meal. He wondered if they could make some type of nets; he'd speak to Anne about it when he got back.

Troy paddled for another few minutes and glanced down. It was getting deeper here, and he had lost sight of the bottom, and that made his body tingle as a shot of fear coursed through him. He actually felt the exact moment his testicles shrivelled, as they tried to retreat into his body. *Get back out here, you cowards.* He grinned at his graveyard humour.

He tried to remember how far out Tygo was when he had dropped the large ruby; *It had to have been around here*, he convinced himself.

He stroked on a bit more, holding the jade eye in his fist. He was relieved to feel it growing warm and knew that meant he was getting close to his destination.

Troy came up to take another breath and then went down, and this time heard something, a scraping noise, like when you drop a small boat anchor and the tide or current drags it along the sea bottom for a while.

He hovered, looking down and holding his breath. Worryingly, all the fish that had been keeping him company had vanished.

*Dammit, guys, come back*, he thought. *Safety in numbers, guys.* Regardless of the bath-warm water, he suddenly felt cold, and a little shiver ran through his body.

He came up, dragged in a breath and breast-stroked on a little more. The orb in his fist seemed to wriggle and he let himself float as he looked down, opened his hand and saw that it was now pointing downwards.

*Thank god*, he thought. But looking beyond the jade eye, he saw the water was inky black down there, and just as worrying, that damned dragging sound was still happening.

Troy stuck the jade eye in his pocket and tread water for a moment. *Let's get it over with*, he demanded of himself. He then sucked in a few deep beaths, filling his lungs, and dived.

He swam down, the light quickly turning from silver, to grey, and then to gloom. He stopped to pinch his nose and repressurized his ears and then stroked on.

*There. There was a dot of red.*

He hoped it was the gem and powered toward it. It remained constant.

But then it blinked out. But only for a second or two. Or maybe it didn't blink out, but instead something moved across in front of it. That wasn't good.

He hung in the water for a moment, thinking, calculating the risk. He still had enough breath left. *Just get down there, grab it, and get the hell out*, he urged himself.

He started to think about sitting on the shoreline with Anne fussing over him, and he wanted that more than anything else in the world right now. But that would be even better if he had the gem with him.

He stroked down another few feet and it became clearer; it *was* the gem, sitting on the bottom, half embedded in the sand. He gave a few last sweeping strokes and landed beside it.

Troy pulled it out, tucked it under one arm, and turned his face to the surface. Just as something wrapped around his ankle.

Just the touch of the thing scared the ever living crap out of him and he spun, expelling a mouthful of oxygen in an impossible-to-hold yell of surprise. He then received his second shock – the thing that had wrapped around his ankle was a stout and powerful looking tentacle.

He held up the gem for light and it illuminated a scene that would haunt his dreams forever – if he lived to have those dreams – there was a large green and black head, a pair of flat, plate-sized eyes, and a face full of coiling tentacles. Behind its head there was a shell as large around as a wagon wheel that vanished into the gloom.

It was an octopus, or a squid, or something; he bet Anne knew what it might be. He kicked back at the rubbery mass, but all that did was cause another tentacle to grab at his other leg.

Its suckered limbs were rubbery, muscular and strong, and he felt them compress and squeeze his calves.

As he stared, the thing flared open, and in the red light of the gem, he saw the foot long parrot's beak in the center of the tentacles open and close. He had no doubt that it would snap his bones and tear away his flesh with ease.

Down in the darkness, Troy began to panic, kicking and thrashing, and even though he knew he was burning through his oxygen, the animal part of his brain was taking over and it had two options: fight or flight.

Another tentacle coiled around his leg and kept going to snake up his thigh. Almost gracefully the creature was turning him around to try and feed his legs into its maw. Troy felt his lungs begin to burn and his mind was begging him to just open his mouth and take a deep breath – which would have been death.

Troy finally reached down for his blade, pulled it out, but another tentacle looped around his wrist. He strained, but the strength of the thing was titanic, and it began to pull his arm away from his body. Even though he was still on the bottom, his one thought was he must not drop the knife.

As he was being pulled into the flaring mass of tentacles and the waiting razor sharp beak, he dropped the gem. Troy saw the shelled cephalopod's large eye swivel to the glowing object and in that second or two of distraction, he reached across to his knife in his right hand to take the blade in his left.

As the huge eye swivelled back to him, he struck out, piercing the left eye dead center. The honed blade sunk deep into the gelatinous eye and in an explosion of turbulence, blood, and ink, the thing literally spat him out and vanished.

Troy backed away; his breath gone. But in the seconds he had left while his vision was just pops and pinpricks of light exploding behind his eyes he scooped up Odin's Heart, jammed his legs against the bottom, and then speared himself toward the surface.

*Hold it, hold it, hold it* – he had to fight his lower order thinking as it demanded he breathe, ready or not – *5 seconds, 4 seconds, 3 seconds…*

His mouth came open and he sucked in a breath. Not of air, but of cold dark water. Thankfully his forward motion carried him the last six feet as he burst to the surface and coughed, spluttered, and vomited. He then dragged in the biggest breath he had ever taken in his life. He vomited again, and wetly coughed several more times until about a pint of water was ejected from his lungs and stomach.

Troy closed his eyes and lay on his back on the water's surface, until the nausea and dizziness leaked away. Finally, he began to kick toward the shore.

As he slowly stroked one-handed, he noticed that the hand he held the ruby in was covered in sticky black ink, that was like mucous. Also, around him the water was discolored with ink as well as blood.

"Troy!" he heard Anne yell.

He turned and saw her standing knee deep in the water, the gun in her hands.

"*Get out.* Get out of the water." She held the gun up.

"I'm okay," he said weakly, but doubted she heard it.

"Behind you!" she screamed.

\*\*\*

On the forested hill behind Anne and Troy eyes watched them. They didn't blink, they didn't deviate, they just focussed like twin lasers. The muscles in the powerful legs coiled, ready to spring forward.

\*\*\*

Troy spun in the water. And then he saw what Anne did. "Oh shit."

It was a shark fin. A *huge* shark fin. And it was weirdly shaped, like an anvil.

Troy swam backwards. He wasn't that far from shore, but with the gem under his arm and the knife in his hand he was never going to be able to sprint. And after going through what he just did with that weird squid thing, he didn't want to lose the gem. Plus, he knew he'd probably never raise the courage to go through this again.

He gritted his teeth and continued to swim backwards. The anvil shark fin seemed to get even bigger, and he tried to work out from its fin placement exactly where the business end was – the one with all the teeth.

There was a loud bang from behind him, and the water splashed a little just out to his side – Anne was shooting – and she hit water just as far from the shark as it was from him.

The shark continued to come at him but then swam into the water that was still discoloured and immediately became erratic. It turned and swam back through the blood and ink again, and then quicker, and then did it again. The smell of the hurt creature was exciting it.

"That's right, there's food over there," Troy whispered as he continued to edge away using one arm and scissor kicking his legs.

There was another gunshot from the beach, and once again the water splashed, and at least a little closer to the shark this time. But she was burning through the last of his ammunition.

"*Stop. Damn. Shooting!*" he yelled.

The shark did a last power through the chum pool and then dived. It had obviously picked up the trail of the hurt squid and decided that would be a bigger and better meal.

Troy kept paddling backwards, his eyes moving back and forward over the water's surface that was now returning to its glass-like placid state. In seconds more his feet touched the sand and he stood and turned, but his legs buckled, and he dropped the ruby.

Anne was there to grab him. "You're going into shock."

"The gem. Get the gem," he said.

Anne grabbed it and put an arm around his waist to support him.

Troy staggered up the beach on rubbery legs and Anne guided him back to their sheltering tree. She let him down. And she grinned widely as she rubbed his arms.

"You did it." She held out the stone.

He nodded and tried to smile but his lips wouldn't work properly. "I feel a bit sick." Troy began to shiver uncontrollably and had never felt so cold in his life.

Her expression dropped.

"*Troy.*" She grabbed at him.

He blacked out.

# CHAPTER 22

In the lead boat was Tygo, Elle, Hilda, and Aksel Gundersen, their tracker. Just behind them and stroking just as silently was the two huge brothers, Borg and Gunnar Hagen, and joining them was Joren, the sniper. Over his shoulder the man had a large case and sat back with his arms folded and eyes intense and unblinking. He had told them he needed his hands to be undamaged and therefore had refused to row. For whatever reason the two muscular brothers didn't argue with him as he seemed to give off an aura of danger and unpredictability that made both big men cautious.

Tygo had given Elle the dragon's eye and she held it before her, the tiny orb directing her forward.

"I can feel it," she said. "We're close now."

"There." Tygo raised a hand and the boats glided to a stop in the pond still water.

The massive rift in the ice wall seemed to loom out of the thick fog before them. Steam wafted from its entrance, but the man narrowed his eyes and craned forward.

"It looks… smaller," he said.

"We're coming to the end of the warm season," Elle suggested. "Maybe in a few weeks it will have iced over again." She pointed at a few blocks of ice no bigger than bread loaves floating around them. "They weren't here last time."

Tygo grunted. "We don't have much time." He was about to wave them on, but paused, and then turned his head slowly, listening.

"Do you hear that?" he asked.

Everyone stayed still and silent. And then they heard it: there was a faint whine, like coming from a giant mosquito.

"What is that?" he asked.

The two boat loads of people looked upwards and turned their heads slowly trying to find the source of the noise. But the mist was far too thick.

"Maybe a big bug from inside," Elle suggested.

"Say what?" Hilda's laugh was like a bark that echoed over the still water.

"Shut up," Tygo growled at her.

After another moment or two the whine receded and then was gone. They sat still as stone for another 30 seconds, before Tygo shook his head.

"Is gone."

The huge Viking descendent waved them on and began to paddle towards the rift opening in the ice wall. Only Elle sat with her brows drawn together looking back over her shoulder into the billowing mist.

# CHAPTER 23

Aboard the Sjøspray, Anders crowded close to the tiny screen as Oder worked the drone controls. He had the drone up at about a hundred feet in the air and switched it to thermal and could see through the thick mist to the massive rift in the ice wall which on thermal vision was a towering sheet of blue with a flaring red hole at its center.

"Heat coming from in there. A lot of heat," he said.

"This is what we are looking for." Anders exhaled and patted his brother-in-law on the shoulder. "I believe inside there will be the place that Vikings called Lemuria, their mysterious island that has been hidden for a thousand years."

"I'll hover the drone in place on auto and we can track it in the boat." Oder began to pull it back a little and then frowned.

"Something else." He swivelled the camera.

Anders growled deep in his chest. Below them the thermal had picked up two boat loads of people, seven of them, sitting idle in the water as if waiting for something.

"These will be the people who killed Freja." Anders stared for a moment more, noting their warm orange outlines. "Take the drone up a little higher so they can't hear us. I want us to be a surprise to them. Let's wait until they enter the rift, to give them some space."

Oder nodded. "We're outnumbered, but if we have the element of surprise, then the odds might not matter."

Anders remembered the CCTV footage the police had shown him of the huge, bearded man leaving the burning office. "I don't care about them all. There's only one I want. Her killer." He pointed at the large shape in the front of the lead boat. "That one."

# CHAPTER 24

Troy sat up fast, spluttering. "*Stop shooting.*"

"Hey, hey, calm down." Anne helped him into a sitting position. "You're here, with me."

He groaned. "I thought for a moment…"

"That you were back in the water?" She chuckled. "Come on, you're safe now. And it was just a shark, and it wasn't that interested in you."

He rubbed his face with both hands and then ran them up through his still damp hair. "You didn't see what was happening under the water."

"What was?" she asked.

"Just a giant squid-octopus thing as long as a bus." He exhaled and then looked at her. "And it was in a shell."

"In a shell." Her brows knitted as she looked inwards for a moment as if searching her memory. "Straight shell or curled?" she asked.

"Straight out behind it," he replied wearily.

"Orthocone squid," she said. "Very ancient sea predator."

"Just some other monstrous thing living here that should have long been extinct," he scoffed. "Welcome to the madhouse."

"Yeah, but there are reports circulating on the palaeontology dark web, written by some paleo-linguist called Kearn, or Kearns. He wrote of some oversized Orthocone species that are supposed to live in Antarctica. Or rather, below Antarctica. Deep beneath the dark ice." She smiled. "And they were big and aggressive."

"No shit." He lifted the leg of his pants and turned the calf muscle. There were a few large rings that looked like dark red love bites.

"Okay, I believe you," she said and reached down to measure one of the sucker marks between her thumb and forefinger. She whistled. "Big suckers, big cephalopod."

He exhaled in a rush through pressed lips. "What a day. Giant squid thing in a shell, monster shark, someone shooting at me." He glanced at the massive ruby. "At least we got what we came for."

"You did, and you were fantastic." She smiled. "Just be glad I was here to scare that shark away. It was a big one, and I think I hit it."

He glanced at her to see if she was joking. She wasn't. He nodded. "Yeah, I think you did. Thank you."

"You're welcome," she said brightly.

"How long was I out?" he asked.

She leaned forward and reached out to lift his eyelid. "You were unconscious for about an hour. It was shock."

He nodded. "Still feel a bit woozy." Troy stood slowly and held onto the tree trunk. "We need to get to a place where we can keep a lookout and plan our attack."

She shared a grimace-smile. "I'm nervous. And excited. If we pull this off, we're going home."

He smiled. "And if we don't, we're staying, or..."

"Or we'll be dead," she finished.

***

Troy and Anne heard before they saw the pair of inflatables emerge from the cave in the huge cliff wall and once they were halfway across the expanse of water, they slowed.

Troy had the binoculars to his eyes and felt his heart flip in his chest when he spotted Elle. *Stop it, you idiot*, he thought. *She's more likely to put a bullet in me than greet me with a smile and a hug.*

He scoffed. Put *another* bullet in me, he remembered, still feeling the pinch in his shoulder from the old wound.

He expected them to drop anchor, but instead saw Elle lift a pair of field glasses and turn to scan the forest line.

"Get down," he said, and he and Anne lay flat.

Then his heart sank when he saw what Tygo was doing – he was holding his hand out, and staring at it, and then giving Elle directions.

"Oh shit, they've got another jade eye," he said.

"But that means they'll know it's not below the water." Anne quickly looked from Troy back to the boats. "And they'll be able to track the heart. And us."

Troy slid back a few feet. "They sure will, and they'll come for us. We've got to move."

She grabbed his arm. "Then it's a trade; the ruby for a boat."

He shook his head. "You know what that asshole is like; he'll kill us before we even start to negotiate."

"No, I mean we hide it." Her eyes were wide. "They spend time looking for it, and we double back and take one of the boats."

116

"They've got one of the jade eyes. It'll lead them right to it." He frowned, thinking furiously. And then had a brainwave. "Unless we put it somewhere that is hard to get to. Or takes them time to get to. Even if they knew where it was."

"Where?" she asked.

He smiled. "The dragon's den."

# CHAPTER 25

"Something's wrong." Tygo held his hand out with the eye on his palm. "It's not here. Not where we left it." His teeth were bared behind his thick beard.

"Calm down." Elle, sitting in front of him, looked hard at the green jade eye and where it was pointing. She snatched up some binoculars and put them to her eyes, scanning the forest line. She moved it slowly along the thick line of trees, palms, and fern fronds, one way then the other.

"They must have recovered it," she said, keeping the glasses to her eyes.

"Troyson Strom and the Biology woman?" he asked.

"Of course them; they saw you drop it and where." She lowered the glasses and turned. After a moment, she punched her leg. "*Ach*, I should have killed them both."

"A moment of weakness," Tygo growled. "But what is done is done." He held up the eye again. "It led us to Odin's Heart once before, and it will do it again."

He put the eye in his pocket and gabbed the oars. "We'll find them." He smiled. "And then you can rectify your mistake."

The huge man rowed in long strokes and both boats soon came up on the beach. Joren, their sniper, took his long case and looped it over his shoulder, not yet drawing the long, high-powered rifle from its secure bag.

The brothers, Borg and Gunner Hagen, checked shotguns and their supply of shells. Both had RPG launchers with the tubes thrown over their shoulders. Plus a few grenades strung on their belts

Their tracker, Aksel Gundersen, had a well-used hunting rifle. But his real arsenal was his Model 98 Magnum that was based on a double square bridge action and made from a full block of steel. The big game weapon held four .450 cartridges in the magazine, and delivered speed, reliability, and with enough punching power to even penetrate a bull elephant's skull. His entire belt was packed with spare rounds that looked as long as his finger.

Hilda Bergensen had a sidearm, and diving knife. She had obviously expected to do the underwater work, but so far, it seemed her job was already redundant. Now, she looked nervous as Hell.

Tygo turned to the group who assembled in front of him on the sand. Elle stood at his side and kept glancing at the forest line.

"This is a dangerous place. And it is why I selected you, the best people for the job. But you will earn your money here." He shrugged. "Still, some may die."

He held up his hand and the green orb swivelled to point into the forest. "This will guide us to what we seek." He glanced at Elle. "Everything else is of secondary importance."

He pointed into the jungle, but Elle put a hand on his broad shoulder and turned him to face her.

"If Troyson Strom survived and recovered the Odin Heart, he may be more capable than we suspected. And more cunning." She folded her arms. "Think about it; why would he recover the stone? It's no good to him here."

Tygo began to nod. "Unless he expected to get it home. Or use it to get home."

"I think he knew we would come back for it. *And* come searching for it." She half smiled. "He's been waiting for us this entire time."

"We should take no chances." Tygo's eyes slid to the forest, and then back to the group. "There is a man on this island who will try and kill us. If we encounter him, he must be put down immediately. Understand?"

"Could he have set traps?" Aksel asked.

'Maybe. So that's why a hunter, you, will be leading us in and keeping a lookout for them," Elle replied. She turned to face Joren, the sniper. "He might be watching us even now. I want you to watch for him. See him first and put a bullet between his eyes."

"You got it," Joren replied.

"We need to protect the boats. That's what he really wants," she said to Tygo.

He nodded and turned to Hilda. "You are useless to us. So you will stay and watch our boats." He thought about it for a moment and then looked at the huge brothers. "Gunner, you will support her. Anything that approaches our boats, kill it."

The big man smiled cruelly and nodded once.

Tygo then held up the all-seeing eye one more time to get his bearings. "We remain on this island only as long as it takes to fulfil our task."

He gave the group one last hard look and then nodded to their tracker. "Mr Aksel, that way."

The man began to head into the twilight dark forest and the group followed.

# CHAPTER 26

The small drone exited the cave and hovered over the water. Anders and Oder let the boat glide as they crowded the small screen.

"It's real, it's *really* real." Anders' mouth dropped open. "Lemuria, the hidden world."

"And these people wanted to keep it hidden. Or keep it to themselves," Oder said. "So much so they were prepared to kill for it."

"They did kill for it." Anders began to row again. He shook his head slowly, feeling slightly giddy from the overwhelming scene.

If he didn't see it with his own eyes, he may never have believed it. "Freja would have cried when she saw this. I know bec…" He had to stop talking as he felt a sudden wave of grief choke him up.

Oder moved the drone forward a little and swivelled the camera. "I can see their boats pulled up on the sand." He squinted down at the small screen. "They left a couple of people guarding them. But they're not watching the water, but instead facing the forest."

"Keep watching them. It looks misty, hard to see over distance, so we should be able to move along the cliff wall without being seen. We can pull in further down."

Anders rowed silently and pulled on the oars to move them along the base of the towering cliff wall. He looked upwards at the sheer rock face, but its towering edifice continued up for a few hundred feet and then vanished into a layer of mist and something else that looked like ice.

He turned back to the shoreline and the several hundred feet of water between them and the sand. About 300 yards further down the coast was a clump of trees that extended via a small peninsular or tidal sandbank. That's what he headed for.

As he stroked, something nudged the bottom of the boat causing it to change angles and he looked over the side but saw nothing in the dark water.

He readjusted his stroke to bring the nose of the small boat around and dug the oars in again. This time his oar hit something that he was sure moved out of the way. Once again, he looked over the side but the water was inky black below their boat.

"Hey," Anders said softly.

Oder turned. "Yeah?"

"Bring the drone back and hover it over us to look down at our raft." Anders slowly straightened, resting the oars.

Oder fiddled with the controls and the drone scooted back across the water, rose again to around a hundred feet and then the camera angled down at them.

Oder blanched. "*Ohhh* shit." He looked up. "We need to get out of here, *now!*"

"What is it? What can you see?" Anders reached forward and his brother-in-law turned the small screen around.

Anders' eyes went wide as he saw the shape of something more than three times the size of their small boat. It was whale-sized, but not whale-shaped.

He carefully put the oars back in and began to stroke harder, feeling the thrill of fear make his muscles all jittery. The large creature below the water kept pace with them, and he bet when he looked over the side, not seeing it, it was probably looking back up, and seeing him clearly.

He looked down into the boat and saw one of Olaf's old fishing reels and nudged it with his foot. He wanted to tell Oder to toss it over the side, but then worried that the splash sound might carry across the water and cause the group on the beach to turn around and see them.

"It's getting closer," Oder said in a high voice.

That's it, they had no choice. Anders nudged the reel with his foot. "Pick up that reel. Throw it behind us as far as you can."

Oder lunged for the bright blue reel, and lifted it, drew his arm back and then launched it a good hundred feet back along the cliff wall, where it splashed into the water.

Oder then brought the small screen close to his face again, and his expression brightened. "It's working. It's going to have a look."

Anders turned to the beach and saw that the pair far back in the distance hadn't heard, and he angled the boat's nose in towards the shore and began to pull on the oars faster than he ever had in his life.

Oder kept the drone overhead. His eyes were wide and his mouth open as he stared. His silence was a good thing, Anders thought. And in five more minutes he was approaching the small spit of sand and rock that was his destination.

The sand grated under their boat, and both men leapt out and dragged the small craft up behind the small stand of trees. Anders was still a bit shaky, and he swallowed and waited for his heartbeat to slow.

From deep in the forest a booming call filtered through the massive boughs and fern fronds. Oder looked across at Ander, his expression still pale. "What was that?"

Anders looked back at his brother-in-law. "Lemuria seems to have a lot of secrets. More than we expected."

"We should have brought bigger guns," Oder said softly, his eyes still on the forest.

"We're here now," Anders replied. "These people came here for something called the heart of Odin. If it's an artefact, and I think it is, then Freja would have wanted it for the museum. We get to it first. Or we take it from them." He peered through the trees to the distant figures waiting by the two boats. "And we strand them here."

# CHAPTER 27

**5000BC – Lemuria, Greenland's interior**

It was just three days later that Harald and his small group stood at the edge of the strange clearing with the massive rip in the earth venting steam, heat, and a sulphurous smell into the air.

They had survived encounters with many monstrous beasts and had lost Sune, their best climber, to something monstrous that stepped out of the foliage, grabbed him up with tiny arms and began to eat him immediately, and simply turned to barge away before any of them could react.

The most frightening aspect was that several of them had walked right past the beast as it had stood invisible and silent, waiting to ambush them. It had chosen Sune, perhaps because he was tallest, or maybe Odin had decided his time had come.

Harald hoped the man was with Odin, as his screams had continued for several minutes from far out in the forest, and he knew that his torment would have earned him his place in Valhalla.

Harald stared down into the rip, the glow from down below bathing his face and coloring it a devilish red. He turned to his group, all of whom stood silent with grim expressions, but there was no fear as all their hearts were stout.

"Whatever happens," he began, "it is Odin's will."

He turned back to the rip and began to climb down.

# EPISODE 12

*To choose to climb into Hell you need courage. Or foolishness.*

# CHAPTER 28

Troy put his finger to his lips and then got down on his belly. Anne did the same beside him.

They were close to the huge rip in the ground with steam still billowing from inside. So far there was no sign of the dragon. As yet, they hadn't peered in, but just the thought of what might be in there made his stomach roil.

"What's the plan?" Anne whispered.

"We need to get the gem inside the rift, but far enough down that it takes time for Tygo and his team to extract it." He turned to her and grinned. "And while we're doing it, not get eaten or melted by a dragon monster."

"Okay, I like that plan – especially that bit about not being melted." She nudged him. "I'll keep a lookout."

"Gee, thanks," he replied.

"What? You've got longer legs and can run faster if something goes wrong." She held out her hand. "Let me have the gun again."

He shook his head. "No chance. For one thing, it'd be less than pea shooter against the dragon. And two, you missed my head by inches when I was in the water."

She frowned. "Only because you moved."

He got to his knees. "You're on lookout duties. If something comes, call me, or throw something." He looked toward the rift. "I need to find a good hiding place for the ruby. But I'm only going to scale down a dozen feet or so, and then only if nobody is home."

She grabbed his arm. "Be careful."

He grabbed her hand and squeezed it. "Believe me, I intend to."

Troy quickly looked about, and then with the giant ruby tucked under one arm like a football, he ran to the edge of the rift. Looking down was a little glimpse into hell as there was some sort of volcanic heat source down there that gave off a Hadean glow. He could feel the heat against his face, and he had to narrow his eyes against it.

He saw the massive rift was easily large enough for the drekka to slither in, but still the edges were smoothed undoubtedly by the massive land leviathan's hide as it grazed the walls.

The rift fell away around a hundred feet, and obviously had a huge hollow area for the thing to nest. He just didn't know how big it was down there.

Troy got down on his knees and peered in. There was a ledge about twenty feet down and guessed if he could get to that, and hide the ruby somewhere around there, it would hopefully hold Tygo and his team up long enough for he and Anne to secure one of the boats.

Troy briefly glanced back to where Anne still lay, and she gave him a thumbs up. He nodded, and then turned back.

He hesitated and chuckled nervously. *Here I go, diving into the unknown once more.* After the swim in the sea and tangling with the squid-ortho-whatever, he hoped he had used up all his bad luck. *Hoped,* anyway.

*I'm either very brave or very stupid*, he thought to himself. *Here goes nothing.* He quickly charted his path, and then threw a leg over the side.

*"Be careful."*

He heard Anne loud-whisper, and he turned to her and put a finger to his lips. He then edged in and slid down to the first ledge. He had the gem in the pack strapped over his back, so his arms were free. He also had the gun tucked into the back of his belt, but as he had said to Anne, it'd be useless, and so was there more to bolster his courage.

Troy got down on his belly on the edge and tried to see further inside the rift. But the angle didn't allow him to see if the drekka was inside or not. At least for now he couldn't see or hear it, and that was a good thing, he guessed.

He had to go lower and find a place that was deep enough to cause Tygo and his team to burn up time as they dropped in, and then burn up more time searching for it. He really hoped that asshole met the dragon – that's a fate he deserved.

He climbed down to the next ledge, and then dropped down another five feet to the one after that. He looked up. He was about twenty feet down, and where he wanted to be.

Troy looked around but saw nowhere suitable to hide the gem, but just six feet lower was a small ledge with a good-sized hole at its rear – that'd be perfect.

As he readied himself to jump down, a small rock bounced down. He glanced up but saw nothing. He ignored it, and then another rock bounced down. The same size, in the same place.

Was it a coincidence?

He froze. Or was it Anne trying to warn him?

Shit, that's exactly what Anne would do if there was trouble. He scrambled down to the lower ledge and pushed himself back into the hole as far as was physically possible.

Troy cringed as from above the lights went out as something covered the hole. Something big. He hoped the smells from inside the cave masked his own scent. He drew his gun out. He knew it'd be useless, but just holding it made him feel a little less vulnerable.

As he watched, something fell past. It was big, bigger than a person, and bounced off the edges of the crack in the earth as it fell. Then the drekka climbed in, head first, its massive claws digging into the rock and holding fast as it pulverized stone and dislodged boulders with its massive size and strength.

The monstrous beast seemed to take ages to pass by him, and when the light returned, Troy gave it several minutes before edging forward. He peered down. There was no sign of the dragon but lying down at the bottom of the cave was a medium-sized dinosaur, its neck crushed almost flat. The thousands of pounds of meat obviously the dragon's dinner for the evening.

Troy eased the backpack off his shoulders. He could still plant the gem and be gone, and hopefully make it back to the beach with plenty of time to work out how to steal one of the boats. In fact, the dragon being down there might work out to be a better roadblock than he could have hoped for.

Another pebble came down, and then a handful rained down to bounce around the ledge. *What now?* he wondered and looked up. His mouth dropped open. Anne was climbing down.

"Troy," she said, trying to find him.

"Here," he said softly. "What are you doing?"

She continued to scale down and he quickly glanced over his shoulder. "Anne, what the hell are you doing?" He reached up to grab her legs as she slid the last few feet.

She turned her face grimly to him, her eyes wide.

"Tygo. And his crew," she breathed. "They're all here."

\*\*\*

Tygo held out his palm with the eye pointing directly at the huge rip in the ground with steam billowing from it.

"So, is this where they are hiding from us?" he said.

Elle looked around, her green eye glinting with suspicion. "I don't like this place. It feels... bad." She walked toward the edge of the hole and kicked at something with the toe of her boot and then watched it fall.

She then turned to scan the forest for a few moments before walking in a large arc still with eyes on the surrounding trees. Finally, she stopped and pointed. "Look around us. The trees are all broken off. And the ground here looks crushed, pulverized. I think this is where the drekka lives."

Tygo cursed under his breath.

"You asked if this is where they are hiding." She looked back at him. "Maybe they are hiding in there, or has only Odin's Heart been hidden down there?" Her brows came together as she seemed to think it through. "If they wanted to slow us down, they would put the heart where it would take us time to recover. It's what I would do." She looked up. "Because every minute they steal from us, they give to themselves."

Elle spun and pointed to their tracker, Aksel Gundersen. "Get back to the boats; they may be trying to double back on us. Kill them on sight."

The man nodded, turned on his heel, and then vanished into the forest.

Tygo grunted. "It matters not. The stone is here, and it is our duty to recover it." He put the jade eye in his pocket and turned to the remaining brother. "Borg, prepare the ropes. We will scale down and recover the heart of the All Father."

Elle held up a hand. "No, Borg will scale down by himself." She smiled. "It would be better for him if we were able to cover him from the high ground. Or if something went wrong, then we can pull him up quickly."

Borg looked suspicious, but Tygo gave her a small smile. "As you say. Because we have a crack shot with us who would prefer the high ground. Correct, Mr. Karlsen?"

Joren Karlsen took the rifle case from his shoulder and began to draw forth the long-barrelled, high-powered gun.

He nodded at Tygo. "Higher is better." He began to load one of the finger length rounds into the chamber.

# CHAPTER 29

Aksel Gundersen easily followed the tracks back to the beach. He'd been in plenty of thick forests before – the jungles of the Congo, Amazon, and New Guinea, and he could follow a trail in pouring rain or even in darkness.

He hoped their adventure wasn't coming to an end so quickly, as the briefing they received from Tygo had prepared them for some significant adversaries and so far, he'd only heard creatures little more than things the size of dogs scurrying through the underbrush. He spotted their tracks but had no idea what they could be. And that just fired up his curiosity even more.

He stopped and looked around slowly. It was a cool but not cold temperate environment. Water dripped from large ferns and palm fronds, and the heads of the towering trees were lost in the mist high above him.

Aksel sniffed deeply, smelling damp soil, plant sap, and, interestingly, fresh animal dung. *What sort?* he wondered.

He guessed he had plenty of time so decided to check it out. After all, he'd be damned if he was going to travel all the way to some hidden, mysterious island, and then do little more than walk a few miles into the forest, about face, and then head straight back out.

He pushed aside a veil of hanging vines and headed into an area more like jungle. He moved through layers of dense green and came to some open areas. And there in a pile as high as his knees was bundles of droppings.

"Amazing," Aksel whispered. He'd seen elephant and rhino droppings before, and they weren't anything like the size of this pile.

He looked about and then crept closer. He could tell by the shape and by the macerated vegetation and seeds still in the shit that it was left behind by a plant eater.

*But by what type?* he wondered.

He lifted his head and followed the tracks of something heading away from the dung pile. It was big, heavy, and a quadruped. By the look of the track depth the thing had to be heavier than a bull elephant and wider, given the gait.

He stopped beside one of the prints in the softer soil and saw the large foot with short claws. It was like nothing he had ever seen in his life. As a hunter, this was an opportunity too good to pass up. And if he could take home a trophy, then he'd be happy.

Aksel crept forward, staying in the shadows, even though the jungle made everything a dim twilight, his instincts told him that stealth was the key, so he treaded carefully.

He looked back over his shoulder, seeing nothing other than the mist-filled tunnel pushed through the vegetation he was following. He turned back and then froze. He heard it. There was a sound of squelching caused by heavy feet coming down on damp soil. And then branches snapping.

He used the sound to mask his own movements as he went forward a little faster. In moments more he came to the edge of a clearing with curtains of silvery light filtering down, and ringed by massive tree trunks. His face broke into a huge grin.

There was a creature, at least 25-feet long and he estimated about 9 to 10 tons. It was using a beak-like mouth to pull tough reeds from the ground and chew on them like a cow would. The head was broad, and down each of its sides were large spikes, and all finishing in a long tail that was out, stiff behind it. It sort of reminded him a little of a large armor-plated cockroach.

Aksel straightened and grinned broadly. There was no way he'd be taking that thing back, and even the head would be a challenge to remove with all that armor covering it. He guessed the head alone probably weighed in at around 150 pounds.

He looked it over; the thing continued to eat, its dumb, glassy eyes like dark, soulless marbles. He decided; he couldn't take the head, but maybe just one of its unusual feet would do.

The creature paused to sniff. Then it lifted its head and sniffed again.

It turned, sniffing twice more and then quickly spun to face him. Its tiny bead-like eyes blinked and Aksel bet it was like a rhino in that it had picked up his scent even if it probably hadn't yet seen him.

It hissed and took a few steps back.

Aksel smiled and held up a calming hand. "Easy there, big fella." He walked foward. He bet it was more scared of him than he was of it.

Aksel held his high-powered hunting rifle in one hand as he checked his blade. He gripped the gun again and took a few more steps forward. "Just take it easy." He smiled. "And this won't hurt a bit."

The thing was a serious sized animal, so knew he'd need a head shot to bring it down. Best placement was one of the eye sockets to get right inside the skull to the brain.

The creature hissed again, furiously this time. It didn't retreat, but now turned side on.

"That's it. Nice big target," Aksel said, now having a better shot.

The creature hissed and then snapped its beak together. It lowered its head and Aksel brought the barrel of his gun up.

As he did, the massive animal had obviously had enough of the creature closing on him. For something so big, it half turned again, leaving its back half rooted to the spot for a moment, before swinging it around. Fast.

The tail it had been dragging finally appeared and whipped around from behind it almost faster than Aksel's eyes could follow. On its end was a massive ball of hardened keratin and bone the size of a double medicine ball. It didn't miss, as even as Aksel aimed and fired, his bullet glanced off the armored head, just as the tail club smashed into him, and drove him back into the tree with the club going with him.

The force of the strike shook the massive tree causing a pile of debris to rain down. But Aksel had been caught between a literal rock and a hard place. From the waist to the chin his body had been squashed to the consistency of paste. On his face was a shocked expression, made ludicrous as both his eyes had popped out of their sockets to rest on his cheeks.

The ankylosaurus snuffed once with disdain, and then turned to vanish into the misty forest.

But Lemuria wasn't done with Aksel just yet. From out of the forest several small creatures that looked like long legged chickens, but with short snouts full of razor-sharp teeth, were attracted by the smell of his blood.

They quickly found him and leapt up onto his body; their movements were quick and darting and exactly bird like. They snatched away his eyes first and trilled their delight.

More appeared, and then more. Soon, like a school of feathered piranha, they were scrabbling for the scraps as they quickly took the obliterated human being down to its bones.

# CHAPTER 30

Elle lifted her head to face the forest "What was that?" she asked.

"Gun shot," Tygo replied.

"High powered hunting rifle," Joren Karlsen added. "Like the model carried by Aksel. Maybe he ran into your friends."

"Two of them; but there was only one shot," Tygo said.

"Maybe he ran into something else." Elle made a guttural sound in her throat. "Borg, we need to hurry." She nodded to the hole. "Get down there."

The big man hesitated for a moment, but then glanced at the implacable expression on Tygo's face and stepped forward. He took the pack from his shoulders and lay it carefully on the ground. He had enough grenades to level a city block and Tygo had made him carry all of them. He also had a good length of rope which he withdrew.

There were no suitable trees or rocks close to the hole as everything looked to have been crushed to gravel. He then returned to the pack and drew out a large spike two feet long, and then used a stone to hammer it into the ground. He tied the rope off to it.

Tygo came and lifted it and held it in both hands. "I will support you. And tug twice when you have it."

Borg nodded.

"Wait," Tygo said. He held out the green jade eye. "You know what this does. Use it to locate Odin's Heart."

Borg was a big man and knew how to look after himself, but Tygo stepped closer, looking down on him and his voice got low and mean. "Do not lose it."

Borg nodded and then Tygo stepped back. "Ready," he said with his massive legs braced.

Elle turned to Joren. "We'll watch him, you watch our backs."

Their sharpshooter nodded and turned to face the forest. Elle walked closer and watched as Borg began to ease down into the hole.

She kept glancing back over her shoulder at the forest for a moment, and then turned to stare down into the hole. Down there it glowed blood-red and a thick mist rose from its hellish looking depths. She waved some away; there was a hint of sulphur in it, but for the most part she guessed it was steam, maybe from hot springs.

But there was something else; a strange animal odor that she had smelled before – inside Odin's fortress and just before the drekka had arrived.

It had been here, she knew. But was it here now? She glanced back over her shoulder again, looking at the forest line, and choosing several rapid escape routes if the monster suddenly appeared.

She wouldn't tell the oaf descending. If the dragon wasn't down there, they'd get the stone. If it was, then more than likely Borg was as good as dead. And while the dragon burned him down and ate him, it would give the rest of them time to escape.

She watched Borg descend to a ledge, briefly hold up his palm with the green jade eye, get his bearings, and then prepare to drop down to the next. He hesitated for a moment, as though seeing or hearing something.

"Hurry up," she hissed.

Borg looked up, his brutal face running with perspiration and showing something it had not expressed in probably years, or ever – fear.

***

Troy and Anne scaled down to another rock platform, edged along it, and Troy peered over. From their vantage place they couldn't be seen from above, but it allowed them to see more inside the dragon's lair.

Anne crawled up beside him. "What do we do?"

He exhaled, and then held up a finger. Above them they heard voices; Tygo and his team had arrived. He looked back down.

"Our choices are we leave the gem for them to find, and they take off. Not great as it means we've given up our biggest advantage for nothing. And they head back to the boats with a head start. We could be stranded again."

"We *would* be stranded again. This time for good," she whispered.

"Probably," he said. "Or, we climb down, shelter inside, and when they come down, we take them out one at a time."

"Kill them?" Her eyebrows went up.

"Of course not; we reason with them. They seem to be sensible people, right?" He grinned.

She nodded. "Oh right, hardy har. Okay, so we kill them."

"Them or us." He turned to peer over the ledge.

134

Small pebbles skittered down and bounced around them.

Anne grimaced. "Someone is coming down."

"That's our cue. Follow me." Troy threw a leg over the ledge and reached out his other leg for the next platform.

Anne watched him as he touched down and crouched. She followed and he grabbed her legs and swung her in close to him. The ledge they now found themselves on ran all the way down the ravine and dropped them at the bottom. They followed it around until they were just a dozen feet from the cave floor. Troy leapt down and held up a hand to stop Anne where she was. He turned slowly. After another moment, he called her to him.

Now, on the floor of the cave they could see the true size of it – it was huge and tunnelled out under the surface and its end was lost in the distance. They now saw where the hellish red glow and mist was coming from as pitted about the cave were the cracks of volcanic vents looking like open, weeping wounds. Around the edge of the cave water dripped, and there were small pools of the clear liquid.

"If I was a giant reptile, this is exactly where I'd want to live," Anne whispered. "Where it's nice and warm. And safe."

"Safe from what?" Troy asked.

Anne shrugged. "Other drekka?"

"That's a nice thought. Keep your eyes open and stay alert. The dragon is in here somewhere." He nodded towards a large smear of blood on the cave floor. "The dead dinosaur is missing; it came back for it."

"I hope it's not hungry anymore, but I'm betting it's territorial, so if it sees us…" Anne shrugged.

"Yeah, I get it." He exhaled and then looked along the cave. "Do you think there could be other ways out?"

Anne nodded. "Sure. I'm no geologist, but most animals that live in large dens like an escape hatch."

Troy nodded. "Tygo will be using the eye to locate the ruby. We place it, and then get out of sight. When they go for the gem, we strike."

As Troy searched for an appropriate place to leave the fantastic ruby, he brought an arm up to wipe his streaming brow. It was like being in a red-lit sauna and he began to feel the sulphur coating the back of his throat to make it feel slimy.

The rocks around were mostly slick with mineral drips and constant humidity that fed an array of multi-colored mosses and the thick miasmic stench hung heavily in the air. Some of the fresh cave-in rocks were sharper edged and where Troy perched, one of them seemed to dig into his calf.

He shifted his boot. But the digging sensation in his calf stayed with him. He frowned and looked down.

"*Shit.*" He shook and then violently kicked his leg.

There was a 10-inch long insect gripped on there. Its six legs were sharp and wrapped around him, and its body was flat, heavily ribbed, and armor plated.

"What the hell is this thing?" Troy whipped out his knife and sliced down at it.

He hit the bug, but his knife glanced off it as the carapace was like iron. In turn the thing drew its head back far enough for Troy to see a hypodermic-like spike extending from its face.

"The hell you will."

Troy furiously grabbed its back and ripped it away from his leg, taking the pants material with it and deeply scratching his skin. He threw it down hard onto the ground, and then stamped his boot on it.

The thing barely cracked, but when he lifted his boot, it flipped itself over and scuttled away.

"Holy mother of god," Anne said breathlessly.

"What was that thing?" Troy rubbed his leg hard. "Was nearly indestructible."

"I think it was a flea." Anne scanned the cave floor.

"That was no damn flea," Troy replied.

"I think it was. All creatures have parasites, and dinosaurs were no exception. I think it was a *Pseudopulex*, a genus of extinct, primitive flea that lived between the Middle Jurassic and Early Cretaceous periods."

"It didn't jump," Troy said. "But that little bastard was as tough as hell."

"Only the latter, smaller species evolved the long jumping legs that we know. The *Pseudopulex* hunted solo. Just be thankful you got it off before it stuck that sharp stylet into you – it probably could have drunk a pint of blood before you even knew it."

"God, I hate this place," Troy said between his teeth. He then found what he was looking for and pointed. "Over there."

There was a small plinth type rock with a flat top. And two dozen feet from it there was a cluster of rocks perfect for hiding behind.

Troy crept forward and balanced the large ruby on the rock. Its own glow was overwhelmed by the orange red illumination from within the cavern. He and Anne then went and ducked down behind the boulders to wait.

He kept his eyes on the ruby. "I'll watch the gem." He glanced over his shoulder at her. "You keep a lookout for any more of those damn dino-fleas."

***

Borg abseiled down, landed on one shelf, checked the eye, and then jump sailed down to the next ledge.

His progress was good, and he only wished he had his brother with him. Tygo scared him and he didn't trust him for a minute. At least if he had Gunnar with him, together they could have resisted the giant and not be used as little more than cannon fodder.

Borg sailed down to the last ledge above the cavern floor and looked down. He checked the green eye and it still pointed downwards and slightly to the north. He hoped this thing called Odin's Heart was easy to recognise and recover, and once recovering it, he could climb straight back up.

He sniffed; the cave smelled funny – not just of sulphurous vents, but more like a damn bear cave.

Borg placed the jade eye back in his pocket and slid down the rope the last 30 feet to the cave floor. He left the rope dangling and clung to it as he looked up. He was reluctant to let go and it seemed a long way, and he knew it would be a lot harder to climb out than it was to climb down.

On the cave floor he consulted the eye again, turning slowly. It felt warm in his hand and it swivelled quickly to point and stop. He looked up.

"Yes." He smiled; there it was, the huge red stone. This was going to be easier than he thought.

He crossed to it quickly and stared down at it. The thing was huge and he wondered at its value. He felt a tingle in the back of his jaws and knew that if there was a way to secure it for himself and his brother on the way home, they'd do it faster than that big asshole Tygo could blink.

He smiled dreamily as the glow from the gem bathed his face. He'd talk to Gunner when he got back. Maybe they could kill Tygo and his green-eyed bitch when they slept. Then it was all theirs, and he doubted anyone else onboard would stand up to them.

He took his backpack off, opened it, and reached out and grabbed the ruby. He held it up, transfixed by its beauty for a moment as he felt its warmth against his face.

Borg paused, his brows coming together. He half turned.

*What was that?*

***

Troy chose his knife for the attack and held it in his right hand. But also had his gun in his left. He'd try not to use it unless he had to as he only had three bullets left and guessed he might need them for the others when he got topside. Plus, they'd be less on guard against a human attacker if they didn't hear a gunshot. He also hoped to obtain the man's weapons and anything else they could use from him.

Anne watched with round eyes as he stood preparing to speed from behind the tumbled boulders and cross the 40 feet between him and the man to then take him out with a single neck thrust of the blade. He coiled his muscles and began to move just as Anne lunged at him and grabbed the back of his shirt.

He spun, frowning. "What are...?"

She dragged him down. "*It's here*," she mouthed.

Tory didn't need to know anything more and immediately crouched low and carefully peered back into the cave depths.

Through the billowing clouds of mist the massive head of the drekka loomed forward. Its monstrous yellow slit eyes were on the man as he held the gem in his hand.

Troy marvelled at how something so colossal could move so silently as it gradually came closer. And only when it was just a hundred feet from him, the man must have sensed something because he spun.

The big man froze and stood staring with mouth dropped open.

The giant dragon seemed to shiver, but Troy knew what it was doing as he had seen it done to his friends before. No one deserved the fate about to be inflicted on the big brute. Not even one of Tygo's men.

The man's open mouth finally worked, and he screamed long and loud.

"*Get out of...*" Troy began.

From the dragon's mouth a long gout of the steaming greenish bile was ejected, that coated the man, his pack, and the ruby. His scream then became shrill as the agony of the super-heated acidic bile coated him and its torturous burning began.

Borg reached up a hand to his face, but it was too late as the skin began to drop from his arm. The glistening red bones of fingers appeared, and there was a plopping sound as huge gobbets of flesh slewed away.

In seconds more he went to his knees, and then the screaming went from shrill, to wet gurgle, and then when his lower jaw and tongue liquefied, it was shut off completely.

Troy grimaced as he watched everything else that was the man collapse into a pile of mush, with a few sharp bones sticking out. Finally, there were just two rounded objects remaining in the center of the puddle of melted flesh and blood – his skull and the ruby.

From above there were yells from voices Troy recognized: Tygo and Elle. But he wasn't the only one who heard them; the dragon looked up, and then surged upwards to meet them.

Troy eased out and carefully looked upwards. Then crept out a little further. The dragon was exiting the rift, and he judged it safe to rush over to the mess that was once Tygo's man. He looked down at the mess and felt his gorge rise; even the skull was softening and flattening into the blob. It left the ruby standing alone and he used the tip of his boot to push it from the pile.

Anne joined him and got down on her haunches. "It should be okay," she said. "Ruby is a type of gem that is called a corundum, and is very hard – in fact, a 9 on the Mohs scale. It also can take up to 1800 degrees without being damaged."

She looked up and half smiled. "If a diamond is a girl's best friend. Then a ruby is her second best."

Troy rolled the ruby on the ground to try and wipe the still steaming bile from it. He then dug his hands under it, lifting the ruby and the dirt to shield his hands and carefully took it to one of the small pools and dropped it in. He quickly glanced up again and saw no sign of the dragon.

Anne did the same. "I hope it melts and eats all of them," she said.

"Yeah, me too." He worked on the stone, rolling it around in the pool, washing it clean, and then he lifted it out. "You're right; undamaged." He wiped it on his shirt and then put it back in his pack.

"What now?" she asked

Troy looked back at the puddle. "So much for getting some extra weapons." He then glanced across to the cave floor under the rift hole and saw the pile of rope that had dropped down. Troy's head jerked upward as the light from above was shut out.

"Oh shit, it's coming back." He grabbed Anne's arm. "*Run.*"

***

Tygo had his legs planted and held tightly to the rope, but was at ease as there was no strain, meaning Borg was still searching for the stone down below.

Elle stood on the edge and peered down. "Oh no." Her eyes widened. "*The dragon!*" she yelled, and without another word turned to sprint away.

"*Ach!*" Tygo dropped the rope and also turned to run. Only Joren, who had his back to the pit while watching the forest line, paused to turn.

The massive truck-sized head emerged first. Yellow slit eyes went from the fleeing Tygo and Elle, to Joren who stood momentarily transfixed by the bus-sized head that had appeared from the hole.

It opened its mouth to spray a stream of steaming bile toward the fleeing people, barely catching them, but then managed to cover Joren who only just began to back away while lifting his sniper rifle.

He held his hands up as the viscous liquid covered him. And then the screaming began.

Elle felt spots of the liquid on the backs of her legs, and it stung like scalding water. But the sounds of agony from Joren told her it was nothing compared to the sniper's fate.

*Good,* she thought. It would mean the monster would be kept occupied for a few minutes.

She couldn't see Tygo as he had run in a different direction. But for now, she just needed to find a place to hide.

However, there was no way she was leaving without that gem, and she hoped it followed Tygo, as then she could safely double back to the dragon's lair.

She ran in an arc as she couldn't hear any more sounds of pursuit and doubled back along a line of huge trees. She stopped behind one of them, dragged in deep breaths, and peered around the huge trunk. The dragon was sucking up what was left of their sniper.

She looked across the clearing and could make out Tygo hiding behind a large tree trunk. He nodded to her.

The massive beast snorted a few times and turned, slowly scanning the surrounding forest. It then returned to the massive rip in the ground and began to scale down.

When it had fully vanished inside, she stepped out. Same for Tygo. And the pair crept to the hole in the ground in time to see the dragon vanish at the bottom. Tygo joined her.

She spoke without turning. "Odin's Heart is still down there."

"And now so is the all-seeing eye. If the stone is moved, we'll never find it again." He looked at her from under lowered brows. "We have no choice; we need to go in."

She smiled and walked to where Borg had left his spare explosives and then to the still pegged rope. She tossed the heavy bag of explosives to Tygo who caught it and looped it over one broad shoulder. She then lifted the rope and walked to the edge of the huge rift in the ground.

"Then what are we waiting for?" She began to quickly scale down on the rope.

Tygo laughed softly and waited a few moments, before grabbing the rope and joining her.

***

Anne and Troy ran down the huge cavern, staying as close to the wall as they could while trying to avoid falling into the pools of steaming mineral water. Behind them they could hear grinding stone as the land leviathan crushed rock on its way down. Troy tried to find somewhere to hide, but so far there was nothing that would shield them enough from the monster.

As they ran, he grabbed Anne's hand to drag her forward. The heat was building, and he could feel the perspiration dripping from his chin. Around the edges of the cave, the pools of water bubbled, and balloons of gas exploded that surfaced – the heat was building the further in they went.

The smell of sulphur was getting thicker and made them gag as it slid down their throats and pooled in their stomachs. They rounded a corner just as from behind the sound of pursuit abruptly stopped. Troy and Anne also skidded to a halt. And just stared.

Spread before them, everywhere, there was ancient bones - human - and broken weapons. Anne stepped forward as Troy went to peer back around the corner.

"It's stopped for now," he said between puffing breaths.

"This was a war. Here. A battle," Anne said.

"More like a killing field," Troy remarked.

"A last stand maybe." She bent and picked up a corroded axe head and looked down the cave. The bones seemed to go on forever. "There were hundreds of them."

Troy briefly glanced back down the huge, dark cavern and then joined her. "They descended into the dragon's lair to make war on it." He kicked at some of the bones. Many were splintered, pulverized, and some seemed smoothed through the melting they were now more than familiar with.

She picked up a human mandible and rubbed it with her thumb. "It's old, perhaps many thousands of years. Maybe even neolithic."

"That old?" he asked.

"Easily," she replied. "This could be some race that predates Vikings by many millennia. Or were the very first Vikings."

Troy looked around. "This right here could be where all the legends came from. Warriors fighting dragons. And this is where one such battle took place."

Anne let the bones slip to the ground. "It spread all around the world. There once was a land of dragons. And it was called Lemuria." She looked up at him with a broken smile. "And not so magical."

They heard a soft dragging sound coming from back in the caves and both of them turned to stare with held breath.

Finally, Anne turned to Troy. "What do we do now?"

"Two options; we hide out here until the dragon is gone…"

"If it goes," she interjected.

He nodded. "It will. And when it does, then we try and climb back out." He turned back to the steaming caves before them. "Or we continue on and see if there's another way out."

"We could get lost." Anne exhaled through pressed lips. "A choice between two bad options." She continued to stare down into the steaming, red-lit cave. "But I have a bad feeling about what's down there."

"Couldn't be worse than what's in here," he replied.

Beneath their feet the ground shook and they backed up another step. Both stared back the way they'd come. There had been a soft warm breeze blowing down the cave as the hot air rushed up and out to escape. But now it stopped dead, as if something was blocking the cave.

"And here it comes again," Troy said.

He looked about and saw a small depression in the rock at the base of one wall. "Here, quick."

He and Anne went and lay flat in the depression that was just deep enough to hide them. Troy hoped that the sulphurous smell would mask their scent.

Sure enough the huge land leviathan came down the tunnel. It was on all fours and had to crouch even in the huge cavern.

Troy could only stare. The creature's scales alone each measured five feet around and were covered in ancient mosses and weird growths as if it was part of an ancient moving mountain that had existed for as long as the Earth did.

There were backward curving spikes on its back all the way to its head, and in amongst them there were rips and old scars attesting to a life of fighting. Perhaps thousands of years ago some of those wounds were inflicted by the army it had obliterated. But he doubted it.

It stopped close to them and turned its head. The massive yellow slitted eyes moved slowly over the surroundings and Troy held his breath lest it somehow smell his exhalations. But in those devil-slitted eyes there was more than the gaze of a dumb brute. He saw intelligence, and that made it a hundred times more dangerous.

Then the massive creature moved on, and in a few minutes, it vanished into the thick steam.

Anne got to her knees. "That just made our options choice easy – we go back the way we came."

"Yep." Troy grabbed her hand, and the pair ran back along the cave trying to be as silent as they could manage. Troy kept looking back, but then Anne stopped dead and tugged hard on his arm.

"Oh, shit no," she groaned.

Coming down the cave was Tygo and Elle, and Elle had a gun up and pointed right at him. He had no illusions that this time she would shoot him dead. And he doubted Anne would fare any better.

"Stay where you are," Elle yelled.

"*Like hell,*" he whispered, and quickly pulled Anne to the side. He drew his gun.

"I'm armed, and you know I'm a better shot than you," he yelled back.

Tygo and Elle spread a little, and before the big man edged behind a rock he reached into his pack and tossed something to Elle. He then grabbed one out into his own hand.

"Americans make good grenades. We now have an M67 each." Tygo held the silver cannister up. "It is a fragmentation device and contains 180 grams of composition B explosive. I chose them myself. Just one of them will be enough to obliterate both of you."

"There's methane down here. You detonate that, you're liable to blow us all up, you included. So you can just piss off." Troy knew that wasn't true but hoped Tygo didn't know it.

Tygo laughed. "I commend you on your survival skills, Mr Strom. And because of that, I have confidence you will survive even longer on this island. If you give me Odin's Heart, you will live. If you do not, you will die here, now."

Elle spoke from behind a stalagmite. "He means it, Troy; he'd rather die than live without the heart. Throw us the stone and let us leave."

Troy cursed softly. Beside him, Anne turned to him and mouthed: *What do we do?*

"The explosion will bring the dragon. But we'll be dead by then." He sighed. "We have no choice."

"You'll give it to them?" She frowned.

"Live to fight another day." He half leaned out. "Take the stone but leave us a couple of grenades; we'll need them."

"No," Elle replied.

"Then no deal," Troy cursed. "Whoever steps out to throw the first grenade, I'll shoot them between the eyes." Troy knew he was gambling and hoped they wouldn't call his bluff.

"It doesn't matter if you kill me. Or my chieftain," she replied.

"My chieftain?" Anne scoffed and her mouth turned down. "She's insane."

Troy shook his head and felt a squirming in his gut at her deferential reference to the ogrish man with her.

"If you kill one of us, the other will recover the stone from your body. Or its parts," Elle replied.

Troy tried to think of new options, but Elle changed her tone to beseech him.

"Please Troy, I don't want any more people to get hurt." She groaned. "I'm sorry things worked out the way they did. I wish they were different."

"You mean you wish you killed me and left with Odin's Heart months ago," he scoffed.

"No, you were special to me. You still are," she implored. "I just can't change who I am."

Troy hesitated.

"Oh bloody hell, Troy, don't you dare listen to her," Anne seethed. While keeping her eyes on Elle, she leaned closer to Troy. "Shoot her."

"*No.*" Troy held up the pack with the huge ruby inside. "All I want is a boat. That's all. You get Odin's Heart, and we all walk away happy."

Tygo laughed corrosively. "And where do you think you will you take your little motorboat?" He laughed some more. "We have the ship. And you are not getting onboard that."

He held out a hand from behind the rock and made a show of pulling the pin from the grenade. "How about I just take the heart from your dead hands. You have five seconds."

"Run for it?" Anne whispered.

"Elle would shoot us down." He sighed. "Checkmate."

"Two seconds," Tygo said.

"*Wait!*" Troy yelled back.

# CHAPTER 31

Oder reset and recharged the drone. He attached the new coupling and turned to Anders. "Now, let us have a little fun."

He and Anders were a quarter mile down the beach and concealed behind a small headland with bushes growing on it, providing further screen.

"First, we harass them. Then we strand them. And then…" He looked to Oder with a grim face. "Then we finish the big man."

"Agreed," Oder said enthusiastically. "And we're away."

He worked the controls and the drone lifted off. On its top in a special carriage was a 9mm handgun, pointed forward, also remote controlled. The drone's soft whine could barely be heard above the sounds of life emanating from the forest, and Oder moved the flying device into the trees, and guided it skilfully along behind the green wall to where the two people guarded the boats.

After a few moments more he and Anders crowded around the small screen as the drone approached the pair. It hovered just between two tree trunks and watched as the man and woman talked. The man was big, like a barroom brawler, and lazily smoked a cigarette. The woman was small, athletic, and had what looked like a dive knife strapped to her thigh.

"Here we go." Oder smiled.

The drone fired two shots, and one of them punctured one of the boats. The woman dived into the water, and the man sprinted down the beach and jumped behind a washed ashore tree trunk and took out his gun.

Oder hovered the drone in behind the tree momentarily, and then eased it out to watch. The woman swam around to get behind one of the boats and then crawled on her belly out of the water.

Oder took the drone down the beach to hover close to where the man lay. He sighted on him, and the small screen was then overlayed with a targeting bomb site.

"I could put a bullet right between his eyes," he said softly. He half turned. "Just say so."

"No," Anders said. "I only want the guy who killed Freja to pay. Not these nobodies." He straightened. "Scare him again."

Oder turned back, adjusted the aim to the tree trunk just beside the big man's face and fired again. The big man rolled away, and then a gun appeared in his hand and he fired several rounds into the forest – left, right, and straight ahead – he had no idea where, what, or who to shoot at.

Oder fired once more, and this time grazed the man's shoulder, leaving a line of scarlet blood showing through his ripped clothing. That was it, the man rose to his feet and ran into the water where he dived under and swam down along the beach towards the boats.

"Take out the boats," Anders said flatly.

Oder drew the drone back into the forest, zoomed down behind the trees and eased it forward. The woman was looking up over the top of the boats, and Oder then pumped three rounds into one boat, and two more into the already deflating other boat.

The woman shrieked and ran down the beach with hands over her head. The big man tread water, staying a few feet from the beach.

"And that's that," Anders exhaled contentedly.

"What now?" Oder said, and Anders noticed he still had the target centered on the man's face. He seemed determined to take him out.

"No, leave him. We'll..." He frowned and jerked toward the screen. "What is happening?"

Tentacles rose form the water around the swimming man, wrapping around his neck, head, and undoubtedly, torso. The man screamed, and as the pair watched, a massive body rose from the water, with a head several feet wide, and what looked like some sort of shell behind it. It also had one large, damaged eye. But the other dish-sized orb was fixed on the man, and though he was a big person, he was outweighed by hundreds of pounds, and worse, he was in its kingdom.

In seconds more he vanished beneath the water, and never resurfaced. Down the beach the woman watched with her hands up to each side of her head, and mouth open. In seconds more, she ran to retrieve something from one of the boats and then sprinted into the forest.

"Oh my god," Anders whispered, as they watched the water return to its placid lake-like stillness.

"Monsters," Oder replied.

Both men turned to their left to glance at the water, so close by, and so impenetrably dark.

"We finish our job. And then we leave," Anders said softly.

Oder looked up to where the woman sprinted into the forest. "Do we wait here for them to return?"

Anders thought about it for a moment. It was a good plan, but they had no idea how long that might be. Plus, the woman would warn them, and they could spread out and locate them.

He shook his head. "No, we follow her. She should lead us right to them."

They already had their backpacks on, and Oder piloted the drone in after the woman. They'd watch her, and tag along.

# CHAPTER 32

Troy had his gun in one hand and the backpack holding the massive ruby in the other. He knew he was a better shot than either of them, but against two adversaries, the odds of he or Anne getting hit were high.

He could think of nothing else he had to trade. The only upside was they got to keep their lives. He seethed; he had played this one badly. He hadn't expected them to arrive so soon, and he was outgunned and outnumbered.

"Here it is." He tossed the pack.

Tygo put the pin back in the grenade. Elle watched from behind her rock with her gun held loosely in her hand. But neither made a move for the huge gem, and the seconds ticked by agonizingly slowly.

Then Elle stepped out, with her hands up. Her gun was tucked back into the top of her pants. Troy pointed his gun, but she walked toward the pack with hands up and a small smile on her lips.

"*Shoot her, shoot her,*" Anne urged.

"She's unarmed," Troy said.

"Dammit, then give me the gun." Anne tried to lunge for the weapon, but he held her back.

Troy knew then there was no way he could kill or even wound Elle, and she calmy picked up the bag and backed away. The smile never left her face.

"I'm sorry, Troy," she whispered. "I wish…" She never finished.

"*Bitch,*" Anne said tightly.

They'd get away cleanly, with everything, unless he brought in another party to even the game. He couldn't shoot her, but maybe he didn't need to. He half turned to Anne. "Get ready to move fast."

Troy had only four bullets left, and they were the most valuable things he had. But the time had come to use that value – he snapped the gun up and fired twice, and then got back behind the rocks.

The gunshots were loud and echoed up and down the huge cave. Elle cursed and now held her gun in two hands as she backed away.

Tygo guffawed. "He missed."

"He wasn't shooting at us," Elle said through gritted teeth. She half leaned around her rocks to yell: "You've killed yourselves, damn fool."

From behind them there came the sound of thunder as something titanically heavy was dragged over stone.

Elle and Tygo ran to the opposite cave wall, and Troy and Anne sprinted down the far end of the cave.

In seconds more there came a roar blasting throughout the cave that shook the rock around them.

"That's your plan?" Anne said. "We don't even know if there's a way out down there."

"But we're in front of those two. So let them deal with a monster." He waved her on and pointed to a small side cave. It was only large enough for them to enter half a dozen feet, but it curved to the side, so pressing themselves in, meant they were hidden from the large cave. Troy and Anne folded themselves in and waited and listened.

In just a few minutes more there came the sound of an explosion and dust rained down on them.

Troy grinned. "Looks like our parties have just met."

But then there came multiple explosions. Then the sound of heavy rocks falling. Immediately the flow of air shut off. Troy groaned, tilted his head back and shut his eyes.

"What just happened?" Anne asked. "Did the dragon get them?"

"I don't think so." He laughed darkly and then opened his eyes. He sighed and looked at her. "I think they blew the cave leading to outside. Knowing Elle's luck, they managed to get out, and trapped the dragon in here." He looked at her. "With us."

She began to nod slowly. "Yeah, this was a good plan." She stepped out and looked up and down the cave. "Large predatorial creatures that live in burrows or caves usually have another way out of their lair. But we need to get there first, or we could be trapped in here for days, or even weeks." She stepped out another few steps. "And we don't have that long."

From deep in the cave, there came the sound of grinding stone again.

"Now or never," she said.

"Then now it is," Troy replied and together they began to run.

***

Troy guided them down the cave, swerving around bubbling pools that gave off a salty mineral smell, and he was sure that if they fell into

149

one, it would scald the flesh right from their bones.

And speaking of bones, they continued to come across fragments of skull, hip bones, and some corroded weapons. The battle that had occurred back in the caves had obviously continued.

Troy wondered if they were pursuing the dragon, or more likely, were they being pursued and forced into the depths of its lair?

He couldn't imagine what it must have been like for these long dead, brave warriors, lit only by burning torches, taking on a monstrous acid-spitting beast with nothing but wooden shields, swords, and spears. It must have been Hell.

He remembered a quote from one of his favorite authors about courage: *To choose to climb into Hell you need courage. Or foolishness.* He guessed it was a bit of one and a lot of the other.

Anne tugged on his arm. "Slow down, I can't breathe."

He looked across at her and saw her face was beet-red from exertion. But there was something else; the air wasn't that great in the caves. Troy knew that as well as sulphur, volcanic vents gave off all manner of toxic gases like carbon dioxide, sulphur dioxide, and hydrogen sulphide, and he bet they were sucking in every one of them, and at a time they were putting their lungs under pressure from exertion.

Troy stopped and turned, listening. The sounds of pursuit had stopped. He didn't know how long for, but every second they had was an opportunity to outpace the dragon. He placed a hand on Anne's back who was bending over, hands on her knees.

"Are you okay?" he asked.

She nodded, and then coughed. "I feel like that time in college when I smoked an entire pack of cigarettes."

He laughed and rubbed her back. "You were such a wild child. Let me guess, while sucking down tequila shots?"

She turned her head a little to look at him with one eye. "You were there?"

Troy looked back down the cave. "I don't think it's following. But we've got to keep going and try to find a way out."

"And if we don't?" She straightened.

"Think positive." He took her pack from her and placed it over the opposite shoulder to his own. "Let me know if you need to rest again."

She nodded and they continued.

The cave remained huge, and they could see in some areas where it narrowed slightly that the walls and ceiling were gouged undoubtedly by the passing of the dragon's body. They continued to pass by crushed human bone fragments and weapons.

"Whoever they were, they brought an army," Anne observed.

"But did any make it home?" Troy asked. "If they did, you'd think there'd be some sort of record, story, or legend."

"Like I said, this is very ancient." As they walked, Anne picked up one of the corroded axe heads. "And maybe they did make it back and left a legend. It's just that over the millennia it travelled around the world, and each culture added to it, or took something from it." She looked up. "Ever hear of St George and the dragon?"

He bobbed his head. "Vaguely."

"The legend has it that this creature was terrorizing a village, and they offered it sheep, first, and then children next. Then they started giving it adults, and the final straw was when they offered it a princess. So brave St. George decided to go and slay it."

"But this here was long before that legend, right?" Troy asked.

"Yes, but that legend can be traced all the way back to Babylonia, 1800 BC. And who knows where it was drawn from before that." She dropped the axe head. "This ancient battle might be the genesis of those stories of brave warriors going to a foreign land to fight dragons."

"If that's true, then at least some of them made it out. And made it home. We can too." Troy lifted his pace. "Come on."

They walked for another half an hour, and the heat was getting to them as there were more hot pools bubbling like cauldrons. Water ran down the walls and their ragged clothing stuck to them. The humidity was off the charts, but the pair began to lose a lot of water through perspiration.

Troy stopped and turned side on. He closed his eyes, and then began to smile. "Do you feel it?"

Anne did the same and began to nod. "Yeah, a cool breeze."

He opened his eyes. "And it's getting drier. I think this is it."

The cave narrowed a little more and then they came to the wall. There were stones piled upon each other. They were mostly tumbled now, but they probably made a wall blocking off the cave.

"Did it keep the dragon out?" Anne asked.

"The cave's smaller here. Maybe the narrowness kept it out rather than the people and their puny wall."

They stepped through an opening and saw it had been in use for a while as there were ancient fireplaces and even graves in an area near the wall. But what caught their attention was one large flat wall that was covered in paintings.

The colours were still vivid, and understandably, because the people living here were close to volcanic vents, they had access to mineral salts in just about every hue imaginable.

"The dragon," Anne said and pointed up at the representation of the massive beast. "It's perfect."

"Like it or not, for a time they had to live with it." He half turned. "Maybe to them, living with their god was a good thing. An honour." He walked along the wall. He had experience with ancient Viking murals and writing before and as he took in the images, he gave Anne his impression of what he was seeing.

"They lost nine tenths of their warriors, men, and women. A high price." He pointed at a marooned ship and turned. "Hey, maybe these were part of the group who got stranded in the dried river cave."

"They must have had other ships as there were so many of them," she remarked. "They would have needed a fleet."

Troy stopped at an image of ice walls and read the runic writing. "It seems they had been trapped here for years. Stuck here as the massive rift walls through to Odin's Gate, and their way out, iced over."

"But they made it out eventually. How?" Anne asked and stood with hands on hips before the final image. "And what does this mean?"

There was a picture of a mountain, its top lost in the mist.

He frowned as he tried to draw the meaning from the image. "Someone came to save them. Or tried to save them." He hiked his shoulders, as he wasn't sure he was translating correctly. "Or maybe warn them."

There were only a few words underneath it and Troy read them carefully. "*Harald den store kommer att leda oss till Himlens Moder.*" He stood back and rubbed his chin.

"Well?" Anne asked.

"*Harald the Great travelled through the Mother of the Sky to call us home.*" He began to smile as he turned to her. "I think there's another way home."

# CHAPTER 33

**5000BC – Lemuria, Greenland's interior**

Harald got down on his belly and peered down into the red crack in the earth. The smell was of strange fires and bad water. But also wood smoke and roasting meat.

He looked up. There were more cracks in the ground, some small and no bigger than a man's head. And others much larger. He had sent Sif to go and scout and she had come back and told them there was a mighty hole with fire at the bottom. Also, she found evidence of a great beast living inside.

"It will be the drekka. It would be best if we don't meet." Harald got to his feet. "But I believe the missing clan is below us somewhere. Let us bring them home."

He then led his group to a larger hole, this one with a way to climb down. He looked up and grinned. "Slowly now, lest we survive the beasts, but be killed by our own surprised kin." He slid in and began to scale lower. The others followed.

The group followed the smells of cooking and after 20-minutes spotted the first sentry.

Harald called to his team to wait while he stepped forward to announce himself. He left his weapons behind and faced them with arms open wide.

"Hail, warriors from Lemuria." He lifted his voice. "I am Harald from the clan of Ragnar. I come to talk with you."

The two guards stared. Harald noticed they were tall, very tall, and at least half a head bigger than he was, and he was one of the tallest in his clan. This missing clan had been lost in the mists of time, perhaps for two centuries. He wondered what foods they had eaten to grow so robust.

The two men conferred and then one of them ran back along the cave. Harald waited.

In minutes more a group approached, a war party, and a lot more warriors than Harald had. He stood firm, and in fact walked forward and stood with legs planted and fists on hips, waiting for them.

A grey-haired man with a cloak of strange fur or feathers came to the front. He looked Harald up and down for a moment.

"Call your people out," he said softly.

Harald turned and called to his small clan, and they came and stood shoulder to shoulder with him. Once again, Harald waited.

"I am Bernhild, chieftain of the drekka cave clan. You are welcome here, and we invite you to our camp. It has been *forever* since anyone from the home world has come to us." He grinned, showing long and strong teeth. "We thought the world outside had ceased to exist."

Harald smiled in return. "It exists, and still talks of you. But only in legend." He stuck out his chest. "I am Harald, warlord of the Ragnar clan from the land of mountains. I bring greetings from the king, and we seek you, the lost clan of Lemuria. We have much to talk about. And we offer you a way home." Harald came down from the tumbled rocks and walked confidently toward the group.

"The way home is ice locked," Bernhild remarked. "There is no way home."

"It is. But there is another way for those who can brave it." Harald approached the chieftain, and once again was startled at the man's size. The old man was taller than he was and even the few women warriors with them were enormous. He wondered if his own people stayed longer, would they grow even taller as well?

The group embraced and Bernhild addressed them. "Come with us and tell us of the outside world." He smiled that toothy smile again. "We will feast, and I promise, you will all be enjoyed."

With that, Harald's clan was invited back to the settlement. They passed through a strong stone wall and saw there was a village made up of wooden structures built inside the cave. There seemed to be hundreds of them, men, women, and children.

"We have been here a long time," Bernhild remarked. "We live close to the drekka. It cannot reach us here, but its very presence wards off the other beasts of the land above."

"Does it not attack you?" Harald asked.

"In the beginning it did." He smiled, his lips lifting his grey beard slightly. "But we have an understanding now." He waved them on. "Come, we have much to talk about."

154

Harald's group followed them to the chieftain's great hall. And Bernhild called for meats, ale, and bread. It was a great feast, and there were many questions about the path they took to find the secret passages through the Mother of the Sky Mountain.

Bernhild seemed most impressed and promised to remember them in their songs and art. The feasting went on for hours and following it, for the first time, Harald slept peacefully.

The next day, the chieftain offered to show Harald some of the remarkable gifts the drekka had given them and the wonders that had been revealed. The others of his clan would stay behind to learn more about the village, and perhaps ready them for their trek home, but only for those who wished to go.

Bernhild took Harald down the long cave, and then through a crack in the wall the pair slithered through – easy for Harald, harder for the big Viking chieftain. Bernhild carried a lit torch and at the entrance to the new cave he paused and carefully poked his head in, and on seeing it was safe stepped out and waved Harald with him.

"This is the den of the drekka. It is out hunting now." Bernhild waved him on.

Harald noticed some heavy iron rings set into the cave floor and made a mental note to ask the chieftain about them. But for now, he was on guard about the monster.

Bernhild took him to an area of the cave that had a massive pit in its center. He looked down. And then nodded toward its core.

"The drekka brood," he said almost reverently.

Harald stared down into the dark heart of the massive pit. It looked like a giant dish of melted stone, as if something unbelievably hot had been there. He looked up and saw that the ceiling was different here, closed over and it too smoothed, as if a giant bubble had risen and then cooled to seal over the cave within it.

At the base and in the direct center was a group of egg-shaped objects, all of them softly glowing. In fact, it looked like a clutch of giant glowing red eggs.

"They are gifts from Odin himself." He nodded as he stared almost trance-like. "We will be allowed to take one and build a temple in honour of it. All will come and pay deference."

"How will they know about it?" Harald asked.

Bernhild turned. "Because you will tell them." He smiled. "And you will take one as well. When you leave."

"Would you not come with us?" Harald asked, confused now.

"Why? Everything we want and need is here. Our army was defeated here, but we were spared when we promised to keep these precious things safe." He faced Harald. "Tell them it is the heart of Odin. Tell them to come."

Harald wasn't sure he understood. But he didn't come to argue. He had come to rescue them, but he never thought that they might be content to stay.

Bernhild quickly climbed down into the pit and brought back one of the egg-shaped objects. Seeing it up close, Harald needed to narrow his eyes as it made them water and also made his teeth ache. But it was the most beautiful thing he had ever seen. It was a gem of great value and he was honored to be given such a gift.

He was then led back to the village, and on arriving, the clan was strangely silent. Harald looked for his people, but there was no Birger, Srgne, Inga, or even the beautiful Sif.

"Where are my people?" Harald asked.

Bernhild turned and put his large hands on each of Harald's shoulders. "You are a brave warrior, and from now on you shall be known as *Harald the Great*. Your name will live on." He stared hard into Harald's eyes. "But your people must stay."

"But I will need…" Harald began.

Bernhild shook his head. "They are needed here. We need new blood. Take the stone and tell all the clans of the world about Lemuria. And tell them that only those brave enough and strong enough will be worthy of Odin's love and respect… if they can find our land."

Several tall and formidable warriors came and stood at his shoulders, and Harald knew he had no choice. He tried to see past them to spot any of his people, but there was no sign.

Bernhild then handed him the large stone wrapped in a soft hide. "May all the gods be at your side." He nodded. "Farewell, Harald the Great. Thank you for coming to our land; you have truly proved yourself worthy of the All Father's love, respect, and to be by his side in his Great Hall."

Harald took the wrapped gem and placed it in the bag over his shoulder. He then turned and was escorted back to the entrance where he had dropped down into the cave. He turned one last time, but it seemed already the village life had forgotten him as they went about their daily life.

He sighed, and then began his long climb back home.

*\*\**

Inga slowly lifted her head and half turned to the sound. "Do you hear?" she whispered.

"Yes," Sif replied wearily. "It comes then."

Both women were naked and bound with a soft rope made from

animal hide to an iron ring embedded into the cave floor.

"Good. Then it will be over soon," Inga replied, and then her words grew bitter. "I will tell Odin of these creatures and what they are doing to his children."

Sif nodded. "And I will tell him of Birger and Srgne." She started to sob. "And tell how they had their throats cut and were then hung to be bled out like hogs."

"Stop it, don't think of it, or remember it," Inga said.

Sif sniffed wetly. "And I will tell Odin how they were cut up to be cooked and served like fresh lamb." She turned to the dark cave depths. "And now I don't know if they were the lucky ones."

"And where is Harald?" Inga asked. "Did he escape?"

"I hope so," Sif said softly.

The roar from the dark depths made them both cry out.

A small movement caught Inga's eye and she turned to see the old warrior, the chieftain named Bernhild, watching them from a crevice in the rock wall.

"*Curse you!*" she yelled.

The man shook his head. "No child, it is an honour."

Then, dragging itself from the cave darkness came the titanic creature, its yellow slit eyes fixed on the morsels left for it. Bernhild eased back into his viewing crevice, and both women at first shrieked, but then dropped their heads and squeezed their eyes tight, not wanting to see anymore.

The dragon was used to this offering and came slowly, confident they could not flee. It sniffed them once and then opened its mouth to vomit a stream of greenish bile over them.

The agonized screams of the women did not last long, and soon the dragon was licking up the puddle of melted flesh, viscera, and bone.

Bernhild nodded, satisfied, and pulled back from the scene. He had been right; Harald's clan had been needed – every morsel of them.

# EPISODE 13

*The voices of the ancients call to us. Sometimes we hear them.*

# CHAPTER 34

"What does this mean?" Anne pointed to more images on the wall.

Troy stood before them, and after a few moments shook his head and sighed. "These... don't make much sense."

Unfortunately, there were few runic symbols and the images themselves were perplexing – there were several pictures with one of them showing a large depression and a group of the red orbs like Odin's Heart at its center. The next was of a single warrior holding one.

"It looks like he left by himself. But this seems to indicate he took Odin's Heart with him." He half turned. "Unless there was more than one." Troy thought it through. "And if that's the case; what happened to the one he took to the outside world?"

Anne looked around. "This settlement looks like it predates even the earliest Vikings. Maybe they were survivors of the great battle down here. It might be 8,000 to 10,000 years old. But the last images of the lone warrior seem to be made later; perhaps only five to eight millennia."

"Over five thousand years ago." Troy folded his arms. "A gem that big would surely have surfaced somewhere over all that time. It would have been the prize of emperors."

"St George," Anne whispered.

"What?" He turned.

"Want to hear a crazy idea?" she asked.

"Yeah, sure." Troy waited.

"What do they look like?" She pointed to the drawing of the group of red stones in the depression and of the lone warrior leaving while holding one of them.

Troy turned back to the image, remaining silent. There were also images of some people tied down before a dragon, and others being put, piece by piece, into a fire. Sacrifice? And surely, they didn't cook and eat the others. He remembered the huge warriors telling him he was food, and knew it was possible.

*This was a brutal place*, he thought. Troy sighed and looked back at the image of the clutch of large red gems. "Okay, I'll bite; what do you think they look like?"

"It's obvious; eggs." She snorted softly. "And now for the crazy part. What happened to the one that was removed? I think it hatched."

"And you think it might have grown into the beast that was eventually killed by St George?" Troy scoffed. "You've seen the monster here; how does a single guy with shield, lance, and sword kill that?"

"He obviously killed it before it got too big. I think these drekka, or dragons, were dinosaur killers. While they're small or only in few numbers they aren't a huge threat. But if they grow big, then we, human beings, might end up the next species to go extinct."

"I'll grant you it looked like an egg, but the stone was a ruby; hard and clear. There was no embryo suspended inside it."

She shrugged. "Lots of creatures have clear spawn that turns opaque when the animal begins to form inside." She turned about slowly. "Somewhere, either down here, or somewhere else, there might be that clutch of eggs. We have no idea about this creature's life cycle. It might stay dormant for centuries, millennia, or many millennia. And only when the environment is just right, they hatch, grow, and begin to consume."

Troy didn't like what he was hearing, because it was plausible as hell, and scared the shit out of him.

Anne grabbed his arm. "And it's another reason not to let Tygo or your damn ex-girlfriend leave the island with the stone. I mean, egg."

He nodded. And then moved down to the last image, that seemed as though it was painted years after the original cave art. "Looks like the clan that lived here also decided to leave. Hey, I wonder if these guys might have been the forebears of the clan in the hills we met."

"Possible." She still held onto his arm. "Troy, this is serious. I've seen what introducing a new predatorial species into an environment does. Sometimes, it forms a balance. But most times it wipes out all its competition. That'd be us. So we need to recover that gem. I don't know how, but we can't let them take it from the island."

"Yeah, that was kinda always the plan," he replied.

She let go of his arm. "And we can't take it either."

He sighed. He knew she was going to say that. Did he really plan on enduring all of this and go home with nothing more than torn clothing and some good stories to tell his grandkids one day?

Not a chance.

"First, we need to climb out of this hole. Then we have to find a way to get home. The upside is, we have a plan-B for escape; we follow Harald the Great through the Mother of the Sky to get out of here." He began to smile. "If he could do it, we can do it."

"Or die trying." She smiled and nodded.

Troy took one last look at the images. They still unsettled him and left him with a feeling of disquiet in the pit of his gut. He turned to look back down the cave. Somewhere back there the dragon was stopped. But he didn't think for an instant the cave-in Tygo and Elle created would have crushed or trapped it. Given its size he bet it could have burst out anytime, anywhere it wanted.

They headed further down the cave, and though it had constricted by more than two thirds from when they first entered, it was still a few dozen feet over their heads.

"This is promising." Troy slowed.

There was the beginning of a few cracks appearing in the ceiling, but no way to reach them. That was until they came to the dangling rope.

He slowly walked toward it and stopped to look up. There was no one up there, and he grabbed the rope and tugged. Nothing fell or jumped in, and no face appeared. But the rope was a modern design, he bet hung recently, and he thought it looked like the rope that Tygo's man had used to scale down.

"Has this been hung for us?" Anne asked.

"It is now." Troy grabbed it.

"Wait." Anne peered up. "Do you think it's a trap? Maybe they're waiting for us to poke our heads up, and then..."

Troy nodded slowly and looked up to where the rope came over the lip. "We don't have a choice." He adjusted the gun at his belt. "I'll check it out first. Then I'll haul you up." He looped it around one leg, and then began to climb.

It only took him a few minutes, but when he got to the top he stopped, slowly peeked out, and then turned in a full circle. There was nothing and no sounds of any person or creature close by.

*Maybe it wasn't a trap,* he thought. *Maybe Elle really threw it down for him because she had some sort of pang of regret or guilt.* He hoped so.

Troy levered himself up to sit momentarily on the edge of the crack and took a better look around. Close by in the dirt near the rope was a few footprints, large, and in the shape of the boot-type moccasins he remembered the giant Vikings wearing.

He chuckled softly. So probably not Elle after all. He looked up. "*Yrsa?*" he whispered.

*Was she following them?* he wondered. For now it didn't matter. He turned on his belly and poked his head back down into the hole.

"Come up, coast is clear." He knew after their ordeal, they were both weakened, and he doubted Anne could climb the rope under her own power. "Wrap it around your chest and under your arms and hang on tight. I'll pull you up."

She did as asked, and when ready, he braced his feet and began to drag on the rope. It came up foot by foot, and though his muscles strained, they had both lost weight, so he had her at the surface in moments more.

She grabbed onto the rock edge and climbed out and then rolled over onto her back. She lay there and undid the rope that had pulled tight, constricting her. When undone she took a deep breath and let it out with a whoosh.

"I've never been so glad to see daylight again." She looked up at the wintery white sky. "Sort of daylight."

Troy reached into his pocket and pulled out the green eye. It swivelled to point into the forest.

"Magic eyeball says this way." He looked across into the dark wall of fern fronds and massive tree trunks. "I think we'll be too late, but we have to give it a shot, right?"

"We sure do." She exhaled, signalling her exasperation. "But they'll never believe us about the threat the gem poses."

"No," Troy replied. "And I'm not fully convinced either. And bottom line, Tygo sees us, he kills us." He wiped his hands and stood, lifting her up as well. "Step one, we get to the coast. Step two, we work out how to stop them, or get the gem from them without getting shot or blown up."

"Step three and four. We take their boat, sail home, and then lay in a hot tub sipping expensive wine." She smiled up at him.

"That's the easy part." He grinned back.

She shrugged. "Life goals."

"Then let's make it happen." He took one last look around, wondering whether Yrsa was there somewhere, watching them, or it had just been a coincidence. It didn't matter now. He turned and headed into the forest.

# CHAPTER 35

Hilda Bergensen ran, leaping over fallen trunks, and swerving around huge trees that were like redwoods except were draped with curtains of roots and vines that were hung with grape-like bulbs that might have been fruit or seed pods.

The people firing at her, puncturing the boats, and then seeing Gunner grabbed and dragged down by some monster in the water was too much for her rapidly fragmenting sanity. But now there was something else – she was being pursued – the thing was out to her right side, crashing through the underbrush, and keeping pace with her.

She was scared witless, and her heart hammered in her chest as she ran almost blindly. And in the background, there was the continual faint whine of something from behind her. It was high up and in this place her mind conjured images of some sort of giant mosquito monster just waiting to drop down on her and suck out her blood.

She wasn't ready for this, and guessed she never was. The entire place was a madman's fever dream.

She had been running for ages, and now doubted she was even going in the right direction. Hilda was out of ideas, but as panic set in, logic was fast escaping her.

"Tygo! Elle!" she yelled. "He-*eeelp*!"

The sound of pursuit gathered pace and she knew whatever it was, it was now moving to intersect with her. She briefly glanced to the side and saw something snaking through the underbrush, smashing ferns out of its way, and she could tell it far outweighed her.

It was a race, and she knew it was one she would lose. Hilda had been given a gun, and she was no expert with firearms, and had only shot one a few times. She reached for it, fumbling it out, and sure enough it flipped from her hands.

She paused for a few seconds, but it had gone into a clump of plants, and if she spent just a few moments looking for it, she knew she was dead. Instead, she jinked, and sprinted off again.

The thing closed in on her, and she heard its bulldozing pursuit just a dozen feet from her. "Help!" she screamed. "*HELP!*"

She burst from the forest line into a clearing, and there before her was Tygo and Elle. The green-eyed woman stood with her legs wide and gun held in two hands.

"Get down," she said with a calm voice.

Hilda dived, as Elle fired twice.

There was a tumble, and slide, and then the sound of the creature vanished. Hilda quickly rolled over, breathing hard and feeling like she was going to vomit. She scrambled on her hands and knees to the pair.

She climbed up Tygo's leg who batted her away, and she simply pointed, not able to speak yet as she dragged air into her tortured lungs.

Behind her with a bullet in its head and a now missing eye, was a giant lizard, like a Komodo dragon, but around twenty feet long and as broad around as a draft horse.

"Stand straight," Tygo ordered as he frowned down at her. "Why are you here? Where's Gunner?" he demanded.

She pointed back the way she had come. "Dead. Killed."

"You were supposed to watch the boats," Tygo growled and grabbed the front of her shirt, lifting her from her feet. He shook her and her head bounced on her neck. He stopped and leaned forward almost nose to nose. "What. Happened?"

Hilda gulped and blinked a few times, now looking rattled but at least less terrified. "Gunner was in the water. A giant octopus thing came and grabbed him."

"Why was he in the water?" Elle asked calmly.

"Because we were being shot at." Hilda swallowed.

Elle and Tygo glanced at each other, and Elle shook her head slowly. "No, it can't have been Strom or his friend. And no one else was left alive."

"Who shot at you? Where did they come from?" He let Hilda go. "Did you see them?"

"No, they stayed in the forest. After Gunner got taken, I just ran," she said as her voice trailed away. "I think they followed me."

"I see." Elle half turned her head, and then with the speed of a snake-strike she whipped out her gun, aimed and fired into the forest.

The drone just at the tree line dipped as one of its rotors was clipped. It wasn't enough to knock it out of the sky, but it withdrew and vanished into dense greenery.

Elle lowered her arm, still staring venomously into the forest. "So, we have a new player." She turned back to Hilda. "The boats?"

"They had holes shot in them," Hilda replied meekly.

"You useless insect." Tygo pushed the small woman back a step, lifted his gun and shot her dead center in the chest.

Hilda was blown backwards off her feet. Her face was screwed into a pained grimace, but gradually it relaxed and then she was gone.

Elle stepped over the woman. "We've got what we came for. We can repair the boats but need to get the hell out of here." She looked around. "And we need to watch out for whoever it is that has decided to make war on us from the shadows."

"We see them, we kill them," Tygo said and holstered his weapon.

The pair began to jog back through the forest toward the beach.

# CHAPTER 36

Oder had needed to work the controls furiously to keep the drone from smashing into the trees. Three remaining propellers still meant it could stay up, but its manoeuvrability was shot as they moved it back into the forest.

The pair of men were about 300 yards even further in, and Oder swivelled the machine in the air, and watched from within the canopy of a large tree. Then they saw the man they were after shoot the woman in the chest.

"*Helvete!*" Oder exclaimed.

Anders seethed through clamped teeth. "Seems the pig has a taste for killing women."

"They will head back for the boats now. They will find them punctured. But they can be repaired," Oder said.

"Then we need to get there first and slash them to ribbons," Anders said. "Can the drone still fly and shoot?"

"The gyros are still working, but I do not have great air control. I can harass them, and if I'm lucky, hit one." Oder looked up. "But its main weapon was stealth and ambush. That is now gone."

"There's only two of them left." Anders nodded and slapped him on the shoulder. "Let's get back. Then we can plan our final attack."

\*\*\*

Anders led them back through the forest, while Oder kept one eye on his brother-in-law's back, and the other on the drone's tiny screen.

"They're gaining on us," he said.

"We'll make it," Anders replied. "If we pick it up."

The men began to run harder, and Oder took his eyes from the screen to jump over a large log.

Anders tried to remember if they were headed the right way, as most parts of the dark and dense forest all looked the same. This area had massive trees with trunks as large around as a house, and broad limbs that reached out around them like a titan's umbrella. For now, he followed what looked like an animal trail.

Five more minutes in, he detected something and sniffed. He slowed, smelling something that was a mix of vinegar, rotting almonds, and cat's piss. And he was sure the branches above him moved as though there was a slight breeze, where there was none.

Behind him, Oder grunted, as Anders concentrated on navigating the thick forest. "Can you still see them?" he asked.

There was no reply. "Oder, are they still behind us?" Anders said over his shoulder.

Again there was nothing, and for that matter, not even any sound of Oder trailing him anymore. Anders slowed and turned. Then stopped.

His friend wasn't behind him anymore.

"Oder?" he asked.

Anders tilted his head. "*Oder?*" louder this time, and then he began to walk back along the trail.

The forest had become eerily quiet. The bird calls, and even the insects seemed to have shut down.

There, ahead on the grass, he saw the remote and, in a few strides, crossed to it. He lifted it and saw the camera was still working, but the drone without its pilot had fallen from the air.

He held onto it but lowered his arm. He turned slowly. "Oder?" but he spoke quieter this time.

The man might have stopped to piss, or emergency defecate, but whatever reason, he'd call to Anders to let him know what he was doing. And he would never discard the drone controls.

From above him there was a snap of twigs and the sound of heavy sliding. Anders lifted his gaze.

He frowned, trying to understand what he was seeing – one of the huge limbs of the tree glistened as if it was slippery. It was banded in green and black tiger stripes, and as he watched, it moved as if there were muscles at play.

"What is…?" he whispered, confused.

He moved his eyes along its length and came to the head of a snake, five feet long and nearly as wide. He felt a shock pass right through his system as he saw his brother-in-law's boots sticking from the mouth.

The massive neck worked, and in another gulp even the shoes disappeared into the maw and the forked tongue, probably as long as he was, snickered out as if to lick its lips.

Anders' mouth dropped open. As he watched he saw the outline of

Oder move along the long body as it was swallowed down.

"*Gaa.*" He backed up. "*Gaa.*"

The giant snake turned its head, black, glassine eyes swivelled to watch him. Then its head lifted, clearly interested. Perhaps it had more room in that 50 foot long body for another person.

Anders kept backing up, and as he moved, the snake eased forward. He didn't wait. He threw the drone control at the thing's head but didn't wait to see if it connected and instead turned to run.

He sprinted faster than he had ever run in his life, and after five minutes he began to hear bird song again, hopefully signalling he was out of the domain of the giant reptile.

"I'm sorry, Oder," he whispered pitifully.

As he thought about the man, into his mouth shot a bubble of bile and he spat it onto the grass. He'd had enough of this accursed place.

He slowed and sucked in a deep breath.

And then the shot rang out.

\*\*\*

"*Ach*, I missed," Tygo spat and lowered the gun.

His target, the single man, dodged away and vanished into the thick, green growth.

"Forget him," Elle said. "Our priority is the boat."

She pushed into the forest and led Tygo back to the beach.

\*\*\*

Anders dodged around a tree and saw the water through the foliage. He didn't stop and charged out onto the beach, got his bearings, and then sprinted with his last bit of energy to where he and Oder had left their boat.

As far as his plans went, he had failed. His brother-in-law was dead, the hated man still lived, and though they had holed the boats, he knew with a simple patch and reinflation they would be underway in an hour.

When he got to the boat he didn't wait, he immediately pushed it into the water, leapt in, and started the engine. In seconds more he was heading across the expanse of inland sea to the cave.

Another shot rang out, but he stayed low and doubted the bullet even came close to him, and in seconds more he was in the cave, and kept the throttle wide open as speed was the goal, not fuel consumption or silence now.

He then rocketed out from between the mighty walls of ice, and he immediately noticed that it was cooler, and even in the short time he had been inside, there was a few small icebergs dotted around. The cooling time was returning, and it wouldn't be long until the walls of ice narrowed, and the sea ice locked it all away.

He had Captain Olaf wait for them in a direct line, a quarter mile out from the ice rift. If he kept on his current bearings, he should find the man's boat.

He counted the minutes and doing quick math in his head estimated he was hopefully coming up on Olaf's position.

The mist was as thick as ever and he eased back on the throttle. He expected to see the lights glowing, but so far there was silence, and nothing but steel grey water, with a few bobbing bergs thankfully only as large as basketballs.

"Oh shit," he breathed. "Please no."

Anders felt his spirits sink. He couldn't go back, and if Olaf was gone, then he couldn't go forward, as the small boat would run out of fuel hundreds of miles before he found any substantive land mass. And added to that, if those killers found him, they'd shoot him dead on sight.

"Think," he demanded of himself. But after several seconds he had nothing and slumped forward with his hands over his face.

Then he heard the soft thrum of an engine and his head jerked upright. He turned about, and finally, through the heavy mist there came a halo of light, and the sound of an old boat engine he recognised.

"Thank you, God," he breathed.

In minutes more the boat came closer, shut off the engines and glided up beside him. Olaf came out on deck. "Hail there. Lucky I saw you on the radar. It still don't work too well in these parts."

"Where were you?" Anders asked

Olaf pointed. "There's a boat moored just a quarter mile down the coast. No one on board. I went to check it out."

"Really?" Anders' mind worked.

Olaf frowned as he threw a rope. "Where's your brother-in-law? What happened?"

Anders grabbed the rope and looked up. "He didn't make it." He sighed. "It was horrible."

Olaf nodded. "Sometimes legends should stay legends." He lowered the winch ropes to haul the inflatable boat onboard. "Come on up and get yourself warm."

Once on deck, Anders turned to the old man. "We need to leave quickly. But first, show me this boat."

# CHAPTER 37

It had only taken Tygo ten minutes to patch the boat, but they needed to wait another 15 minutes for the rubber sealants to set and cure. It was painful as they were impatient, but both knew that if they put the inflatable under duress, it was liable to burst the patch, and the last thing they wanted was to be taking on water when they entered the freezing sea outside the caves. After many more minutes, Tygo scratched at the patch and announced it ready.

"Wait," Elle said. She reached into the other still damaged boat and removed the spare tank of gas and the flare gun. She began to douse it from bow to stern and then stood back.

"Just in case that meddlesome Troyson Strom and his bitch survive." She fired the gun into the deflated craft and it went up with a whump of billowing orange flame. Black smoke boiled upwards as the rubber and synthetic materials caught fire.

In minutes more, Elle and Tygo sped toward their destination of the exit cave. Tygo held up the huge ruby and stared into it with an almost dreamy expression.

"I wouldn't do that." Elle smiled without humour. "Remember what happened last time."

Tygo's face dropped. She was right, and he turned back to the receding forest as he lowered the gem. But he refused to let his spirits dim as they finally had what they came for and had disposed of their crew without any trouble at all. They had served their purpose, and neither Elle nor Tygo would think about them again.

They shot through the cave, then along the massive walls of ice, to then burst into the outside world. As they neared what they hoped was their moored boat's position, they saw the glow through the mist. Tygo accelerated and headed directly for it.

"What is this?" Tygo demanded.

"Oh no," Elle whispered.

As they drew nearer, they saw that the glow wasn't the strong fog lights they had left blazing all over the ship, but the entire structure of the craft was in flames. Already it was riding lower in the water.

"Bastards!" Tygo yelled. "*Bastards!*" He screamed so loud the veins in his neck stood out like cords. He stood in the boat, his huge size making it unstable.

"Another boat," Elle hissed.

Tygo spun fast, spotted it, and then reached for his gun.

Elle did the same but kept it below the gunwale.

The older boat came closer, but then slowed about 50 feet from them and then put their propellor in reverse to stop the craft.

"Who are they?" Tygo said in a low growl.

"I have a bad feeling about this," Elle whispered. "Be ready."

There was the crack of a rifle and water splashed up to their port side. Tygo immediately sat down.

"Can you swim?" the voice boomed across the water via the loudhailer.

Tygo growled and his hand gripped his gun so hard the handle popped from the pressure. "*Who are you?*" he yelled back.

"The one with the hunting rifle with sniper scope pointed at your head," came the calm reply. "And the one you tried to shoot."

"Shit," Elle groaned.

"You sunk our boat." Tygo pointed at the flaming wreck now with just the rails and cabin above the water.

"So what; you killed all your crew," the voice replied.

"You need to take us onboard. Otherwise we will die out here," Elle beseeched.

"You killed my Freja in Oslo. At the museum." The voice had an edge now. "So, you do not deserve any sympathy. Or mercy," the voice replied with a deadness to its tone.

"The husband or lover of the Museum woman," Elle said softly. "We are in trouble."

Tygo just sat, fuming for a moment. "What do you want?"

"I want you dead. Just give me one reason why I shouldn't kill you right now." The voice was remorseless.

Elle could tell one wrong move or word and they would both be killed. Or sunk. And she didn't like the idea of trying to swim back to the island. They'd never even make it to shore.

"A trade," she said and held up the bag.

"What are you doing?" Tygo's eyes bulged, and he lunged for her.

Elle put her boot on his chest and pushed him back. "Saving our lives."

She opened the bag and took out the massive red stone. "Can you see?" It shone with a warm red hue as she held it up. "It's the largest ruby in the world and worth around one hundred million dollars."

"I'll kill you for this," Tygo said between gritted teeth.

She looked him dead in the eye. "We just recovered this stone from a hidden prehistoric island, populated by monsters. Do you really think we can't retake it from some skinny museum guy?" she lowered the stone. "But we've got to be alive to do it first."

Tygo sat back.

She turned and held out the stone. "Do we have a deal?"

There was silence for many minutes as whoever was on the boat conversed. She looked out over the water, and the impenetrable grey surface gave away nothing of what was below. She hoped his parting gift wasn't to sink them, as there were now a few small bergs at the surface, and the temperature was enough to kill them. And if that didn't, then some beast living in Lemuria's seas would.

"We have a deal," came the reply, with a humourless laugh. "Besides, the island will kill you in ways far worse than one of my bullets between the eyes."

"Probably," she replied.

Elle waited some more as the sound of some sort of work went on their deck. Then silence hung over the water again except for the soft lap of waves against their hull. She turned her head to speak softly to Tygo. "Be ready."

The older boat's engines restarted, and it glided closer.

When it was within a dozen feet the engines reversed again. Both Elle and Tygo gripped their handguns, waiting for their opportunity.

"Look up at the wheelhouse," the voice said.

Elle could just see another figure there, hiding behind a window corner. And the barrel of a long gun pointed right at her. She cursed, as she knew they were exposed, and the shooter wasn't. It also meant he wasn't alone. If it came to a gun fight, they had nowhere to hide.

From the rear deck something was thrown over the side that floated toward them. It was a round life buoy with a rope attached. She saw at its center it had a fishing net tied there creating a cradle of sorts.

"Place the gem in the net. That is all," the voice, eager now, ordered.

"Wait…" Elle began as the buoy floated closer.

The man in the cabin fired again; this time she felt the bullet whizz past her head. She cringed and bared her teeth.

"Stop that, dammit." Frustration burned within her.

"Place the ruby in the net." The voice had an edge of impatience now. "Or next one is into your boat. Or you. I don't care which."

Tygo made a strangled noise in his throat, and Elle saw his face was scarlet with rage. His hand vibrated as he gripped the gun, and she looked at him with dead level eyes.

"Don't even think about it," she seethed.

The buoy was close now and she reached out to pull it closer and then placed the stone in the net bag at its center.

She watched with a sinking feeling in her gut as it was reeled in. It was pulled around the back of the boat where they couldn't see. *Smart*, she thought. Because when whoever went to gather it up, they would need to take their eyes off them. And she wanted to shoot them both more than anything else in the world right now.

She looked up again at the cabin and saw the gun still pointed at them. She judged distance and angles. She was a good shot, but she knew if she missed by only a fraction, the return fire from a shooter with a scope would be deadly.

The boat began to reverse away, slowly at first, and then it picked up speed. It continued farther and farther, until it was indistinct in the mist.

But then it seemed to hang there like a faint ghost, as if watching them.

Elle and Tygo sat silently for a few seconds. She looked to Tygo who was like a volcano that could explode at any second. She could usually control him, but when he was in his rages, she usually just got out of the way. In a tiny boat she didn't have that luxury.

"What was lost, will be found," she said.

He looked up at her, his eyes red rimmed with rage. For the first time, she didn't trust him. And she bet, he didn't trust her.

"We'll get it back." She dragged in a deep breath and let it out slowly and then gave him a crooked smile. "Time to go home."

The shot rang out, and *thwacked* into the side of their boat. Immediately, air started to escape.

She spun around, eyes wild and with bared teeth. "You *fucking*..."

She stuck a hand over the hole, but the bullet had gone in at the top and exited somewhere under the hull.

Laughter rang out over the water as the ghostly boat started up again and slowly vanished into the mist.

Elle pointed at Tygo while keeping her other hand over the hole she could reach. "Start the engine. We have only minutes."

# CHAPTER 38

Troy saw the whisps of black smoke rising over the treetops and then smelled the heavy, acrid odor of melted plastics long before he reached the beach.

He stopped to look up and down its coast and then immediately spotted the incinerated inflatable raft that had burned down to leave a scorched mark on the sand, and a trail of melted material running into the water like rapidly cooling lava.

"Those bastards," he yelled.

"They've gone." Anne stopped and put her hands on her knees, breathing hard from the exertion. "We missed them. Again."

Troy walked to the burned boat and kicked some sand up onto it. "This happened in the last hour or so." He looked over the raft's interior. "There's nothing left. Nothing salvageable." He kicked up more sand.

Anne went and sat beneath a tree with fronds leaning over her like an umbrella. Troy eventually sat beside her and rested his forearms on his knees. He looked across at her.

"*Déjà vu?*"

She snorted softly and smiled. "You sure know how to show a lady an exciting time."

Troy lay back and closed his eyes for a moment. "On a scale of one to ten on the insane life choices index, I'm putting this voyage up at about an eleven."

Anne slapped a hand on his thigh. "Come on; if you were back home now all you'd be doing is eating fatty food, drinking too much expensive wine, and stressing about your next big business deal."

Troy sat up. "I'm sorry, but I could live with that."

The pair sat in silence for a while, each lost in their own thoughts. Finally, Anne began to nod.

"I'm hungry," she remarked.

"Me too." He turned to her. "Got anything to eat?"

She shook her head. "Nope."

Troy looked out over the calm water with a few vapours rising from its warmth in the cool air like little ghosts. After a moment, he frowned and tilted his head, listening.

"Hey." His brows came together even more.

"Yeah?" Anne turned to him.

"You hear that?" He straightened.

Anne closed her eyes and listened. After another moment she began to nod her head. "That's an outboard motor." She looked towards the cave in the massive cliff wall across the water. "*There, there.*"

Sure enough, from the mouth of the cave came a small boat. But there was something wrong with it; it sat low in the water and was moving sluggishly.

"Who the hell is that?" Troy got to his feet.

As they watched, the person in the front of the boat started to fire at something in the water. And then they could make out what it was; something travelling alongside it, that surfaced and dived, but then came back again. It bumped them, causing the small boat to be swamped even more.

"Whoever they are, they've got problems. Some sort of predator is tracking them." Anne squinted. "And they're sinking."

"They're not going to make it," Troy said.

Anne walked a few paces down the sand, but as the boat slowly approached, something about the shape of the two people in the craft set off alarm bells in Troy's head.

"No, stay back. Let's see who they are first." He drew her back under the tree fern's hanging fronds.

It became clear that the person in the front was a woman and she moved from one side of the boat to the other, firing into the water. Eventually something like a gigantic, smooth alligator reared up, a long pointed snout opened to snap at her arm. It missed, and then dived back down, but didn't go away.

Judging its size next to the raft, Troy estimated the creature to be about 30 feet long and looked to be a powerful predator. So far, the woman's aim had struck home, possibly annoying it enough to be an irritant but not a deterrent.

"Big mosasaur," she remarked. "They go down any more, and they'll be swamped."

"They go down any more, that creature is simply going to slide over the side of their boat." Troy watched as the boat was down to travelling at about 2-knots, little more than a slow walking pace.

The creature circled them now, and even Troy could guess it was looking up from below the water and judging the best place to pick one of the warm bodies from the boat.

"That's Elle," he said and felt his stomach knot with worry for her.

"Then she's about to get what she deserves." Anne smiled as she watched.

Troy shook his head. "Maybe Tygo. But she doesn't deserve that." Troy pulled out his gun.

Troy knew he had two bullets left and little chance of hitting the thing from still several hundred yards. But as he watched, the big guy in the back who had to be Tygo, held the engine's handle in one hand and pulled something from his pocket.

Just then the massive sea predator launched itself from the water and latched onto the raft close to the outboard and began shaking its head like a dog with a bone. The engine cut out completely and the raft began to be pulled beneath the water.

"And they're dead," Anne said calmly.

Elle dived over the side and started swimming furiously. Tygo turned and tossed something into the floor of the sinking raft and then also went over the side.

As both people were swimming the raft vanished below the surface in a swirl of agitated water. But then there came a massive *whump*, and a gout of foam shot into the air.

Elle and Tygo seemed unaffected, but the creature had undoubtedly absorbed most of the shockwave and had vanished, obviously realizing this prey was proving too painful to consume.

"They're going to have to swim for it," Anne observed. "The mosasaur was scared off by the blast. Let's see if anything else is hanging around."

Troy half turned. "They only have about 400 feet to swim, but there's one thing I learned about ocean predators was that loud noises meant distress. And there's nothing that attracts predators like another creature being in trouble."

"True." Anne nodded. "I wonder how fast they can swim." She grinned.

Troy noticed her eyes were lit with excitement.

He turned back to watch Elle. "So, Odin's Heart returns home after all." He reached into his pocket and drew forth the green eye and held it in his palm. He expected it to reorient itself and point at the approaching pair or at least to where the boat was.

"Wait a minute." As he watched, the eye turned to point away from them. "They don't have the ruby. What's going on here?"

Anne looked over his shoulder. "They've lost it somehow. They dropped it overboard."

"No, it's moving, moving away." He held up his palm and watched as the green jade eye twitched and moved fractionally. "They've lost it alright, but to someone else."

"*Ha*." Anne slapped his arm. "The robbers got robbed."

"But by who?" Troy moved some more fronds out of the way to watch the swimming pair. He glanced over his shoulder at Anne. "Hey, maybe it was the people who dropped the rope down to us."

"Maybe." Anne folded her arms. "So what now? We can't share this place with those guys; they're killers."

Troy's eyes narrowed. "I can kill him without so much as blinking." His lips pressed into a line for a moment. "But…"

"But? But what? You can't kill *her*?" Anne scoffed. "Because she was led astray, and you still think somehow it was all a mistake." She laughed. "Even when she put a bullet in you."

He glanced at her, not wanting to admit what she said was probably true, even though hearing it out loud made him feel as dumb as it sounded.

"Okay." She lightly punched his arm. "You shoot him, then give me the gun, and I'll shoot her."

He shook his head and grinned. "You're not a killer."

"For her, I'll make an exception." She lifted her chin.

He turned to her and shook his head. "It stains you."

"How would you know?" She lifted an eyebrow. "You're a tech business guy. The only thing you've killed is your business."

He looked her, his face expressionless. She had no idea of his past. *Good*, he thought. As he looked down at her, she must have misinterpreted his look.

"I'm sorry." Her mouth turned down. "I didn't mean that about your business. But you seem to have a knack for making bad decisions."

He gave her a lopsided grin. "Look around you; remember where we are. My business, or ex business, is the last thing on my mind right now." He turned back to the water and saw Elle and Tygo wading to shore.

"What do we do with you two?" he said softly.

"If they live, we'll always be hiding from them," Anne replied.

"Why?" he asked as he watched the pair. "If Odin's Heart is gone, then there's no reason for us to be in competition. No reason for them to harm us."

"Because they're psychopaths." She sighed. "We watched them kill most of us, and they didn't even blink. And your girlfriend led us to the gallows, while leading you by the nose."

"Yeah, you're right. But you're forgetting something." He turned slowly. "We can't let that stone, or egg, or whatever it is, get back home and then hatch." He looked back to the pair now on the beach. "And those two are the only ones who know who has it."

Anne tilted her head back on her neck. "Ah shit, that's right." She lowered her head to follow his gaze. "Then just kill one of them."

Troy took his gun out and checked the magazine – his faithful two rounds still sitting there. Not enough to make war, but just enough for what he had in mind.

"Then let the party begin." He half turned. "You stay here."

"Wait." Anne snatched at him, but he had already stepped out from under the tree.

Troy walked fast down the beach. If, *when*, they spotted him they both began to fire from a distance, his only option was to try and drop both – kill Tygo, and wound Elle. Hard, if they were far away, and had more ammunition.

But he hoped they'd remember he was a good shot, and the surprise might make them hesitate long enough for him to get closer.

Elle and Tygo looked back out at the sinking boat. It was about a hundred feet from the shore and only the front still showed above water.

In their wet clothes he couldn't help admiring Elle's tall and athletic figure and he remembered her in bed with him. He had a pang of loss, and his ego still whispered that he could get her back. He just needed to understand what happened to make her change.

He also saw the bulk of Tygo, and he was also reminded of how the guy was an extremely fearsome human being. However, after meeting with the giant Vikings, everything was now relative.

The pair began to turn, and he increased his pace and held up his gun arm.

"*Hey!*" he yelled.

They spun, froze for only a second in surprise, and then both went for their guns.

"*Don't.*" He stopped, and drew a bead on Tygo, right between his eyes. From this distance it'd be an easy shot.

The big man froze, but Elle kept moving. Troy shook his head. "I'd hate to do it, Elle, but I will if I have to. I still owe you a bullet."

She lowered her hand. Both stood just watching now. Troy came a little closer but continued holding his gun ready.

"What happened? Something not go to plan?" he asked.

Elle half smiled. "First up, and believe it or not, it's good to see you."

"Yeah," Troy said. "You came back for me, right?"

"No. We both know that's not true. But I prayed that you'd be safe here. So…" She looked around, scanning the forest line, "…I assume your puppy dog made it as well." She began to smile. "Ah yes, there she is." She waved. "Hello, Anne, come and join us."

He half turned and saw Anne boldly step out. He groaned, and turned back in time to see Tygo begin to move.

Troy flicked the gun up. "I will shoot you dead, asshole. Just give me a reason." He glared. "Maybe I should do it anyway. Call it risk mitigation." He pointed his gun. "Both of you, remove your weapons, just two fingers on the grip."

Anne came and stood beside him.

"Toss them to Anne. All the way," he said.

Tygo and Elle glanced at each other, and Troy knew if they were going to try something it'd be now.

"*DO IT!*" He roared so loud, Elle's head flicked up from the surprise.

Both froze and then slowly held their weapons out pincered between thumb and forefinger. They flicked them toward Anne who crouched to scoop them up.

Troy took one of the guns from her and glanced down to check. He scoffed softly. It was his Sig Saur P228 that Tygo had taken from him months back. And still near fully loaded.

"Thanks for looking after it." He stuck it in his belt.

"Now what?" Elle asked and went to fold her arms.

"Who said you could move?" Anne held her new gun in two hands. It wobbled slightly as she pointed it at Elle.

Elle smiled. "Oh, the puppy dog has teeth now?" She didn't drop her arms.

"Tell me what happened?" Troy asked.

"A new player," Elle said. "Someone else who managed to follow the clues and track us here. They killed most of our crew using an aerial drone. Then waited outside the cave on the ocean to ambush us." She shrugged. "They sank our support ship. Then gave us the option of handing over Odin's Heart or being killed. They were ruthless."

"And then they shot your boat anyway," Anne chuckled. "I'd say they were a pretty good judge of character."

Elle smiled tightly at her.

"Who are they? Where did they come from?" Troy demanded.

"Oslo," Tygo said, but then hiked huge shoulders. "Don't know who they are."

"Then how did you know they were from Oslo?" Anne asked.

"They told us," Elle replied. "Why do you ask; going after the heart maybe?" she asked with a suspicious glint in her real eye.

"Yes, but not for the reason you think," Troy replied. "To return it here, or destroy it. While we can."

Tygo's bushy eyebrows snapped together. "Over my dead body," he growled.

"Your terms are acceptable," Troy replied deadpan.

"Why?" Elle asked. "After all we've been through to get here and find it. Why would you want to destroy it? It's…"

"Because it's a damn egg," Anne interjected.

Elle snorted derisively. "Oh bullshit."

"It's true," Troy said. "The last time an egg made it outside was sometime between five and eight thousand years ago, it hatched and caused devastation across many countries. And the creature was only a juvenile. We can't let the things get out and repopulate the world again."

"Then why is there only one here?" Elle asked. "And why hasn't it killed everything in here?"

"We don't know," Anne said.

Tygo laughed softly. "You just want Odin's Heart for yourself. I have looked deep inside the heart and saw nothing but my future." He grinned. "Besides, we don't have a boat, you don't have a boat, so all we can do is sit here and sing songs until we die."

"You can do that. But Anne and I…" Troy stopped himself, deciding not to tell them anything. He smiled instead. "But Anne and I quite like it here now."

"Really?" Elle's brows drew together a little. "You know I know you, Troy. I can see inside your soul." She levelled her gaze at him, the real eye glinting. "What are you up to?"

Both Troy and Anne remained mute.

Tygo growled under his breath. "They know something."

"Do you have a boat?" Elle asked.

"You had all the boats and kept sinking them," Troy snorted derisively and then pointed to the burned out raft. "Or burning them."

Elle made a sound of annoyance in her throat. She turned back. "Then what; what have you found out?" Elle's gaze seemed to increase in intensity. Her eyes narrowed, and then her brow relaxed. "You've found another way home, haven't you?"

Tygo began to grin. "Then I propose a truce. Let us work together to get home." Tygo slowly lowered his hands. "And I think we should do this with some urgency."

"You keep your hands up," Troy said but noticed that the man's eyes were focussed over his shoulder. "As far as I'm concerned, you two can live, but stay as far away from us as possible. Any intrusion on our camp will be met with deadly force."

"Uh, Troy…" Elle whispered.

Troy didn't want to take his eyes off them and fall for the old, *look over there trick*. But he leaned toward Anne. "What's behind us?"

She turned. And then bumped into him. "Oh God. There's three raptor-sized theropods that have decided this is a good time to come down to the water and see what washed up. Or what they can catch."

"Give me a gun, quick." Elle held out her hand.

"Not a chance," Troy said.

Elle and Tygo began to back up. Troy chanced a look over his shoulder and saw three roughly man-sized creatures with their familiar box-like bony heads, black and brown striped bodies like camouflaged tigers, and tails held out stiffly behind them.

They also had oversized powerful legs with a big toe sporting a large single raptorial claw. He knew these things were built for speed – he had to fight one just like them.

He watched their jerking bird-like movements and their heads came down to point arrow straight toward them as they began their stalk. Troy knew what they were doing – selecting a target, and right now, Anne was the smallest of them. And she knew it.

She raised the gun in two hands.

Troy had two guns now, one in each hand, and Anne leaned back toward him. "Nice and slow," she said in a voice that was little above a breath. "Nobody move suddenly as it'll trigger an attack."

The raptors kept coming, their bodies from nose to tip of tail a straight line pointed at the small woman. They didn't blink and their mouths opened a little and the way they were built made it look like they were smiling and revealing rows of backward curving, wickedly pointed teeth.

Troy glanced to his side; they were close to the forest line which at least afforded them some cover. "We can make it," he said softly.

"*Run!*" Tygo shouted, and he and Elle sprinted to the forest.

That was the trigger as the creatures then exploded forward. Anne fired and missed. Troy, did the same with both guns, and both shots hit home.

The powerful raptors had never felt the pain of a bullet before, but worse, the sound of the guns freaked them out.

They wheeled away and trotted down the beach, chirping like large birds, and obviously deciding to stick to looking for something that washed up or something with a little less firepower.

Troy turned to where Tygo and Elle vanished into the forest. "Bastard."

"Yep, you can sure trust them," Anne sighed, but then spun back to watch the disappearing raptors.

"I should have known he'd try something like that." He placed one of the guns in his belt.

"Troy, get with it. She went as well," Anne cursed softly and shook her head. "And I'm betting if they had their guns when we were distracted, they'd have shot both of us."

"He would have." Troy started up the beach to the forest.

"Don't trust them, don't trust her, and don't get yourself killed." She followed him. "Because if you get killed who's going to get me to that *Mother of the Sky Mountain* place?"

"Don't worry. We have all the guns now, remember?" He wiggled his eyebrows.

"One question." She caught up with him. "Just how many grenades did they have between them?"

He exhaled, knowing he'd forgotten about them. "Ye-*eeeah*, good question."

"So they're out there with explosives." Anne looked up, seeing the darkening sky. "Yep, we'll sleep well tonight."

***

An hour later Elle still walked alone through the dark forest. All she had was a bush knife strapped to her belt and that was it. Tygo had kept the last few grenades, and frankly, he had brought them, her, nothing but bad luck. *Time to make some changes*, she thought.

She paused beside a tree trunk, and let her eye move over the thick walls of green surrounding her – there was no movement or sound, but that didn't mean a bus-sized predator wasn't lurking close by, standing stone-still, and waiting for a tasty morsel like her to wander by.

After another moment, she heard the soft sound of voices. They were whispering, but the forest was graveyard quiet, and noises carried far. She suspected Troy wouldn't light a fire and she crept forward on her toes.

In another moment she saw the pair sitting close to each other. Her brows knitted slightly – were they a couple now? She doubted it. Elle saw in their brief encounter that Troy was still interested in her, just by the way he looked at her. And she bet he'd forgive her. Anything. And that was what she was counting on.

Elle sucked in a deep breath and walked out into the open.

***

Troy cut the skin from the long plant root, removing the rough green texture, and exposing the moist center. It tasted a little like a cross between a melon and a cabbage. The upside was it contained a lot of water, and vitamins. The downside was it wasn't very filling and smelled

182

like bad body odor.

"We'll need to hunt again tomorrow. We need more protein," he said.

Anne took the sliver of plant root and nodded as she bit the end off. "Good idea. This stuff is not nearly nourishing enough." She looked down at herself. "But the Lemuria diet has done wonders." She grinned and held up an arm, flexing her bicep. "I even have muscles now."

"If only you can get home, you'll be able to show them off at the next museum Christmas party." He grinned and then continued to eat his cold dinner.

Troy swallowed, and then went to take another bite, but froze.

"I don't suppose…" Anne saw his face and then quickly looked to where he was staring. "What the…?" she scoffed.

Elle stood at the edge of their camp area underneath a big tree with her hands up.

"I come in peace," Elle said softly. "And I'm alone."

"*Piss off*," Anne said and fumbled her gun out.

Troy held a hand up in front of Anne. "Easy there, Annie Oakley." He turned from Anne to Elle. "Where's your boyfriend?"

"Not my boyfriend." She shook her head. "It's complicated."

"I'll bet it is," Anne's laugh was like a bark.

"He made me do it," Elle said. "He was blackmailing me." She bobbed her head. "You do know he was my ex-husband, don't you?" She shared a crumbling smile. "I told you he was violent."

"Where is he?" Troy asked, drawing his own weapon.

"We parted company. I wanted a truce, for us to work together. He wanted to attack." She shrugged. "I told him to go to hell and left. Been looking for you for hours."

Troy got to his feet. "Come in slowly."

"No." Anne scowled.

Troy turned to Anne. "Get me some rope out."

"Fine, and I'll make a noose," Anne muttered as she did as she was asked.

When Elle was close by, Troy had her kneel down, and to hold her hands behind her back. He tied her wrists together, and then the hands to one ankle, basically hog-tying her.

"You get to stay where you are while I do a quick scout for Tygo," Troy said. "Anne, watch her." He pointed a finger. "And do not hurt her."

Anne just gave him a broad, fake smile.

"I mean it," he warned.

Troy then took off into the forest. He moved quietly and fast, staying low. He had his gun drawn, and he planned on doing a large circuit around their camp. If Tygo was watching them, he wanted to find him before they tried to get some rest. As it was, he knew now, he and Anne would need to take turns on watch.

But he was prepared to hear Elle out. One part of him whispered to not trust her for a New York minute. The other said that Tygo, her ex-husband, had manipulated her. He'd question her some more when he got back. In his former job at the CIA they had developed plenty of psychological techniques to ferret out and catch people in lies. He hated to do it to her, but he had no choice, as their lives depended on it.

***

Anne and Elle sat staring at each other. Elle had a calm expression on her face, and a small smile curving her lips.

"I can see right through you, you know," Anne said.

"If you can see inside me, then you will know I'm telling the truth," Elle replied softly.

Anne snorted. "You may have Troy conned, but I'm onto you, and no matter what you say or do will change my mind. I'll be watching you like a hawk."

"Fine with me. All I want to do is help get us all home. And you know I *can* help." Elle looked away.

"By putting another bullet in Troy? I was there, remember." Anne's frown creased her forehead.

"That wasn't me. Not really." Elle turned back. "I wish I could take those stupid actions back. I can't. So all I can do is apologize and try to make it up to both of you."

Anne laughed. "You deserve an Oscar."

"My actions will prove me," Elle replied.

"Time will tell," Anne said.

Troy came back into the camp. "Seems all clear."

"I told you," Elle replied and jerked her arms to one side. "Can you take these off. It's very uncomfortable."

Anne shook her head. Troy got behind her and undid the ties to her legs. But that was all.

"For now, that'll do," he said. "It'll allow us to rest easier tonight. Tomorrow, we need to set off and we'll need all our energy. Also, we need to hunt on the way."

"Set off to where?" Elle watched him.

"Hopefully our way home," Troy replied. He took one last look around and then lay down with his head on his fraying pack. "Get some rest."

Elle continued to watch him. And Anne continued to watch her.

184

# EPISODE 14

*All things have a beginning. And sometimes that beginning is the end of something else.*

# CHAPTER 39

Anders held the huge gem up to the light in the small wheelhouse. "Strange, I thought it was clear. But it's not. Or at least not clear anymore." He squinted. "Sort of milky now. And there's something in the center." He brought it close to his nose and peered into it. "Two somethings."

"But is it still valuable?" Olaf asked.

"They said a hundred million. Even if it's only worth a tenth of that we'll be rich beyond our dreams." He turned to smile at the old fisherman. "But this is a pre-Viking artefact, so to the museum its value is beyond priceless. And that's what Freja would have wanted."

Olaf took the pipe from his mouth. "And my cut would be…?"

"Your cut is the eternal gratitude of the Oslo Museum. If it ever goes on display, in the provenance notes, I will ensure your name gets a mention." He nodded. "Now that would be something to show the grandkids."

Olaf slowly turned back to the wheel. "I don't have grandkids. Or kids. There's just me and my sick brother."

Anders patted his shoulder. "He'll be proud."

He took the gem back down to his cabin room and sat on the steel framed bunk and held the stone up again. *Was it worth it?* he wondered.

He'd lost Oder, his brother in-law, and Freja, his beautiful lover. He continued to stare at the gem. It didn't glow anymore, and it seemed every time he looked at it, it got duller, and more and more opaque.

He put it on the bench top as it was hurting his arm to hold it. He got down low and rested his chin on his hands and stared into its depths. He then quickly reached into his pack and drew out a small flashlight. He shone it inside and was sure there was something at its center, that was bigger than before.

Just a flaw in the stone, he bet.

He put the light down and sat back. The accursed thing had cost him a lot. But at least that monster of a human being and his green-eyed girlfriend were marooned on that hellish, mysterious island. He wanted nothing but torment for them.

He thought again of the frightening island and had to crush his eyes shut. Though he feared and hated it, he knew that Freja would have been captivated by its uniqueness, its mystery, and its untouched prehistoric beauty.

*Should he tell the world about it?* he wondered. If he did, then the world would come, and it would never be the same again. He'd think about it as right now he was the only person on Earth who knew about it. And escaped.

He'd catch some sleep and then decide. Anders went to push the gem back a bit on the bench top, and as soon as his hand alighted on it, he snatched it back.

He sat forward, staring and flexing his hand.

It was hot. Red hot.

He lay down, his eyes on it. In the cold cabin he could feel the warmth of it on his face. It felt good.

In moments more his eyes began to droop.

***

In another few hours the blood red object had turned milky. In its center the once clear looking ovoid swirled and at its heart the objects there grew large. Larger. And then twitched and wriggled.

In another couple of hours, a crack could be seen running from the top to the bottom. And then a thick crimson liquid began to run down its sides. In more time still, a piece the size of a man's fist broke off and fell to the desk top.

The two creatures emerged. They were each about eight inches in length and longer rather than wide. At one end of them there were small spines and spikes, along its sides were four small not fully formed legs, and at the rear a grub-like tail.

One explored the bench top it found itself on, and the other lifted its front end and tiny yellow slit eyes opened. It saw the creature sleeping, and the dark hole of a mouth open wide, and snoring. It made its way along the bench top to that warm dark hole.

# CHAPTER 40

Troy opened his eyes to the cool and silvery light of morning. He sat up, groaning through the new aches and pains from the day before.

Anne still slept and he quickly turned to Elle. She was already sitting up, hands still tied behind her back, and watching him.

"Hey, did you sleep?" he asked.

She smiled. "On this island, I don't sleep. I don't need to."

"I see." He nodded. "That doesn't sound healthy."

She shrugged. "Do I look unhealthy?"

He looked her over. Her eyes, or eye, was clear. Her complexion perfect, and her muscles full. In fact, she looked, *vibrant*. "No, you look fine. Hidden prehistoric islands must agree with you."

He continued to stare. She looked better than fine, but he knew what she was trying to do. And staring at her made him want her. And she knew that. He looked away.

"Tell me more about your plan to get us home," she asked.

He faced her again. He wanted to trust her, but just wasn't sure he could. She half turned her body.

"Can you take these off now? They hurt." Her large green eyes mesmerized him.

But not enough for him to take that kind of risk. Not yet, anyway.

"No, I think Anne and I would feel better if we didn't need to worry about you slitting our throats in the night."

She shook her head. "Never. Never ever." She leaned forward. "I didn't shoot you. Or mean to; I only wanted to wound Anne to slow you down. It was you that dived in front to take the bullet. Very honourable, but very stupid. You could have gotten killed."

"Yeah, I could have." He shook his head. "If only those bullets weren't so hard or moved so fast."

"You know what I mean," Elle said softly. She then let her eyes wander to the sleeping Anne. "Is she your girlfriend now?' Elle raised an enquiring eyebrow. "She always wanted you back, so being marooned here was a gift to her."

"You marooned us here. To die," he said evenly.

Elle ignored him. "I asked, is she your girl?"

"No, we're good friends. The only friend I've got or need right now." He rubbed his grimy face.

"I'm your friend," Elle said softly. "More than you know."

He snorted. "Yeah, right."

They sat in silence for a few moments before Elle brightened. "So, tell me about your plan."

He looked at her and decided that telling her wouldn't hurt. He took out the roll of hide that Yrsa had given him and unfurled it on the ground in front of her.

He traced it with his finger, along a river valley, and to a mountain at the top right corner of the map. "There's a place in this land called *Himmelens mor...*"

"Mother of the Sky," she added quickly.

"Yes." He went on. "Thousands of years ago, a clan of Vikings climbed a mountain on Greenland's surface and in it found a passage beneath the ice ceiling. All the way down to this island." He tapped the map. "It's toward the summit of this geological formation here. We think we can find it and climb back out."

She nodded, her lips pursing in thought. She looked up. "And then what?"

"*Huh?*" he looked up at her. "Then we get out."

"You're not thinking this through." She smiled again. "This is why you need me."

"What do you mean?" He sat straighter.

She looked up. "When we came in this time, there was more ice. The cold season is coming on us again. Maybe soon, the entire rift leading to Odin's Gate will ice over, sealing this land in again." She tilted her head as she looked at him. "Do you know what's above us?"

He followed her gaze, seeing the layer of mist like thin cloud and the glint of ice crystals through it. She went on before he could answer.

"There's an ice layer above us, and then on top of that is snow, more ice, and freezing temperatures. You're wearing light clothing, or what's left of them. You climb out into that, and you'll last about half a day. Or maybe just hours." She smiled sadly. "And climb out to where? I'm guessing it'd be somewhere a long way from the coast or a settlement."

He sighed, getting it then. "Shit, you're right, we'd freeze."

She shrugged. "Just means we need more warm clothing, more supplies. That means more to carry, and if it's a raw climb, then that's going to make it much harder."

"Well, I guess step one is to make sure the secret passage to the outside even exists. If it does, then we establish a camp, and obtain our extra supplies." Troy smiled. "And if it doesn't, then this is home."

"What's going on?" Anne sat up, quickly wiped her eyes and then glanced suspiciously from Troy to Elle.

"Trying to make plans to get home," Troy said, turning to her. "If we can find the passageway up through the mountain, we might find ourselves out on the Greenland ice when it's about 20 below. We need to be ready for that."

Anne's mouth pressed into a line for a moment. "You told her?"

"We're all in this together now," Troy replied.

Anne glanced at Elle who looked back with a hooded gaze. She scoffed softly. "I doubt that, Troy."

Troy got to his feet. "Anyway, breakfast. I'll try and catch us something, and then we head out. I want to be as far away from here as possible in the next hour."

"And as far away from Tygo as possible," Anne said, keeping her eyes on Elle.

Elle just stared back.

***

A hundred feet out, beyond a large tree, the ground moved. Just a little.

Tygo lifted his head, and the leaves, moss and soil fell from his shoulders. He watched the group with an unblinking gaze. He had been in place for hours, and even lay still as Troyson Strom walked right past him when he did his initial scouting. Right then he could have killed him easily. But he needed to know what he had planned.

His gaze shifted to Elle. She was still bound, and he saw them talking for ages. Could he trust her?

It didn't matter, he trusted no one. She said she was his soul mate and the reincarnation of Brynhilde. But so far, it seemed the luck she had brought him was all bad. Maybe the prophecy was wrong.

He narrowed his eyes and continued to watch. For now, she was useful. But his priority was to get home and reclaim Odin's Heart. Killing the museum woman's husband would be a bonus. Killing Troyson Strom would be pure enjoyment.

# CHAPTER 41

Troy entered the forest and paused. He had become adept at hunting and trapping animals. The upside of being a small, soft, two-legged biped in this primordial forest was that the scent and shape of humans was so alien to the local creatures many never understood the threat until it was too late.

The downside was that he could never stop watching for predators, large and small. Against them he was near defenceless, and their camouflage was perfectly matched to the shadowy forest.

He let just his eyes move over the undergrowth. It was quiet, and he was under pressure to make a quick kill and get back to camp so they could get moving. He had no doubt that Tygo was out there somewhere. *As if we don't have enough problems,* he thought.

There was some movement up ahead, and he crept forward. He parted some of the fronds to see a small clearing. He frowned; there was a small creature, no bigger than a piglet, but with a horned head and tail with spikes on it.

It was lying in the clearing, still twitching but with eyes rolled back. Because it had its throat cut – not torn out by tooth or claw but severed by a blade. Troy looked around slowly. The blood still oozed out; this was a fresh kill.

Did someone just leave it for him?

"Yrsa?" he said. "*Yrsa, is that you?*" he said a little louder this time.

The forest was quiet, and the one thing he had learned was noise was the enemy. Drawing attention to yourself was dangerous. But so was the smell of fresh blood.

"Thank you," he said.

He wasn't sure it was her, but he had no idea who else it could be. He began to move forward to pick it up. But then froze. Or it had been left by Tygo. As a trap.

He lifted his gun, scanning the forest in a circle. On seeing nothing, he went back to the now dead creature, and gently dug around it to ensure Tygo hadn't rigged some sort of booby trap. But there were no wires or anything there.

Troy snatched up the animal and headed back to camp.

In twenty minutes more he re-joined his small group. "Success," he said, feeling a little like a fraud, but he guessed he didn't say how the success was achieved.

For the meal, they allowed a small fire, and he was glad to see that Anne had already started on lighting it – *That was confidence*, he thought.

They sliced meat from the carcass and wrapped it in leaves. Then each of the leaf packs was pushed into the hot coals and covered over with dirt. This way the meat cooked slower, but all the way through, and kept the smell of cooking meat from wafting through the forest. They'd eat some and take the rest with them.

They had used the waiting time to pack what they needed. And then in another half hour, their meat was done. Raking back the coals and sand, and then opening the packs showed a white meat not unlike chicken. Though he'd gotten used to the flavor of dinosaur he still found it a cottony, dry meat with little fat or taste. He would have killed for a little shake of salt.

Against Anne's protestations, Troy had released Elle, who ate ravenously.

"Delicious. What's for dessert?" She smiled.

"More dinosaur meat." Troy smiled back.

Elle stuck her tongue out.

"It's better than going hungry," Anne said.

Afterwards, they packed the spare meat, and left the carcass for scavengers. Troy loaded them up, they got their bearings and they headed into the forest.

He estimated it'd take them several days to reach the mountain. The map sort of recommended following a long dry river course. Everywhere was dangerous, so it was probably as good as any way forward.

"Ready?" he asked to nods from the women. "Then let's go meet the Mother of the Sky."

# CHAPTER 42

Troy, Anne, and Elle stood at the mouth of the cave. Troy held up the map again.

"So that's what this means." He showed Anne. "The path is drawn fainter here; I guess it means that's because it disappears underground." He looked up and saw the broken land and thick jungle; it was a tangle of thorned, green madness above ground.

"Do we follow the map or go around it?" Anne turned from the cave mouth. "We haven't had much luck with caves so far."

He half smiled. "Or above ground, or on or under the water. Everything is dangerous and deadly here."

"We go in. Whoever took the time to make that map charted the best route for a reason," Elle said. "Follow the ancients."

"Hey, she doesn't get a vote," Anne protested.

"All our lives are at stake, so all of us can be heard," Troy replied. "That jungle up there looks near impenetrable. The map says the cave is not huge, just a half mile by my reckoning of the scale. If we move slow and careful, we can do it in half a day."

"Half a day. Shit," Anne muttered and turned away. But then turned back. "And I smell death."

Troy sniffed. "Yeah, something is dead close by." He turned about and then held up his hand. "Wait here." Troy rolled the map up and tucked it away. He walked cautiously toward the cave mouth and vanished inside.

He found the source of their smell – there was a dead creature, a large theropod, and possibly a carnosaur. It hadn't been dead for long, and he couldn't see any wounds. *Maybe the place was like an elephant's graveyard where they came to die,* he wondered.

He pulled out his gun and looked about slowly – if he could smell the dead creature, then it should also attract all manner of scavengers for miles. There was nothing anywhere, and he walked closer. As he stared down at the huge beast an idea came to him.

He jogged back out of the cave. "Hey, come on. We've got a job to do."

They followed him in, and Anne held her arms wide. "Wow, big boy." She pointed. "This is a Tyrannosaurus rex." She walked all the way around it. "Beautiful. But he was old."

"That's what I thought. Maybe just came here to die." Troy stepped closer and crouched. He grabbed one of the long bristle-like feathers and tugged hard. It popped free. He felt along its length, spreading the fibers. He then slowly stood and wiped his hands on his pants. "Yeah, this will do fine.

"Everyone grab as many bristles as we can. We won't be able to find or make new clothes, or even furs, but we can make something to insulate us against the cold with these." He grinned. "If it works for the dinosaurs, then..."

"I like it," Anne replied, and the three of them set to plucking the giant beast.

In another twenty minutes they each had a stack that they bound together, and strapped over their shoulders.

Troy turned then to the dark cave. "And now, we smell like a super predator, and also have the makings for our new clothing." He waved them on.

Anne held one of the remaining flashlights, and its beam was already yellowing. Troy also had one, and some spare batteries. But he would not use it, as he knew they'd need a lot more light if they were to climb up the center of a mountain.

The first thing they noticed was that the cave sloped downward at an angle of about 25 degrees.

"This is weird; there's no life down here," Anne remarked. "There should be something, at least at the mouth of the cave."

"My teeth hurt," Troy said.

"Mine too." Elle felt her cheek.

"Just like when we were inside Odin's fortress," Anne whispered.

They continued, slower now. In ten more minutes they entered a huge area that was broad, roughly oval, but the ceiling was lower and supported by hundreds of columns that at first looked like where the stalactites had reached down to touch and combine with the stalagmites. But on closer inspection it wasn't from dripped water but looked like where the rock had been liquified and then set into stone.

Anne pointed her light down at the ground, eliciting a sparkling reflection. She crouched and wiped her finger through it.

She rubbed her finger and thumb together and then scoffed softly. "If I didn't know better, I'd say this is a mixture of diamond dust, and iridium." She looked up. "Like when a meteorite falls to earth."

"You said that this entire place could have been formed by a meteor strike some time millions of years ago. Could this be where?" Troy asked.

"Maybe," Anne replied. "The entire area would have been molten for weeks. Liquifying the surrounding rock, throwing it up and over itself like an umbrella. These columns could have been where the still liquid rock ran back down from the newly formed ceiling."

Elle had wandered away and seemed to be checking the passageways. She vanished, and it was only when Troy called to her did he hear her voice.

"Over here," she yelled.

They joined her and there at the center of the deepest point of the depression was a mass of broken rocks that might have been pure diamond. But there was something else that held their attention – two football-sized gems, huddled together.

As they looked around, they saw there were more, scattered about. Anne made a small noise in her throat.

"Is this where the giant ruby, Odin's Heart, came from?" Elle asked.

"Not a stone." Anne turned. "An egg." She turned back, frowning. "But they don't look like they've been laid. More they were at the base of an impact, and that's why they're scattered about." She faced Troy. "Remember what you said the Vikings told you? That they thought the dragon had been here forever and had fallen from the sky? Maybe this is where it, they, landed."

"It's not native to our world. It came from somewhere else." He shook his head. "And maybe where Harald the Great was gifted his," Troy said softly.

"There's enough for all of us," Elle whispered.

Troy turned to her and saw that her single green eye was near luminous with excitement, or desire, or something else he couldn't fathom.

"We're not touching them," he said evenly. "And if we ever get home, we'll do our best to bring the other one back."

"Or destroy it," Anne added.

Elle turned quickly and her initial hostile expression immediately softened. "Yes, of course, you're right, that's what we'll do. But first step is we get home."

Troy nodded and was about to turn away but saw Elle's brow furrow.

"Something wrong?" he asked.

"Yes, you seem sure they're eggs. And that we shouldn't take them." She pointed. "But here they are. Why haven't they all hatched in all these years; in fact millions of years you are implying?"

Troy turned back. She had a point.

"Could be something on this island. Maybe the iridium. Or the constant cool temperature. Or the small landmass. Or something else we're not aware of. But whatever it is, there's something here that's keeping them in check."

"One dragon is enough, I guess." Troy turned, but then paused. He lifted his hand to his jaw. "Or maybe whatever force is making my damn jaw ache."

As they stared, the ground, the cave walls, and ceiling all shook. Just a little, but enough to cause dust to rain down on them.

"What was that?" Anne asked.

"Earthquake?" Elle suggested.

"No, I think Greenland is geologically very stable. Even the volcanoes are inactive now." Anne hiked her shoulders. "I could be wrong about that because no one's ever charted the geological morphology of what's below Greenland."

"Whatever. Touch nothing. We're done here." Troy turned away. "We've got to keep going."

\*\*\*

Tygo stayed low and watched the group as they vanished into the depths of the cave. All he had was a couple of glow sticks and the one he used now was a rapidly fading yellow light, giving him little illumination.

But he didn't fear the dark. And after seeing all the massive gems strewn about, he knew he needed to worry less about the one stolen from him.

He smirked. He'd still track the thief down and kill him. Slowly. For the insult he had inflicted upon him. But for now, his future was assured.

He lifted two gems, one in each hand. As before, they glowed softly, pulsing, like the hearts they were meant to be.

He smiled and tucked them into his pack and shouldered it. The extra weight would be a burden, but one he would gladly carry.

He spun at a noise, and quickly held up the glow stick.

Its glow did little to dispel the gloom and he was sure a large shadow pulled back behind some rocks. He was also sure he heard it before as if someone or something was following him.

One half of him urged him to go and confront who or whatever it was. But he knew his destiny was ahead, and he should save all his strength for the fight that was to come.

He hefted the pack, and turned away, creeping once again after Troyson Strom. And Elle.

*\*\*\**

On the surface, the massive dragon paused and pressed its huge snout to the ground. It inhaled, drawing in a huge breath, took another step and inhaled again.

Without seeing them, it knew the humans moved through the cave below. The dragon followed on the surface.

# CHAPTER 43

Troy emerged first and looked at the huge mountain rising before them. Its top was hidden in the clouds, but he guessed it rose higher than that and hopefully punctured the ice layer.

He checked the map, and then looked back up again. He squinted, concentrating.

"That might be it."

"The way in?" Anne asked.

"Yeah, see that crack about 1500 feet up? I think that's where we need to get to."

Elle craned her neck upwards. "And then we need to climb all the way through its center. And then who knows how much more we need to scale before we break through the ice layer." She looked back down at the map, and then pointed. "What does this mean over here?'

Troy looked back at it and slowly shook his head. "Some sort of big fish, I guess."

There was something that looked a little like a shark on the coast.

"But I think this means it's on land," Elle remarked.

"This map was probably drawn hundreds of years ago. I doubt the current owners even knew what it was. And we certainly can't ask them now." He rolled it back up. "It's not relevant to us right now, so let's not worry about it."

The trio began to climb. To begin with the slope was quite easy, but soon they exited the vegetation layer and were on bare rock. And then it got a little steeper.

They climbed for another hour and the gentle slope had turned to a significant gradient that meant they were climbing on all fours more than walking, and even Troy was beginning to feel a little light headed.

"Break time," he said and looked up. The small crevice they needed to reach was still another thousand or so feet, but the last hundred feet of the climb was near sheer rock.

There were handholds he could see, but it was going to be tough if they were tired. It was still only midday so they could afford to take some time out.

He sat between Elle and Anne, and they ate some of their dried meat reserves, and sipped water. Then they set to spending some time using some fibrous vines they had collected on the way and using their knives to put holes in the quill end of the giant feathers. They threaded them close together, and soon, they had shimmering cloaks of feathers that they hoped would give them some insulation against the brutal cold they could expect when they emerged onto the Greenland ice.

"These will work," Troy said and stood to throw his around his shoulders.

Elle threw hers on as well and struck a pose. "The colours don't suit me, but it'll do." She smiled warmly at Troy.

Troy smiled back and Anne glared, more at Troy than Elle. She also tried hers on and ran a hand down the side, nodding. "They should provide good insulation. At least for a while. But a wind chill will cut right through them. We need to find help within 24 hours, 30 max."

"For that we'll need one more critical element," Troy said.

Anne raised her eyebrows. "Which is?"

"Luck." Troy shrugged. "We've had it so far, right?"

Anne smiled back as she nodded. "I hope we left a small portion of that in reserve."

The trio removed their cloaks and tied them into a bundle. They then strapped them to their shoulders.

"*Do we have everything we need?*"

The strange voice spun their heads around.

Rising from behind some rocks was a vision of hell – it was Tygo, covered in plants and creepers to create some sort of natural ghillie camouflage suit. At his shoulder he hefted a long spear, and had his arm drawn back, with the tip pointed right at Troy's belly.

The big man's beard, all run through with twigs and leaves, lifted at the sides as he smiled. "I won't miss, Mr. Strom."

"We can work together," Elle said.

"Why?" Tygo scoffed.

He then faced Troy. "Lay down your weapons." Then faced Anne. "You too, little bird."

"You'll never make it alone," Troy said deadpan as he took his gun out. He lay it on the rocks.

Anne did the same, and Elle picked them up.

"Told you," Anne whispered.

Tygo smiled triumphantly. "I think I will do just fine." He shrugged his pack off and showed them two of the massive rubies inside. "Who knew there was more of them." He looped the bag over his shoulders again. "And now I have two fine cloaks, and your food and water. Plus weapons."

He lifted his spear again.

"Don't kill him," Elle said.

Tygo turned. "He's nothing to us, my Brynhilde."

Elle shook her head. "He has honour."

"What he has, is more lives than a cat. While he lives, he will be a thorn in our side." Tygo began to smile. "Prove yourself to me."

Elle lifted her chin.

Tygo's stare bore into her. "Shoot him."

"Do you?" Elle asked.

"Do I what?" Tygo's huge brows began to come together.

"Have honour?" She stared back.

His jaws clenched for a moment before he spoke through gritted teeth. "I have the honour of the Viking clans dating back a thousand years to the great Ulf Skarsgard. I have honour, strength, and courage to do what must be done."

Tygo turned back to Troy and drew his arm back. Troy went to dive out of the way but slipped and sprawled. Anne screamed and Troy's body tensed as he waited for the large spear to pierce his gut.

Instead, a gunshot rang out, and the big man clutched his side. He turned; his face twisted in shock. That morphed into disbelief and then sadness.

"Why?" he asked.

Elle stood with the gun in her hand. She said nothing.

To the left side of them the mountain moved.

And then the mountain roared, so loud, it was like a physical force blasting across the landscape and into the atmosphere. The ice ceiling above them contained the sound and bounced it back at them.

"*The dragon!*" Troy yelled.

He saw they were exposed on the bare rock. Troy quickly looked down the mountainside – too far. And then up – they had no choice. They were so close.

"*Up, up!*" He pointed and began to scramble.

Anne, Elle, and he started to climb, scaling like monkeys in their haste. Tygo stood, and still holding one hand over his wounded side, tried to launch the spear, not at Troy, but at Elle.

It missed, and she stopped, smiled serenely back at him, and then let her eyes slide to the dragon for a second, before smiling again, and then she turned away to continue her climb.

"*Vile whore. Betrayer!*" Tygo yelled. He picked up a fist-sized rock and launched it at her. "I'll kill you."

Tygo turned back, and perhaps knew he had no chance of scaling upwards with his wound and instead began to climb and slide down the steep, rocky slope, and across away from the approaching behemoth.

Either because Tygo was the biggest animal, or maybe because of the scent of blood, the dragon focused its attention just on the fleeing man. For something so big the dragon moved swiftly, and the mountainside was crushed and abraded by its many hundred ton body as its long claws dug into the rock as it came after him.

It came faster now, and Troy looked back over his shoulder. Tygo was only about 200 feet up and to the side of the creature and slipped and slid. The dragon's slit eyes fixed on him, and it opened its mouth. He didn't want to watch but couldn't tear his eyes away.

Tygo must have known his plan of escape was hopeless, so he simply stood, pulled out his knife, and chose a Viking's end.

The man held the knife high and with a long roar of "*O-ooood-iiin,*" dived.

The dragon opened its mouth to receive him, and Tygo vanished inside the train tunnel-sized maw. The gullet worked, and Troy knew the huge, bearded man was on his way down to the gut.

He shook his head and turned back to focus on his climb. The trio were just reaching the last point of the climb. A little more than a hundred feet to go, but it was the near vertical part.

Elle's athleticism put her easily in front. He was next, and about 10 feet back was Anne. And she was struggling.

He stopped climbing to allow Anne to catch up. "Keep going, you're doing great," he urged.

Troy looked back over his shoulder and a jolt of fear ran through him. The massive creature was digging in 6 foot long claws and climbing up behind them. Of course, Tygo was too small a morsel to satisfy it.

Its neck was extended, and its eyes firmly fixed on them. Anne went to look back as well.

"*No!*" he said sharply. "Keep going, keep looking up and stay focussed."

She nodded, sucked in a deep breath, and lifted herself another 3 feet.

It was a race, and he knew that they were moving far too slow.

Anne skidded on some rock, and she squeaked in fright and clung to the rock face for a moment.

"There's not enough...I can't..." She rested her head against the stone.

"I'm coming." Troy scaled across and got behind her and used his hands to push her, making himself the footholds she needed.

The rock face jumped beneath his hands and the massive creature took a single step as it clawed its way up after them. Gravity was massively dragging on its colossal weight, but its huge form meant muscles so big, it could keep going easily to where they needed to climb into the crack in the rock wall.

He glanced up and saw Elle manage to reach the crack in the rock. She paused for a moment, staring in, before she vanished inside as though pulled.

"Keep. Going. Hurry!" he said, and pushed on one of her heels, levering her up another few feet.

"I'm nearly there," she said.

"You can make it," he said, as his own fingers were becoming abraded, and the blood was making them slippery.

Troy locked his fingers into a small lip of rock and used his other hand to push her one last time. Anne gripped the edge of the crevice and disappeared inside, but as he did, the strain was enormous on him, and on the small lip of stone.

It broke away and he slipped. He slid down about 10 feet. The tips of his fingers were on fire and he lost a fingernail. But he managed to stop his slide and hang on. Just.

"*Ah, shit,*" he whispered.

He didn't want to turn around as he could smell the odor of the drekka, the leviathan creature of legend, so close behind him now its hot foul breath warmed his neck.

*What a way for it to end*, he thought.

"Not yet," he demanded of himself and gritted his teeth.

He tried to move, but he couldn't help himself and he had to look back. He wished he hadn't.

The massive dragon was right there, yellow slitted eyes on him, and massive mouth opening.

Troy looked back up at the crack in the rock face; he was close, just on about 6 feet, but not close enough. *Make it quick*, he prayed and shut his eyes and waited for the blast of acidic bile that would turn him to liquid.

But then he felt his wrists gripped, and he opened his eyes to see Yrsa hanging out of the crevice, using her long legs and muscular thighs to lock herself in place.

He looked up into her crystal blue eyes shining from within the black band of warpaint across her face. The giant Viking woman's arm, covered in green clan tattoos, bulged from the strain and her hand wrapped entirely around his wrist.

"I have you," she said calmly and then began to pull herself back into the small crevice, taking him with her.

The dragon roared and shivered as it readied to spit bile at its vanishing meal.

Yrsa dragged him all the way inside the crack in the rock just as the monstrous beast ejected its bile toward the hole, hoping to cover them all inside.

Yrsa yanked Troy behind herself and pulled the large round shield from her back, braced her legs, and held it over the opening.

The bile hit her, but most of the hot acidic stream was deflected by the shield, however some splashed her legs; she yelled and pulled away the hide pants covering them.

Troy saw the welts; even after only receiving drops of the bile they were already going from a viscous red, to lifting into painful blisters.

Yrsa threw the dissolving shield aside and ignored the blisters as she pushed all the people away from the crevice opening and then sat to rip open her kit, pulling out a long orange root that she broke open. Sap welled up, and she rubbed it on a few spots of the steaming liquid that had penetrated her clothing. They immediately stopped sizzling, and she lowered her head for a moment, breathing easier.

Elle stood behind her, mouth open, staring, with Troy's gun pointed right at the back of Yrsa's head.

Troy waved her down. "No, don't, she's a friend."

He stood and went to her and held his hand out to the sitting woman. It was more a courtesy as there was no way he was going to be able to pull to her feet a woman that probably weighed close to 300 pounds and stood nearly 8 feet tall. He remembered he'd already had her on top of him, and knew what it was like.

"Oh my god," Elle breathed.

"Hello, Yrsa," Anne said. "Thank you."

"You are either very brave or very stupid," Yrsa said, looking down at Troy. She had eyes for him and him alone.

"I'm a bit of both, I guess." He still held her hand. "Thank you. That was close."

In turn, she turned his hand over and looked at the scraped fingers. "Painful," she whispered, and once again took out the orange root and squeezed some of the sap onto his wounds. She smiled into his eyes as she massaged his fingers. "I think you need someone to care for you. All the time."

Anne lifted her chin. "What did she say?"

Troy looked over his shoulder at her. "She said I need someone to look after me."

Anne scoffed. "Hell-*ooo*? How do you think he's survived this long?"

"What is that plant?" He nodded at the root.

"*Ormarot* root," she replied. "It grows near the swamps. It takes away pain. And heals." She finished. "Better?"

Troy flexed his hand, noticing his hand and finger abrasions had dried and stopped hurting. "Much better, thank you."

Yrsa's eyes slid to Elle, who had dropped her gun arm, but eyed the female giant with suspicion.

"And who is this green-eyed woman?" Yrsa asked.

"She's a friend. Also," Troy replied.

Her eyes slid back to him. "You seem to collect women friends, Troyson." Her eyes narrowed. "I don't trust this one."

The mountain shook, and a huge claw raked at the entrance, gouging out a large shard of stone and widening the hole. The four of them leapt to each side and then kept backing up.

Yrsa spun back to the now bigger hole. "We need to move from here. The drekka wants us and will not stop till it digs us out."

Troy also stood again and looked upwards. "Then we need to climb."

Yrsa shook her head. "No; this is forbidden. We should not even be here." She looked toward the entrance. "There are more caves at the back. Maybe in a day or two the drekka will leave."

Troy shook his head. "No, going up there is a way out, and our way home."

"We hope," Elle said.

"This will not end well." Yrsa stood in front of him, stopping him. "You came by boat. You should leave by boat."

"Our boats are gone. And no one is coming," Troy replied. He would have liked her to come with them, but the modern world wasn't the place for a neolithic age Viking giant. Especially one nearly 8 feet tall who solved all her problems with an axe and shield.

"You must stay here," he said. He reached up to rub her upper arm. "One day we may meet again."

She looked down at him for a moment or two and then glanced at Anne and Elle. "You will not return. You don't need to." She straightened. "But maybe I will see you in Valhalla." She then tilted her chin to look upwards.

Above them there was a hole in the cave ceiling that led up into the heart of the mountain. Around the walls were cut hand and toe notches. Small, but enough to form a crude ladder.

The mountain shook again, and Yrsa pushed him aside as a jet of bile shot in through the opening to splash the back wall. It missed all of them but filled the cave with an eyewatering stink.

Yrsa sighed. "We must go, now. Because I do not have enough root for a direct hit of the drekka venom." She looked upwards at the tiny hole. "I will climb with you and say my farewells at the top." She smiled. "And if we fall, then I will not need to."

"Don't say that." Troy shook his head. "I promise we won't fall."

Troy wiped his hands on his pants. His fingertips still hurt, but at least they had dried. He hoped it could give him more grip.

Once again, the huge claws of the monstrous beast scrabbled at the exit, furiously trying to dig them out, like an anteater digging into a termite nest.

"Time to go." Troy reached up, gripped one of the tiny ledges and lifted himself. His toe found the first notch in the wall, and he began to climb.

He lifted himself about a dozen feet, before Elle followed him, then a dozen more behind her came Anne. Yrsa quickly crossed to the exit, glanced out, just as the massive snout pounded into the rock crevice, knocking her backwards.

She quickly got to her feet and leapt up, to grab a handhold and lift herself after the group. Though her bigger hands and feet would find it less easy to perch on the tiny grooves cut into the rock, her enormous strength and athleticism meant she could lift herself easily and she seemed to never tire.

It didn't take them long to leave behind the crack in the rock and its silvery light. Troy had hung his flashlight around his neck otherwise the darkness would have become absolute in the shaft.

After scaling up for half an hour, he wondered how far they needed to climb – five hundred feet, a thousand, more maybe? If it was a huge distance, he hoped they found a ledge to rest, as already he felt his shoulders complaining and his fingers had begun to bleed again.

Carefully glancing down he saw Anne had also hung her flashlight, and it illuminated Yrsa behind her, who was the only one of them whose face looked untroubled by the climb. But her brows were knitted perhaps by them being in a place forbidden by their clan.

Time rolled on and Troy felt they seemed to have been climbing forever, and on their way, thankfully, he found a small perch that he rested on. He called back down to the group.

"There's a small ledge here – only big enough for one at a time, but take a few minutes to rest, sip water, and then go on." He carefully reached into his pocket to take his own advice and took out the water bottle, flipped the cap with his thumb, and sipped. He carefully replaced it, and then drew in a breath, and continued to climb. Behind him he then heard Elle get to the ledge to rest a while.

He stopped counting minutes in his head, or the small notches cut in the rock, as it was becoming monotonous and hypnotic. But the cold was starting to seep into his bones, and he was glad of the exertion to keep his muscles warm.

The upside was, it told him they might be passing through the thick ice layer protecting Lemuria from the surface world, and soon he must surely rise above it.

Troy wondered just how cold it would get. And how much he could take, as there was no way he could don his feathered cloak while clinging to the wall.

Far behind him he heard Anne groan.

"How much further?" she called.

He had no idea, and half turned. "Not far now – getting very cold so we must be nearing the top." He was only guessing, but knew he needed their spirits high or they could lose focus, and hope, and then, they might give up and drop. *How far now? One, two thousand feet?*

He raised his hand again, gripped, got a toe hold, and lifted himself another few feet. He did it again, and again. Over and over. And then after what was a robotic motion for a mind numbing amount of time he had no idea of, he looked up to see a glow.

"We're nearly there. I can see light," he yelled. "Keep going."

He sped up. His fingertips were numb and as he looked up a breeze wafted down that was cold enough to sting his cheeks and the tip of his nose.

And then he was pulling himself up through a hole in a cave floor. He rolled and sucked in a few deep breaths that stung his throat and lungs from the cold. Troy flexed his fingers and then rolled back over and leaned into the opening to reach down for Elle's hand.

He grabbed it, yanked her out, and she rolled away to lay on her back, breathing heavily. He then waited for Anne.

"Come on, you can do it," he urged.

He stretched a hand down and grabbed her wrist and pulled her up. She came out, face strained and streaked with tears of pain. And she lay there hugging him.

"I nearly gave up," she whispered into his ear.

"I'll never let you give up," he said back.

"I never will." She looked into his eyes for a moment and then wrapped her arms around his neck to hug him close and kiss his cheek, hard.

Yrsa climbed out, her huge brown muscles rippling with power beneath her clan tattoos. She glanced at Troy hugging Anne and looked away quickly. She went and sat against the cave wall, her forearms resting on her knees and head down. She was barely breathing hard.

"Put your cloaks on," he said.

Elle and Anne did as asked, and he removed his, but saw that of the four of them, Yrsa was dressed in the least clothing. Plus, she had to rip away one leg of her hide pants after being covered in the dragon's fiery spit. And only because she had saved them.

He handed her the cloak. "Here."

She shook her head.

He pushed it toward her. "Just for a while. We can share it."

She looked up into his eyes, and smiled. "Yes, maybe there is room for two in it, Troyson." She held out her hand.

Troy then looked around the small cave. There was debris everywhere. Plus some bones, human with remnants of frozen, desiccated skin tight across their faces, with mouths dropped open in perpetual screams. And there were other things that looked like giant bats with a long beak that had inch long teeth set in their beaks – undertakers, he remembered, that had attacked him in the trees.

Yrsa set to raking all the debris she could gather, plus some of the bones with dried skin attached, into a pile. She used a couple of small stones she had brought with her to strike together, generating a spark, and had a fire started quickly.

The warmth and light spread, and the small group crowded around and eagerly held out their hands toward the small orange and red flames.

"And now we are here," Yrsa said into the fire. "At the top of the world."

Troy smiled. "She said we are now at the top of the world."

"At the top of your world." Anne sat as she stared into the fore. "But just at the beginning of ours."

Elle got up and walked to the crack leading to outside. There was a bitter wind forcing its way in and sleet moved furiously past out there. The sun was only just coming up, so it was still quite dark. She hugged the cloak around herself tighter.

"What can you see?" Troy asked.

"Nothing." She turned. "We wouldn't make a hundred yards, let alone, how many miles, a dozen, a hundred to the coast?" She sighed. "And all on foot."

"Wait until the sun is up," Troy suggested. "For now, let's regather our strength. Eat something, and rest."

The group ate a meagre meal of dried meat and sipped water. And then they curled up close to the fire. And slept.

Perhaps hours later, Troy blinked open sticky eyes and groaned.

Everything hurt – his shoulders, back, arms, wrists, and especially his fingers. But he was gloriously warm, and he saw that Yrsa had crawled up behind to cradle him and thrown one cloaked arm over him.

She still slept soundly so he eased out and sat up. He rolled his shoulders to loosen them a little and then stood. He turned to the exit to see it was now light outside. But a glaring, white light.

The fire had burned down but the embers still glowed, so he left it for now, not wanting to burn more of their little stock of flammable material. He crossed to the crack in the rocks to the viciously cold world outside.

He drew in a deep breath and let it out slowly, releasing a ghost of his breath to be snatched from his lips and ripped away. It was a brutal whiteout, and nothing but white on white on white.

Troy backed up a step and had to narrow his eyes to slits, as the rushing wind was sapping the moisture from his eyes and inside his nose. Elle had been right; it would be damn deadly out there.

"We're not that high up, I think," Anne said from just behind him.

He leaned forward to look down and then nodded. "Yeah, climbable. But do we want to?"

"Out of the prehistoric fire and into the freezing frypan?" Anne replied.

He turned. "Freezing frypan?"

She shrugged and then grinned. "What? I made it fit."

He laughed softly. *After all they'd been through, at least they still had their sense of humor,* he thought.

A huge shadow loomed over them as first Elle and then Yrsa joined them. The huge woman leaned down to look outside. After a moment she shook her head. "I do not much like your world, Troyson."

"It's not all like this," Troy replied. "There are beautiful places, beautiful land, warm water, green forests, with no great beasts to eat you."

"But how will you get there?" Yrsa asked.

"Good question. We can't," Elle replied.

"You can understand me?" Yrsa's brows rose.

Elle held her finger and thumb a fraction apart. "Just a little."

"We can't get there. At least not right now." Troy exhaled and went and sat by the dying fire.

Elle stayed by the crack looking out and Anne and Yrsa joined him by the fire, all sitting cross-legged.

Anne opened all the packs, checking them. "Okay everyone, here's the bad news. Only Troy and I brought food, and I estimate we have enough for another two days, or maybe three days if we ration and share it."

"We share it," Troy immediately replied.

"Of course." Anne nodded. "Elle brought water, so that's three of us. A sip now and then and we can eke it out for..." she bobbed her head from side to side. "Maybe three days for the four of us."

"Okay, not so bad," Troy said.

"But wait, there's more," Anne sighed. "Now, here's the real bad news. We have food and water for about two to three days. But the Greenland snow season lasts for 5 months, and a decent winter storm can last for 3 weeks. The *Kulusuk* and *Tasiilaq* saw winds gust up to 90-miles an hour and the temperature gets down to minus 30. I think even in this cave it'll become deadly."

"Shit," Troy groaned and held his head. He looked up between his hands. "And there was good news coming, right?"

Anne shrugged. "We're all still alive."

"How did this Harald the Great you mentioned do it?" Elle asked. "He arrived here and then if he survived the climb, set off from here."

"He probably had a long boat waiting," Troy replied. "And it was the warm season, summer."

"Do you think we can return in summer?" Elle asked.

"Sure, this is a huge mountain from the ground level. But above the Greenland ice it's relatively small and probably not even on a map. Also, I think we're a lot of miles from the coast." Anne stared into the dying fire as she seemed to think it through. "But, even if we get to the coast, what then? If there's no boat to meet us, all we've done is go from one cold and desolate place to another. Except out there we won't have any shelter."

"So, we're stuck here." Elle lay back.

Yrsa could obviously read their expressions. "You need to come back down," She said.

Troy nodded slowly. "Yrsa said we need to go back down. Do we have a choice?"

"Yeah, she wants *you* to go back down so she can keep you as a pet," Anne scoffed.

Yrsa frowned, not understanding the words but sensing the tone. "What did she say?"

"Ignore her, she's just having a bad day," Troy chuckled.

"We all are," Anne finished with a laugh that was like a bark.

Elle helpfully translated. "She said you want to keep Troy as a pet."

"What is a pet?" Yrsa asked.

"A small animal you keep to amuse you," Elle injected.

"Elle, shut up," Troy frowned.

Yrsa rounded on Anne. "You think Troy is a pet? Or I would keep him as one?" She leaned closer, her huge form almost twice the size of Anne's diminutive shape.

Elle smiled serenely as she watched.

Yrsa's eyes blazed. "You think you can insult me?" she spoke softly. "I could crush you with one hand." She held up a fist nearly as big as Anne's head.

Anne didn't understand the words of the huge Viking woman but understood her message loud and clear. She shrunk back a little. "Be cool. *Uh*, Troy, a little help here..."

"Easy, Yrsa. She meant no harm," Troy said. "We're all just a little on edge."

Yrsa snorted and sat back to sit staring glumly into the fire.

After adding more fuel to the small blaze and lifting the amount of warmth and light a little more, the four of them sat in silence for another 30 minutes, staring into the flames, absorbed by their own thoughts.

Troy felt the glorious warmth on his face and chest, but his back ached from the cold that swirled in from outside. He began to wonder: *What is a worse death, dying of cold in the cave or out on the snow somewhere?* They were the same, but one would just occur faster than the other. But the thing was, the outcome was a certainty for both – their deaths. After coming so far, it was a shitty reward.

Or there was the third option: taking their chances back down in Lemuria. Troy glanced across at one of the skeletons slumped against the wall. If not, then maybe in a hundred years someone would use the remnants of their skin and clothing to start a fire.

"How long will we stay here?" Elle asked.

No one spoke for a few more minutes before Elle continued. "As we now know, even if we make it to the coast, we need a boat. And if we climb back down, we need a boat. So..."

"We need a boat, we need a boat, we need a boat," Anne laughed bitterly. "Wow, in all the time Troy and I have been trapped here, why didn't we think of that? All we need is a boat to get home." She shut her eyes and hugged herself. "More importantly, we need to warn them about what has potentially been loosed on the world."

"We do. But need more than just a boat to get home," Troy said as he continued to stare into the fire. "We need a boat that'll get us home, not just a few miles from the ice packs. Just like trying to cross the frozen land here, we'd still die if we tried to cross the freezing sea." He translated for Yrsa.

The huge woman nodded. "Then you need to go like you came," she said softly.

"If we could, we would," Elle replied glumly.

"I could get the clan to build a boat," Yrsa announced.

"Thank you." Troy nodded to her. "But we need more than just a small boat. We have to cross an ocean."

They sat in silence for a few minutes until Yrsa drew in a breath. "*Nemo*," she said softly.

It took Troy's brain a few moments to register what Yrsa had said. He looked up. "What did you say?"

Yrsa looked up. "Nemo left behind a *Jernbåt*."

"A *Jernbåt* – an iron boat." Troy scooted closer to the large Viking woman and gripped her forearm. "*Jernbåt, Nemo*, where did you hear those names?"

"You know where." Yrsa reached into Troy's pack and pulled out the roll of hide. She untied it and lay it open. Then she pointed at an object at the far corner of the map.

"Here. The *Jernbåt – Nemo's jern fisk*." Her finger tapped on the edge of the map. "I've seen it."

"His *iron fish*." Troy looked down and saw a tiny drawn object, obscure, faded, and what he had thought was just a representation of some sort of shark or fish, because that's what it looked like. But it was right on the shoreline. He laughed softly and looked up. "You've seen it?"

Yrsa nodded. "Yes, Nemo's *jern fisk* lives in a cave. But it is dead."

"The *iron fish* lives in a cave." Elle craned forward to stare at the map. "Just like in the story."

"Jules Verne hiding fact in amongst his fiction again." Troy tilted his head back and laughed.

"What is it?" Anne asked. "What's a *jern fisk*?"

Troy looked back down at Anne. "The Nautilus. Captain Nemo's nautilus."

"Captain Nemo was real?" Anne pushed straggly strands of hair off her face. "He was really here?"

"What happened to him?" Troy asked Yrsa.

She shrugged. "It was many, many years before my life. And I think he might have ended where all like him have ended." She looked at Troy from under lowered brows and shared a half smile. "And almost you."

"I see." Troy sat back. "As *Fœða* – food."

# CHAPTER 44

**1864 – Lemuria, The Mysterious Island, deep beneath Greenland's snow and ice**

Gideon Spilett pounded the cross in at the head of the small grave. He sat back on his haunches and closed his eyes.

"Topper, faithful dog, faithful friend."

He couldn't help the tears that ran down his cheeks. They had looked out for each other, hunted together, curled around each other for warmth some nights, and had seen more in their few years on the Mysterious Island than any living being from the outside world.

And now he was gone. And Spilett was alone.

"What will become of me now, boy?" he ran a hand over the small mound of dirt. "Who will warn me of danger?" His mouth curled into a fragile smile. "All those times I told you to quiet your barking. I'm sorry. Because I would give anything to hear it one more time."

Spilett heard something approaching and for once he didn't care. Because the thing he feared more than death was loneliness.

He stayed there with head down until he felt he wasn't alone and looked up. His mouth fell open. He was surrounded by giants. They were dressed as Vikings, even with ferocious green tattoos, and war axes resting on their shoulders. They spoke amongst each other for a few moments, and then one reached forward to loop a rope around his neck and dragged him to his feet.

Spilett pointed at his chest. "My name is Gideon. How do you do, sir?"

The man who held the rope grinned down at him, licked his lips, and said a single word. "*Fæða.*"

Spilett had no idea what that meant but nodded and grinned, wanting to show he was friendly. The huge Vikings laughed down at him.

*Oh well*, he thought. *At least I won't be alone.*

# EPISODE 15

*"I am nothing to you but Captain Nemo; and you and your companions are nothing to me but the passengers of the Nautilus."*
**Jules Verne**

# CHAPTER 45

**Today – Lemuria, The Mysterious Island, deep beneath Greenland**

It took Troy, Anne, Elle, and Yrsa nearly a week to make it back down the mountain and then all the way to the coast. Along the way, Yrsa had proved her skill in the forest by helping them avoid hiding predators, and her fighting prowess in defending them against ones they couldn't avoid.

Troy was happy that there at least seemed to be peace between all parties, even though he knew there remained a lot of distrust.

He looked across at Elle, and the woman's face was implacable, but she seemed untroubled. He wanted to trust her but knew it would be foolish to do that. At least for now. Faithful and stoic, Anne had paused to examine some sort of bug she saw clinging to a tree. He smiled, remembering when they dated and how she had endless stories about growing up and forever spending her time fossicking in rock pools and turning over logs in the garden to see what lived beneath there. And now she was doing it on a hidden primordial island – if they lived, and then made it home, he bet she'd miss the place.

He turned to look over his shoulder at the towering presence of Yrsa. The huge woman saw him looking and smiled and nodded. Her tall and athletic body was covered in scratches and bruises. The decision to join them had taken its toll on her as well.

It seemed she had decided that she was going to defend him with her life. He wondered what she thought was going to happen. She had left behind her entire clan to embark on this trial and even through all the hardships, she never complained for a second.

"Far to go?" he asked her.

She lifted her head and sniffed deeply. "You smell that? Salt in the air." She lowered her head. "We are nearly there."

Sure enough in another hour, they began to see glimpses of water. But they were high, and this area of the coast ended in huge cliffs dropping down to the water.

Troy could see it didn't shallow as when the sea got close to the rocks it was deep and dark. The group stopped and Yrsa walked right up to the cliff edge. Troy joined her and she pointed.

"Down there."

He saw there was a huge cave at the water line. On one side there was tumbled rocks, and it was wide enough for them to be able to clamber across and enter the cave.

"We need to climb down?" he asked.

She nodded. "There is a path."

She led them down to a narrow cut on the rock face that they had to edge along in single file, backs to the rock face. Yrsa's boots hung over the edge, but her face remained calm.

In fifteen more minutes they were at the water line. Troy didn't like being so close to the deep water because he knew what lived in there, and some of the creatures were more than happy to not wait until you were in the water with them, but instead could pick you right off a boat or dry land.

Yrsa led them inside the cave, and they saw it was a vast water grotto. It had a high ceiling that must have eroded through in some places as shafts of line beamed down like giant spotlights.

They skirted the edge of the small cave lake and Yrsa climbed a mass of tumbled boulders and then stood with her hand on her hips. She smiled and looked back at them.

"There." The huge woman pointed. "The *Jern fisk*."

Troy climbed to the top of the rock pile and stopped in his tracks. "Oh my God." His mouth dropped open but still spread into a wide grin. "It's the Nautilus."

# EPILOGUE

## Norway, Lomsdal–Visten National Park, north-western shoreline

The detectives walked along the beach toward the vessel grounded on the sand. Already there were local police climbing all over the deck and inside the ship.

Senior Detective Bjorn Lomberg turned to his junior partner, Andrej Hansen. "Who's the owner?"

Hansen flipped pages in a notebook and read: "Olaf Linberg, aged 62, semi-retired fisherman and single owner of the Sjøspray." He looked up. "The lodged manifest indicated it was a private charter by a Mr Anders Ostenson, a researcher from the university Malmo and he also had a position with the museum. There was also another passenger, a Mr Oder van der Berg, his brother-in-law."

Lomberg half turned. "Neither of them sound like fishermen, and not exactly the weather for sight-seeing."

"Nope, and they headed all the way to Greenland, and stayed for several days. Headed back, but never made it. Looks like they ended up here instead." Hansen flipped his notebook closed.

Lomberg's brows went up. "They went on a 3,000 mile round trip. In under a week – why would you do that?"

The low tide had left the boat high and dry, and a wooden ladder was leaned up against the side. Both men carefully climbed it and stood with legs wide for balance on the angled deck.

"Show me what you found," Lomberg said to the pair of officers standing in rubber boots, and what he thought were sickly looking expressions. The men briefly glanced at each other and then turned to firstly enter the wheelhouse.

Inside, the small room was all steamed up, and the detectives immediately held their breath. "*Phew*, what is that stink?"

The smell was like sulphur chemicals and vomit. Near the wheel was some sort of mess on the floor that was hard to make out. In amongst the large, slimy puddle in front of the wheel was a shoe, and a pipe, plus what could be lumps of white hair. But that was all.

"I have no idea what I'm looking at here." Lomberg looked up. "Is this supposed to be a body?" His mouth turned down and he looked around for a moment, and then back to the pile. "Get a sample." He motioned to the door. "Show me the other one."

The pair of detectives were then led down a set of narrow steps below deck to one of the cabins. Inside was the same revolting smell, but this time there was an occupant – a body on the bed – sort of.

"Holy shit," Hansen whispered. He put a hand over his lower face, covering his mouth and nose and made little squeaking noises in his throat as he tried not to throw up into his mouth.

The cadaver was literally just a head on the pillow, eyes rolled back and mouth open. But below it the vertebrae bones started but then the rest was just a moulding skeleton covered in the same slimy gelatinous mess.

"What the hell happened to this guy?" Lomberg looked up at the ceiling, and then back at the corpse. "Did something spill on him?"

He carefully reached out to press the man's cheek with a single finger. The indentation stayed in the flesh for a while as the rubbery texture was gone.

"He's been dead only a few days."

"Do you, *ah*, think it's contagious?" Hansen asked.

Lomberg pulled his hand back and half turned. "Thank you, Detective, that question might have come in handy before I touched the guy." He shook his head, and then lifted a pencil from his pocket.

He used the pencil to lift the cadaver's lips and lower the jaw. It stretched, making a creaking motion, but the body had moved on from rigor mortis, so movement of joints was possible.

He then lifted the skin flap at the neck. He noticed that all the blood vessels were sealed over as if cauterized.

Lomberg then brought the pencil close to his face, sniffed, screwed his nose up, and then tossed the pencil on top of the skeleton.

"I'm guessing this is either Mr Anders Ostenson or Oder van der Berg. And the mess upstairs is all that's left of the captain. So we're a body short." Lomberg straightened. "Okay, bag it all, and get it back to the labs. We'll let the science guys work it out."

He and Hansen then went topside and turned to see a police officer waving to them from the beach.

"What now?" Lomberg groaned.

The pair of detectives climbed back down the ladder and trudged up the beach to the policeman.

"What is it?" Lomberg asked.

"This." The policeman indicated drag marks in the sand.

It looked like something the size of a large dog had half-dragged half-walked itself up the beach. Lomberg turned and saw it extended from where the boat had been stranded, and then continued into the brush.

"There's another one further down." The policeman pointed.

Lomberg turned and could just make out another drag mark.

"Maybe something came down to check out the boat or the bodies," Hansen suggested.

"Yeah, that's probably it. Maybe a couple of bears or wolverines," Lomberg said.

"You think we should go take a look?" Hansen asked.

Lomberg looked from the boat to the forest and then slowly shook his head. "No, forget it. We've got enough to do."

Hansen nodded and turned away. But Senior Detective Bjorn Lomberg continued to stare. The thing he noticed was that the tracks only went one way – from the boat. Whatever they belonged to was no bear, big cat, or wolverine, and it came off the boat and headed into the forest.

He stared at where the tracks vanished into the tree line. The National Park was around 500 square miles of thick vegetation, rivers, and mountains, that dozens of people got lost in every year, with some vanishing forever.

Something could live in there for centuries and never be seen. Lomberg drew in a deep breath of the Norwegian, biting sea air. Something about this whole case scared the shit out of him and there was no way he was going into that dark forest.

"Whatever it was, it'll turn up one day," he said softly. "We're done here."

# END

Checkout other great books by bestselling author

# Greig Beck

## PRIMORDIA: IN SEARCH OF THE LOST WORLD

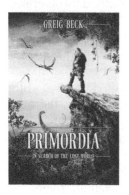

Ben Cartwright, former soldier, home to mourn the loss of his father stumbles upon cryptic letters from the past between the author, Arthur Conan Doyle and his great, great grandfather who vanished while exploring the Amazon jungle in 1908. Amazingly, these letters lead Ben to believe that his ancestor's expedition was the basis for Doyle's fantastical tale of a lost world inhabited by long extinct creatures. As Ben digs some more he finds clues to the whereabouts of a lost notebook that might contain a map to a place that is home to creatures that would rewrite everything known about history, biology and evolution. But other parties now know about the notebook, and will do anything to obtain it. For Ben and his friends, it becomes a race against time and against ruthless rivals. In the remotest corners of Venezuela, along winding river trails known only to lost tribes, and through near impenetrable jungle, Ben and his novice team find a forbidden place more terrifying and dangerous than anything they could ever have imagined.

## THE FOSSIL

Klaus and Doris have just made the discovery of their lives – a complete Neanderthal skeleton buried in a newly opened sinkhole. But on removing it, something else tumbles free. Something that switches on, and then calls home.Soon the owners are coming back, and nothing will stop their ruthless search for their lost prize. Gruesome corpses begin to pile up, and Detective Ed Heisner of the Berlin Police is assigned to a case like nothing he has ever experienced before in his life. Heisner must stay one step ahead of a group of secretive Special Forces soldiers also tracking the strange device, while trying to find an unearthly group of killers that are torturing, burning, and obliterating their victims all the way across the city.THE FOSSIL is a time jumping detective novella where humans soon find that time can be the greatest weapon of all.* THE FOSSIL first appeared in SNAFU No.1 (2014) as a short story. Due to numerous requests, it has now been expanded and released here in its complete, stand-alone novella form.

# Greig Beck

## TO THE CENTER OF THE EARTH

An old woman locked away in a Russian asylum has a secret—knowledge of a 500-year-old manuscript written by a long-dead alchemist that will show a passage to the mythical center of the Earth.She knows it's real because 50 years ago, she and a team traveled there. And only she made it back. Today, caving specialist Mike Monroe leads a crew into the world's deepest cave in the former Soviet Union. He's following the path of a mad woman, and the words of an ancient Russian alchemist, that were the basis of the fantastical tale by Jules Verne.But what horrifying things he finds will tear at his sanity and change everything we know about evolution and the world, forever.In the tradition of Primordia, Greig Beck delivers another epic retelling of a classic story in an electrifying and terrifying adventure that transcends the imagination."Down there, beyond the deepest caves, below the crust and the mantle, there is another world."

## THE SIBERIAN INCIDENT

100,000 years ago the object hit the lake at the deepest point, quickly sinking into its mile-deep stygian darkness. With it came something horrifying that would threaten every living thing on the face of the planetOver the centuries, legends grew of people vanishing, of strange, deformed animals, and of an unexplained luminescence down in the lake depths.When Marcus Stenson won the lucrative contract to create a sturgeon fish farm on the site of disused paper mill on the shore of Lake Baikal, he thought he had hit the jackpot. He refused to listen to the chilling folktales, or even be concerned by the occasional harassment from the local mafia. But then animals were found mutilated in the frozen forest, and people started to go missing. And worse, some came back, changed, horribly.In the depths of the lake, something unearthly that had been waiting 100,000 years was stirring. And mankind will become nothing more than a host.THE SIBERIAN INCIDENT - a tale of invasive Alien Horror from international best selling author, Greig Beck.

Made in the USA
Las Vegas, NV
04 May 2023

71562032R00125